Photographs of Claudia

KG MacGregor

Bella BOOKS

2010

Acknowledgments

This part of the book can be the most challenging to write, not because it's hard to acknowledge others, but because it's hard to do so adequately. I'm going to give it a try just the same.

Thank you to my editor, Katherine V. Forrest, for reminding me of the vast difference between a manuscript and a story. It isn't at all hyperbole to tell you that without her help, this book would not have made it to press.

I wish also to thank my friend Tracy Van Zeeland, a commercial photographer in Appleton, Wisconsin. She was more than generous with her expertise, not only on the technical and artistic aspects of photography, but also on the ins and outs of running a studio business. Though she managed to mitigate some of my ignorance, I asserted poetic license in some places, so please know that any errors are mine.

Thanks as always to Karen, who picked over my carelessness in the final drafts, and to all the staff at Bella Books for putting out a beautiful book. A special nod to editorial director Karin Kallmaker, whose dedication to lesbian romance is an inspiration.

Finally, I owe my deepest gratitude to my partner Jenny, my rock in everything I do.

About the Author

A former teacher and market research consultant, KG MacGregor holds a PhD in journalism and mass communication. Infatuation with *Xena: Warrior Princess* fanfiction prompted her to try her own hand at storytelling in 2002. In 2005, she signed with Bella Books, which published the Goldie Award finalist *Just This Once*. Her sixth Bella novel, *Out of Love*, won the 2007 Lambda Literary Award for Women's Romance, and the 2008 Goldie Award in Lesbian Romance. In 2009, she picked up Goldies for *Without Warning* (Contemporary Romance) and *Secrets So Deep* (Romantic Suspense).

KG divides her time between homes in Miami and Blowing Rock, North Carolina. When she isn't writing, she's either on a hiking trail, a golf course, or if she's really lucky, a cruise ship. Please visit her at www.kgmacgregor.com.

Chapter 1

"I don't suppose I could talk you into trading shoes."

Leonora Westcott eyed the bride's beaded white stilettos and her own Mephisto flats. "Not a chance. The only way you're getting these is off my cold, dead feet." She stepped from behind the camera to arrange Eva Pettigrew and her six attendants for their portrait. The Pacific Ocean shimmered in the late afternoon sun behind their perch on the terrace of the Ritz Carlton at Half Moon Bay. "But I have a box cutter in my bag if you girls want to saw off those heels."

The bridesmaids—youthful and lovely in powder blue chiffon—wore spiked heels that thrust their breasts forward and their rears back. Some of Leo's feminist friends would have decried the look as sexist objectification of women, which made her feel a tad guilty for appreciating it so much. As long as she looked through her camera's eye, no one would catch her ogling.

1

"I saw Todd about an hour ago," said the maid of honor, an Asian woman named Lon. "He looked like roadkill. Jason said they poured Maker's Mark down his throat till four o'clock this morning."

Eva rolled her eyes. "Sweet. So on our wedding night, we're going to sleep together. And I do mean sleep." The soft June breeze whipped a strand of brown hair across her brow. "Okay, which one of you has the hairspray?"

The girl nearest the door broke ranks. "I'll get it."

Leo had seen Todd firsthand two hours ago on the bluff, where he had gathered his bleary-eyed groomsmen for a short series of casual photos. Only one of the men had managed to tie his bow tie correctly, but she had lent a hand to the others before sending them off to greet and seat the guests. Eva wanted casual poses like Todd's also, but her grandmother had insisted on the traditional series for the formal wedding album. Leo was doing her best to accommodate both, snapping off candid and lighthearted images whenever the opportunities arose.

Eva closed her eyes while her attendant sprayed a stream of the sticky product onto her bangs. "How many bottles of this have we gone through?"

"This is our third."

"When I drop my veil, it's going to feel like I'm wearing a space helmet."

"I'm afraid the wind's going to be a lot worse down by the gazebo," Leo said, taking over the task. Though her short black hair rarely got more than a brisk rub from a towel, she knew all about the virtues of hairspray, and makeup too. Helping people look their best for photos was part of her job, which she had been doing for over thirty years. Women as naturally beautiful as these didn't need much help, but weddings always brought out the quest for perfection, whether in style or ceremony.

Not that she was an expert on modern weddings. Early in her career she had shot hundreds, enough to know the standard vows by heart, but the Pettigrew-McCord affair was her first in three years. The last one had been extravagant as well, held in

2

the Japanese Tea Garden of Golden Gate Park in San Francisco, featuring the daughter of one of her corporate clients, a giant in the computer industry.

Most of her work these days consisted of magazine layouts, publicity photos for celebrities and corporate honchos, and even the occasional gallery exhibit. She had reached the pinnacle of her professional dreams, thanks to good fundamentals, perseverance and a handful of lucky breaks. On the rare occasions when she accepted a wedding assignment, it was usually for friends or clients, and more often than not she waived her five-figure fee. Such was the case today, since she was here as a favor to her longtime friend, Maria Long, one of the finest studio photographers she knew and a close friend of the bride's family. Maria had broken her leg in a bicycle accident and didn't trust anyone else to give her friends the caliber of work she had promised. Though it meant rescheduling a two-day magazine shoot in Tucson, Leo was happy to do it and knew Maria would have done the same thing for her.

She stowed the spray bottle out of the camera's view and gestured toward Eva's brow. "If you try to push that out of your eyes again, it'll break off in your hand."

"That's what I call hold."

It was also what Leo called picture perfect. She raised her Extech light meter to Eva's cheek as the sun caught the soft box and cast an almost effervescent light upward. "Hold that pose right there. Could I ask you ladies to step out of the frame for just a moment?"

She stepped behind her tripod and drew a deep breath.

Chapter 2

October 1986

Leo took the index card from a freckled boy with a missing front tooth and matched his name to her list. "Nate Freeman."

"That's my name. Don't wear it out," the third grader whistled cheekily as his friends guffawed.

Rolling her eyes, she guided him to the front of the rural backdrop and positioned his hands atop a faux split-rail fence. "Keep your feet on those feet, please," she said, indicating the yellow shoe prints on a mat on the floor. She had gone through her detailed instructions for school pictures when the class first arrived in the media center, but the children had paid her little mind once their teacher vanished and left them under her supervision.

"All right, Nate. Stop looking at that pretty girl in the red dress and look at me instead." The children within earshot hooted as Leo clicked the shutter to capture a blushing smile.

Nate's parents were going to love that photo.

"I wasn't looking at Alisa," he protested.

"I wouldn't blame you one bit if you did." She shot Alisa a wink that caused the girl to grin with obvious pride. "Now move along to the back of the other line. Who's next?"

One by one, she worked the crowd of eight-year-olds like a comic in a lounge act, pulling out all the stops to get the right reaction, the perfect expression. She loved the portrait side of photography, which constituted the bulk of her business. From the time she was twelve years old she had worked alongside her father in the studio learning what he considered the most important mechanical aspects of photography—lighting and composition. But what mattered most with commercial portraits, he had said, was making people happy with how they looked on film.

She had cut her professional teeth on school pictures, hundreds upon hundreds of children every fall all over the Monterey Peninsula, using each sitting to hone her skills. That had been her father's idea, a training tool so she would be ready to take over the business upon his retirement. Instead, it had become a principal source of revenue while she struggled to maintain the studio after her father's sudden death six years ago. Fresh out of community college where she had studied business administration, she had been forced at twenty years old to put her education to practice in the support side of the studio—marketing, finance and administration. Thanks to steady jobs like this one, Westcott Photography had weathered her father's death, and she now had the chance to focus more on her craft.

"Alisa Workman." Leo guided the girl in the red dress into position and returned to peer through the viewfinder. "All right, say…cheesy sneeze." She snapped the portrait as Alisa laughed at the silly phrase, and got another keeper.

Though she shot hundreds of identical photos in a single week, each was important to her. For most kids, these formal sittings were the benchmarks of their childhood. They would line the walls of their homes and fill the wallets of proud aunts, uncles

5

and grandparents. They were permanent, enduring reminders of progress toward adulthood.

"That one won't come out," a boy taunted from the line. "Nate already broke the camera."

Leo shot him a scolding look, but he had turned away to laugh with his friends. Too bad she didn't have an assistant, someone to help pose the children and keep them in line while they waited. If only the teachers would stay with them, but no. They dropped their students off at the media center and disappeared. And most, like Mrs. Tyler right now, took their sweet time coming back.

"Nate loves Alisa," the children sang.

"I do not!"

Even towering over them at five-nine, she didn't seem to intimidate them in the least. They grew louder by the minute, pushing and shoving in line, and popping one another with the complimentary plastic combs she had handed out when they first arrived. To make matters worse, another class was coming through the door.

"All right, kids. Settle down. I'd appreciate it if you'd stand quietly by the door and wait for Mrs. Tyler." Her pleas for calm had no effect. She could barely hear herself speak above the din of simultaneous conversations. Managing unruly kids was not in her skill set.

"Excuse me, what is your name?" A quiet voice—an adult voice—came from the doorway.

Leo whirled to see a young woman approaching the third graders, focusing on Alisa, who hadn't caused any trouble at all. The woman, petite and slightly built with wavy brown hair past her shoulders, looked barely old enough to be a teacher, but she exuded an amazing aura of authority. Leo thought Alisa was going to be scolded by mistake and was about to intervene when the class suddenly grew silent.

"Alisa Workman," the girl replied shyly.

"I really like the way you follow directions, Alisa. I bet Mrs. Tyler is very proud of you." At once, the other third-graders turned forward and straightened their line. "It's especially nice

6

the way you keep your hands to yourself and listen to Miss..." She turned to Leo and flashed a brilliant smile.

"Westcott." Leo watched numbly, captivated by the way the woman had taken charge.

"To Miss Westcott. I wish you were in my class, Alisa."

So she was a teacher after all, and apparently a respected one. Without raising her voice, she had brought the ruckus to a halt. Every single student in Mrs. Tyler's class seemed to want to please her.

"Thank you," she whispered. "Mrs. Tyler is late."

"I'll be happy to wait with them if you want to start on my group. I'm Claudia Galloway, by the way." The woman held out her hand. "I'm doing my internship with Miss Irwin this semester."

She took the offered hand. So she was Sandy Irwin's intern—that explained why she looked so much younger than the other teachers, twenty-two at the most. Leo couldn't wait to talk with Sandy again and ask her all about this Miss Galloway. "I'm Leo Westcott."

"I know." She stepped away from the children and lowered her voice. "I have a message for you from Sandy, which is to stop in later and say hi if you have the chance."

"Yeah, she and I are good friends." Leo instantly worried that she shouldn't have offered that. Sandy usually kept her personal life private at school. "I know a lot of the teachers because I've been shooting here so long. I have a studio in town."

"Westcott Photography? That gray Victorian on Van Buren Street?"

"That's the one."

"I sometimes cut through Van Buren on my way home. I love all those old houses along there, especially yours. Maybe if I stop by sometime you'll let me peek inside."

"Sure, I'll give you a tour of the whole place." Leo couldn't believe the invitation had come out of her mouth, and to a virtual stranger no less. She was glad to show off her studio, but rarely invited people upstairs to her private quarters.

Mrs. Tyler suddenly bustled into the media center. "Sorry I'm late," she said unconvincingly.

"It's all right. I was just admiring the way Alisa leads your class," Miss Galloway said. "And I'm really pleased to see what good listeners they all are."

"Too bad I don't have more like her. They can't behave themselves, no matter what I threaten them with." No sooner did she disparage her class than the whispering and fidgeting started again. "See what I mean?"

Leo watched in astonishment as the class filed out noisily behind their frazzled teacher. Over her shoulder, she could see Miss Irwin's class standing quietly as they waited to have their pictures taken.

"That was...I don't know what it was. How did you do that?"

Miss Galloway winked at her and smiled. "We all have our tricks."

"Can you teach me that one? I don't have a clue how to handle these kids, and all the teachers keep running off and leaving me on my own."

"Not much to it, really. Sandy and I expect our boys and girls to behave like Alisa." She tipped her head in the direction of the retreating class. "And Mrs. Tyler expects her class to misbehave."

"Which is exactly what they did when she came back." Leo looked again at Sandy's class, astounded by the contrast between the two groups. "You're a magician, Miss Galloway."

"Call me Claudia, please. And there's no magic here. It's a teaching philosophy based on something called the Pygmalion Effect."

"What's that?"

"We studied it in college." Claudia turned sideways and cupped her mouth so her students wouldn't hear. "It's a principle that says students usually do what you expect them to do. So at the start of the school year, we told them how pleased we were that they had given us all the top students."

"So that's it. You got the cream of the crop."

"No, actually we didn't. They're just a randomly assigned group, but they think they're the top group so they act like it."

"Pretty sneaky." Leo looked at the youngsters again. "I think I can manage your class by myself if you want to take a break. I just need to explain the process, and your students look like they might actually listen."

"They will, I guarantee it. But I don't mind sticking around if it's okay with you. Maybe I can help."

Leo was more than happy to see her stay, and not just to keep the children in line. After three days in a row of being with kids, she was starved for adult conversation. As Claudia handed out the black combs with the studio's name printed in gold, Leo introduced herself to the students and walked them through the photo process. Then she assumed her position behind the camera while Claudia directed each student to the footprints on the floor and helped them pose behind the rail.

"That's it. Left hand on top," Leo said.

After positioning the children, Claudia scuttled to stand beside Leo to coax smiles from their faces. With her enthusiasm and help, Leo finished the class in half the usual time.

"I don't suppose I could hire you for the rest of the day."

"I wish I could, but this isn't as much fun as arithmetic," Claudia answered, looking at her students for support. "Is it?"

The children grumbled and rolled their eyes.

"I understand. Nothing is that much fun…unless it's getting your teacher to pose for a picture."

"Yeah!" twenty-five young voices answered in unison.

Leo nodded toward the backdrop. "What do you say?"

Claudia shook her head. "I don't think so."

"Oh, I think so. You're going to want a souvenir of Melrose Elementary. What better one than this?"

At her class's urging, Claudia acquiesced and went to stand behind the rail, which was below the level of her hips. "This is going to look pretty funny."

"It just so happens…" Leo loosened a wing nut on each side

9

and lifted the rail to waist high. "It's adjustable. No more excuses. Now you have to smile." When she positioned Claudia's hands, she noticed an enormous diamond ring.

"It's going to look pretty funny when my picture comes back with the others."

"I won't send these through the school." Eschewing the long-roll camera on her tripod, she took three photos with her handheld favorite, a 35mm Nikon FM2. Then she handed Claudia her pencil and notepad. "Jot down your address and I'll mail them to you. On the house."

"Why don't I just write down my phone number? You can call me when they're ready and I'll come by your studio and pick them up. That way I'll get the tour of your house."

"Sure, that would work." Leo was already looking forward to the call. "I should have them ready by next week."

The next group appeared in the doorway and Leo checked the clock on the wall. Five minutes early, but that teacher didn't seem to care, since she had already disappeared. Claudia turned her line toward the door and in a soft voice directed her students to return to the classroom.

"Thanks for your help," Leo called.

"Anytime." She glanced at her retreating class, then back at Leo. With a sheepish shrug, she qualified her offer. "Except now. It's time for arithmetic."

Chapter 3

Leo loaded the last of her equipment from the media cart into her vehicle, an eight-year-old blue Volvo station wagon. A panel van would have been more practical for the business, but she couldn't afford to maintain two vehicles and didn't want a van for her personal use. The Volvo was like family, over a hundred thousand miles and still going strong.

Her afternoon had flown by, thanks to Claudia Galloway, who had occupied her thoughts through four classes of second graders, the last on the schedule for Melrose Elementary. She had put Claudia's technique into practice, and was amazed at how quickly the children quieted when told they were the best-behaved class she had seen all day. Too bad she hadn't known about the Pygmalion Effect three days ago when she started her shoot at Melrose. It was definitely going into her bag of tricks for future jobs.

From the teachers' parking lot she had a direct view of the bus ramp where excited students were lining up to board buses for the ride home. Claudia was supervising the chaos, and Leo took the opportunity to study her from afar. In her tan skirt and pink oxford shirt she was the picture of professionalism, and at the same time the girl next door.

In just twenty minutes of casual chatting, Claudia had sparked her interest, though the rock on her hand had quickly defined the parameters as friends only. Of course, Claudia might not be keen on being friends once she learned Leo was gay, which some people guessed as soon as they took in her appearance, her deeper than average voice and the way she carried herself. She made no pretense about it, but that didn't mean she felt a special obligation to reveal anything about her personal life, especially in a case like this, since the only real interest Claudia had expressed was in touring her Victorian house.

"That's right. She only wants to see the house," she said aloud, and then looked around as she slammed the back gate of her wagon to see if anyone had overheard her talking to herself.

She lowered her sunglasses and looked back at the bus ramp, where Claudia was waving goodbye as each busload pulled away. Leo wasn't normally quick to make friends and could barely keep up with the ones she already had, but something about Claudia compelled her. She walked back into the building past the media center to the familiar classroom, where Sandy was grading papers at a table in the back of the room. "Hey, stranger."

"Leo! Sorry I missed you today." Sandy, easily the most stylish of Leo's friends, wore a smart green dress with a flowing paisley scarf and brown heels. She pushed her straight blond hair from her brow and grinned over the top of her glasses. "Very sorry, in fact, because I was in a parent-teacher conference with a mom who thinks her son ought to be skipped ahead to high school."

"If anyone's ready for high school, it's the kids in your class. I couldn't believe how smart and well-behaved they all were."

"You can thank my intern for that. She's pretty amazing."

Leo pulled out one of the miniature chairs and perched on

12

the edge. "She told me how you expected them to be the best and they were."

"It was all Claudia's idea, and it's not just the kids. I sit up straighter too!" Sandy laughed as she stood and collected her purse. "Come with me to the lounge so I can have a cigarette."

"Good, I need to talk to you about something. I hope you don't get mad at me."

"Depends on what you did."

Leo waited until they were inside the empty lounge and seated on a vinyl couch. "Where is everybody? I figured all the teachers dashed in here the minute the kids left."

"Nah, they're probably doing their lesson plans for tomorrow. Not everyone is lucky enough to have an intern. I tell you, it's like having a personal slave." Sandy lit her cigarette and took a deep draw. "So what am I not supposed to get mad at you about?"

"I, uh…I sort of slipped and told Claudia we were friends."

Sandy shrugged. "No big deal. I already told her that much."

Leo was mildly surprised. "I thought you tried to keep your personal life under the radar here at school."

"I usually do, but Claudia already knows about Maria and me."

This she found shocking. "You're kidding."

Sandy shrugged. "We spend a lot of time together, so we talk about things. She just struck me as somebody who would be okay with it, and she was."

"I guess that shouldn't surprise me. She's pretty nice. Most of the teachers just drop their kids off and leave me to deal with them but she stuck around and helped."

"You're smitten," Sandy said with a conspiratorial grin. "Too bad. She's got a fiancé. Did you get a load of that three-carat diamond?"

"I am not smitten." Intrigued, she conceded, but not smitten. "So she wasn't freaked out about you and Maria?"

"Seems to be fine. She came over to the house for dinner last week. Matter of fact, I was thinking about asking her to our

13

Halloween party next weekend. You're going to be there, aren't you?"

"Sure, but"—she lowered her voice in case someone walked in—"why would a woman come to a lesbian party if she has a boyfriend?" Maybe it was the Patty Clemons theory. Patty thought straight women who hung out with lesbians weren't really straight at all—they just didn't know it yet.

"I feel sorry for her because she doesn't have any friends here. Her family lives down the coast in Cambria. She's only going to be here for a semester, so why not include her in the mix if she's up for it?"

Leo nodded in agreement, determined now to add Claudia to her list of friends. "She said she liked my house and I invited her over to see it. You think that's okay?"

"Why not?" Sandy nudged her teasingly. "Maybe she'll have an epiphany."

"Very funny." Leo smacked her knee and stood. "See you next weekend."

She scooted out the side door to the parking lot, glancing back at the bus ramp one last time. The kids were gone and so was Claudia. It was silly to be disappointed about the fiancé.

Claudia smiled as she silently shuffled down the carpeted hallway to the classroom. Her first day in charge of the full schedule of lessons had gone better than she had hoped, which she attributed to Sandy easing her into the job one subject at a time. The only hitch had been the incident after lunch when David Spiegel threw up at her feet. At least she had managed to fight back the urge to return the favor.

She was eager to debrief the day with Sandy, but when she reached the classroom it was deserted. "Probably smoking in the teachers' lounge," she murmured. She had half expected to find her talking with Leo Westcott, whom she had seen re-enter the building. Maybe both of them were having a cigarette…nah, she had stood right next to Leo while she adjusted the split rail and hadn't picked up even a whiff of stale tobacco.

The question that really intrigued her wasn't if Leo smoked—it was whether or not she was gay. Not that it mattered one way or the other. She was only curious because Sandy had said she was a personal friend. There were things about Leo that fit her usual image of lesbians—like her short hair, plain attire and sinewy build—but those also described lots of straight women she knew from UC-Santa Cruz. They certainly didn't make her unattractive, especially with those stunning green eyes and long lashes.

Claudia had finished the day with a geography lesson, getting so caught up in talking about Thailand that the final bell had taken her by surprise. Her students had enjoyed her firsthand accounts of the Thai people and their culture, and she was glad for the chance to revisit her memories. As a result, the photos and souvenirs she had collected two years ago in Bangkok were scattered across a table at the front of the room, and she was gathering them up when Sandy returned.

"Nice job, kiddo! I'm going to bring my pillow tomorrow so I can catch a nap while you do all the work."

Claudia grinned sheepishly. "I'm just glad I got my first day behind me. I don't expect it to get easier but at least my nerves will start to calm down. The kids weren't too hard on me."

"If you were nervous, it didn't show."

Sandy drew an emery board from her purse and filed a sculpted nail, another reminder to Claudia that stereotypes didn't hold up very well. She would never have guessed Sandy was a lesbian if she hadn't told her.

Claudia nodded toward the back of the room. "You wouldn't have gotten much of a nap today. Every time I looked back there you were writing something down."

"I made a list of little things you could work on but there's nothing major." Her upbeat encouragement notwithstanding, Sandy went on with a pointed critique that included insufficient eye contact, a tendency to talk too fast and to stand in one place too long. "At first I was worried you weren't projecting enough, but then I saw that everyone was straining to hear and I figured

15

that was good, like they're afraid they might miss something. Maybe you're onto something with that."

For such a glowing review, the list of weak spots was too long for Claudia's satisfaction. She tried to keep a positive attitude throughout the evaluation, but her discouragement must have been obvious.

"Don't get all down in the dumps about this," Sandy said, gripping her shoulder. "A lot of these things are just differences in teaching style. I was back there nit-picking, trying to come up with suggestions so you'd know I was paying attention. You'll be a terrific teacher even if you ignore every single thing I said."

Despite her disappointment, it helped to hear what she could do better and she didn't want to inhibit Sandy's criticism. "No, I want you to tell me what you think I need to work on. I just feel silly for some of this stuff because I know better."

"Of course you do. But this job isn't as easy as it looks. You just need more practice and that's what your internship is all about."

Sandy was right. She'd had plenty of chances in the past two years to stand in front of a classroom, but taking responsibility for a full day was tougher than she had anticipated. It was hard to remember all the little things when she was preoccupied with staying two steps ahead of her students.

"You're still frowning. Quit worrying about it already," Sandy said. "Leo stopped by and said she was going to give you a tour of that old house of hers. She must have liked you because she's never offered to give any of us a tour."

Considering how quickly she and Leo had hit it off, she was surprised. "Hmm…I sort of invited myself. I hope I wasn't too pushy."

"Don't worry about it. She'd have found a way to say no if you weren't welcome. She's not unfriendly, but she does tend to keep people at arm's length, especially at first. I think she's just a little shy."

"Really? I would never have guessed that."

"That's because you saw her with her camera in her hand.

16

Maria says she's a whole different person when she's shooting pictures, all relaxed and confident. She really likes Leo's work. Says she's going to be great one of these days if she keeps learning."

Claudia remembered seeing Maria's photography hanging throughout the house when she had gone there for dinner. "That's high praise coming from someone like Maria."

"Yeah, Leo definitely knows her stuff. By the way, she's coming to our house next Saturday for a Halloween party"—she lowered her voice markedly—"along with about forty other women of the lesbian persuasion. Why don't you come too?"

"A Halloween party?" That answered her question about Leo, but it raised another about why Sandy would invite her to such an event. "It sounds like fun, but honestly, I don't want to horn in on you and your friends."

Sandy scowled. "Oh, that's bullshit. One thing Leo and I have in common is that I don't invite people unless I want them to show up. I'll run interference and make sure they all know you're just a friendly. Just wave that rock under their noses."

She looked self-consciously at the diamond on her hand. It was a whole lot bigger than it needed to be, but Mike didn't do anything on a small scale. "Maybe I should leave this at home."

"I wouldn't do that if I were you. You'll be fighting off horny dykes all night."

She could feel herself start to blush. Getting hit on wouldn't bother her as long as they respected her response, but she couldn't imagine they would waste their time on someone who was straight. "I doubt that."

"Trust me, Claudia." Sandy hooked her purse over her shoulder and flipped off the lights, signaling an end to their workday. "They'd be on you like flies on honey."

17

Chapter 4

Leo spread the photos out on her coffee table. The rest of her film from the job at Melrose Elementary had gone to the lab for developing and wouldn't return for another five weeks, but she had saved the roll from her Nikon to develop at home. It held only the three photos of Claudia Galloway.

She stared at the images with brazen interest, her eyes settling on the outline of Claudia's breasts in the pink shirt. The dip of her neck revealed a small jade pendant, which Leo remembered from their meeting but hadn't allowed herself to study. From the boyfriend, she surmised.

She set the photos aside and propped her feet beside them. After shooting a wedding all day on Saturday, it was nice to relish a Sunday afternoon with nothing to do, nowhere to be and no one to see. She had spent the morning in her basement darkroom and now was toying with the idea of calling the number

Claudia had given her to say her photos were ready. A creeping nervousness had stopped her, similar to what she typically felt before the handful of blind dates Sandy and Maria had arranged. There was no good reason to put her feelings about Claudia into the same category with those girls. This wasn't a test to see if romance could blossom between them. But for some reason it was imperative that she make a good impression on Claudia.

A sudden thud sent the photos sliding across the coffee table.

"Hello, Madeline." She scooped her calico kitten into her lap. "You can't stand it when I pay attention to something else."

The cat responded with a steady purr as she pushed her head into Leo's chin. Her tail twittered in anticipation of her back being scratched.

"How did you get to be so rotten in just six months?"

She swiped at the cat, a birthday gift from Patty, who had joked at her party that Leo needed a little pussy. It was an embarrassing pronouncement made all the worse by its obvious truth. Leo hadn't made love with anyone in over four years, but that wasn't for lack of trying on Patty's part. She proclaimed her undying lust nearly every time they saw each other. Leo played it down with humor, refusing to take her overtures seriously. That only increased Patty's flirtations, but it let her save face while Leo dodged her advances. Patty wasn't her type.

"What do you think, Madeline? Do I even have a type?" She clutched the kitten to her chest as she leaned down and retrieved one of Claudia's photos from the floor. "What do you think of this one? Cute, huh?"

Yes, Claudia could be her type…or someone like her. Leo didn't need to be fantasizing about someone with a boyfriend, but that didn't mean she couldn't use Claudia to figure out what kind of girl she did want. Something about her was intriguing, something that might give Leo a clue about romance. This fumbling through blind dates and talking with friends of friends at parties hadn't gotten her anywhere.

When it came to romance she had been a late bloomer, not

fully realizing until her second year at the community college in Monterey that she was attracted to women. It hadn't come as a complete surprise because the two dates she'd had with boys from her high school had fizzled in mutual awkwardness, and neither had aroused her sexual curiosity. Not so with Melissa, a classmate and off-and-on lover for two years. Melissa had been fascinating and experienced, and had shown Leo the pleasures of lesbian love, but she wasn't long on monogamy. Frustrated by Melissa's dalliances with other women, Leo finally broke things off. No one since had interested her sexually, but what she missed far more than sex was the sheer joy of having someone to care about.

Claudia stared back at her with gorgeous hazel eyes set deep above high cheekbones. Her light brown hair was fine, with soft curls that looked like they defied control. Overall, it was a gentle look that fit nicely with the calm yet commanding way she had handled her third graders.

"I'm going to call her," she told Madeline, reaching for the phone. She pressed the first six numbers and then took a deep breath. "No, I'm not."

Why was she being such a chicken? It wasn't rational at all to be stressing about calling someone to say her photos were ready. She did it twenty times a week. What was the worst that could happen? Her boyfriend could answer the phone and drill her with a million suspicious questions. It was just photos. Calling now would get this over with. Claudia could stop by for a quick tour and pick up her packet, then run off to spend the rest of the weekend with Romeo.

With new resolve, she dialed the number, and was about to hang up after six rings when a ragged female voice suddenly answered. An image of Claudia sweating amidst rumpled sheets filled her head as her mouth went dry.

"Hello? Is anyone there?"

"Uh, Claudia?" The wheels in her brain spun in search of what to say. "This is Leonora Westcott, from Westcott Photography." Way too formal. "Leo, from the school."

"Leo!" Claudia gasped for breath. "I almost didn't get to the phone. I was coming up from the laundry room when I heard it ring."

So she hadn't been in the middle of heated sex after all. "I'm sorry. I can call back if you're busy."

"No, no. I'm glad you called. What's up?"

Leo smiled with relief. "I just wanted to let you know your photos are ready if you want to stop by sometime and pick them up. Or I can mail them if you want to give me your address."

"You have them already? The paper I sent home with the kids said five weeks."

"Yeah, that's because theirs went off to the lab. I switched cameras for you, remember? If I'd used the one on the tripod, it would have lopped off the top of your head." Talking about her work relaxed her. "Anyway, I had some other shots on that roll"—a lie—"and I developed everything this morning."

"Am I funny-looking?"

"No, you look great." Madeline bobbed her head against the corner of the photo. "Even my cat likes them."

"Your cat, huh? I guess that's a good sign, but I was counting on something I could put on the door to scare burglars away."

Leo chuckled, enjoying Claudia's self-deprecating humor. It was hard to believe she didn't realize how attractive she was. "These won't work for that, I'm afraid. It's hard to scare somebody when you're wearing pink."

"So you think I should wear something else for Halloween?"

"I believe it usually calls for black and orange." She wondered if Sandy had followed through with an invitation to her party.

"I'm embarrassed to be caught at home doing laundry on a Sunday afternoon. You must think I have no life at all."

"Then that's two of us, because I'm sitting here on the couch with my cat. But I worked a wedding yesterday, so I don't feel so guilty about putting my feet up for a change."

"It sounds like you work all the time."

"Not really, just odd hours. No one gets married at eight

21

o'clock on a Monday morning." She leaned back on the couch and stretched her foot out to scratch Madeline's chin. This was exactly what she had hoped for, a casual conversation. No tests to pass, no one to impress.

"I was about to suggest that I come over this afternoon, but I don't want to ruin your day off. Why don't you tell me what day works and I'll stop by after school?"

The idea of seeing Claudia today stirred both excitement and anxiety. "This afternoon would be fine. Maybe we can get a bite to eat or something."

"Now you're talking. I'm so tired of take-out, but I hate to sit in a restaurant by myself."

Why would she be by herself? Where was the boyfriend? "Then come on over. I'll give you the nickel tour and we can walk down to Old Fisherman's Wharf. I have two customer parking spaces on the side of the house, so pull on around the corner. My Volvo will be there."

"I'm only about ten minutes away," Claudia said. "But I have to wait for my clothes to finish drying, or someone else will dump them on the floor of the laundry room. Is an hour from now okay?"

"Perfect." Just enough time to straighten up and grab a shower, but not enough to get herself worked up.

Leo paced the parlor, stopping occasionally to peek through the beveled glass that lined her front door. Everything was in order with five minutes to spare. Five minutes she would spend worrying whether she looked okay.

A quick check in the full-length mirror by the studio door helped to settle her doubts. The tips of her hair were still wet from her shower, leaving a damp ring along the collar of her gray T-shirt. Her black jeans fit snugly and her sneakers finished the casual look. Overall, she was satisfied. Not too dressy, not too sloppy.

A car slowed in front of her house and turned into her customer parking area. It wasn't just any car—it was a white

22

Nissan 300ZX and it looked brand new. Its top was open, the T-bar bisecting the cockpit.

From the side window she watched Claudia remove her headband and fluff her hair in the rearview mirror. Then she brushed her sweater, a light blue crewneck that was considerably dressier than Leo's T-shirt. Leo grew suddenly self-conscious when Claudia climbed from the car to reveal navy slacks and polished shoes. It was too late to run back upstairs to change. She could only hope Claudia wouldn't think her a slob.

Abandoning all pretense of nonchalance, she stepped outside as Claudia walked up the five stairs to the porch, her heels landing with a sharp click. Alligator boots. Expensive. "Glad you could make it."

Claudia eyed her up and down. "Damn, I was afraid I'd be too dressed up. I didn't know what you had in mind at the marina so I decided to play it safe."

"You look great. If it's any consolation, I had the same conversation with myself, but obviously it took me somewhere else." She couldn't resist brushing her fingers on Claudia's cashmere sweater. "It wouldn't have mattered anyway. I'm not sure I own anything this nice."

"Maybe we should just swap tops," Claudia said with a grin, briefly gripping the hem of her sweater. "I don't think we could trade pants. Mine would only come to your knees."

Leo chuckled as Claudia pushed past her into the circular parlor, which was the turret on the front left corner of the Queen Anne house.

"Wow, this is so cool! I love old houses. My grandmother's house in Cambria was just like this. It had all this elaborate woodwork and high ceilings. What I remember most was a whole bunch of tiny rooms."

"That's how this one used to be, but we've made a few changes over the years." She was proud of her home, which had been handed down from her grandfather to her father, and now to her. "I'm the third generation in this house. Except it isn't much of a house now...more like a studio with an apartment upstairs."

23

"Now that's what I call an easy commute. I wonder if I could get them to let me live over the school?"

Leo tipped her head in the direction of the parking area. "If I had a car like yours I wouldn't mind a commute. Those are some nice wheels."

"Yeah, I have sort of a weakness for sports cars. I'm just not a four-door kind of gal. You know what I mean?"

She nodded mindlessly, deciding it was rude to ask how a teaching intern could afford such a car. "I have to haul things when I go out on shoots, so I need to drive a station wagon."

"That Volvo? It looks like a classic."

"I don't know about that, unless it's just a polite way of saying 'old car.' It was my dad's."

Claudia studied the detail of the beveled glass that framed the door. "This is exquisite. They don't make houses like this anymore."

"Let me show you around." Leo gestured to the antique chairs and davenports. "This is technically a parlor but I use it as my waiting room in case my appointments get backed up."

"I love these antiques. Are they heirlooms?"

"Antiques...heirlooms." She tried her best to keep a straight face. "You sure have a lot of pretty words for my old junk."

Claudia's eyes went wide before she realized Leo was joking. Then she sneered. "You almost had me there. Show me more." She charged into the next room.

Leo caught up with her and scurried in front to show off her office. "This front part is where we used to have the studio but now it's where I do all the boring stuff, like ordering supplies and sending out bills." A large round table stacked with catalogs and tablets sat between the front window and a fireplace, and an L-shaped oak desk filled the far corner. Samples of her work—among them, family portraits, babies and brides—were mounted on all four walls.

The alligator boots clicked again on the worn hardwood floor as Claudia inspected the displays. "These are beautiful. I bet your customers love you."

24

"I don't know about love, but most of them appreciate what I can do."

"Does that mean you fixed my pointy chin?"

Leo was accustomed to dealing with her subjects' insecurities about their looks, many of them exaggerated. It was hard to imagine someone as attractive as Claudia being insecure about anything. "I bet you're the only one in the world who thinks you have a pointy chin," she said seriously. "You have a very beautiful face."

Claudia's face turned a light shade of pink. "Thank you. I didn't mean to go fishing for compliments. It's just that growing up all I heard was how much I looked like my father. He's a handsome man, but what girl wants to be handsome? Maybe if I had a goatee like his…and a little moustache."

Leo laughed and shook her head. "I can give you both of those if that's what you really want."

"Now you're scaring me." She pointed to the next room. "What's in there?"

"Right, the tour. That was the parlor, this was the formal sitting room, and this in here"—she turned on the lights to her studio—"used to be the dining room. For obvious reasons it's now my favorite room in the house."

Claudia walked to the center of the room and twirled slowly, studying the slate-gray backdrop, the modeling lamps, the reflector umbrellas and the camera tripod. A stylist chair sat before a mirror in the corner. "There's hardly anything in here."

Leo looked around the room and shrugged. "I have different props and backdrops depending on who I'm shooting, but I always like to start with the bare minimum."

"Like an artist with a blank canvas."

"I guess. My dad always taught me that good portraits were mostly about light and composition. I have everything I need for that."

"Is your dad retired?"

"No, he died about six years ago. Liver cancer. We never even knew he was sick until it was too late."

Clearly sensing her melancholy, Claudia patted her forearm. "I'm sorry. I bet you were close."

"We were. But I feel like he's with me whenever I'm working."

"That's sweet. So what about your mom? Where is she?"

"She moved to Modesto to live with her sister, my Aunt Ellie. They were always close, and…well, I can't really say the same about Mom and me. She worked as a receptionist at a doctor's office, so I didn't see her as much as I saw Dad. After he died, she said she always felt like she was on the outside of the circle because we talked all the time about the studio."

"Do you see her now?"

"She visits once or twice a year, and I try to see her on holidays. We love each other but we're not all that close." They fell silent for a long moment. Then Leo cleared her throat and gestured toward a doorway. "That's the kitchen through there. And believe it or not, it's actually still a kitchen."

"Look at these cabinets!" Claudia exclaimed, eyeing the windowpane facings. "I bet they're the originals."

"Probably. They've been here as long as I have." Leo pointed toward a staircase by the back door. No one had ever asked to see her darkroom, and only a handful of friends had visited her apartment upstairs. "Downstairs is the darkroom, and upstairs is where I live. Do you want to see those?"

"Are you kidding? I want to see everything. I would have loved growing up in a house like this. We moved at least six times, always because Mom wanted something bigger and better. They all felt the same to me—empty and bland, no character at all."

"If there's one thing this house has, it's character," Leo said. "Especially when the roof leaks or the bathtub backs up." She flipped the light switch and started down the stairs. "I ran the exhaust fan for an hour after I did your pictures, so it shouldn't smell too bad. Still, we probably ought not stay too long unless we put on masks."

Claudia chuckled. "You only promised the nickel tour, so maybe just a penny or two down here."

26

Leo guided her into the darkroom, where one wall was lined with a sink and developing trays and the other with shelves of equipment and supplies. She indicated her main tool, the enlarger, which was mounted on a counter in between. "I don't use this room much, to tell you the truth. Most of my film goes out to the lab. I do some touch-up with the airbrush once in a while, especially for glamour shots."

"I'm surprised *this* isn't your favorite room."

"No, the studio is where the real fun is. And if I don't do that part right, I don't have a whole lot to work with down here." She pulled the door shut behind her as they walked out. "That just leaves the upstairs, which, I have to warn you, isn't as neat as the rest of the house."

"Will I get to meet your feline photo critic?"

"Madeline? That depends. Some days she's bashful, other days she's your best friend."

They climbed two flights of stairs to emerge on the upper landing, which branched off into four rooms. She started the tour in the back corner, where her double bed nearly filled the room.

"I've been sleeping in this room since I left the crib, but it seemed so much bigger back then. Maybe because I used to have a twin bed."

"This is lovely, Leo," Claudia said, running her hands over the well-worn blue and yellow handmade quilt folded across the bottom of the bed. "It looks so comfortable. I don't know how you ever get up in the morning."

"That's what Madeline's good for."

"Madeline! Where is she?" Claudia spun in the doorway and shot her a grin. "I bet you're wondering what you've gotten yourself into, letting some crazy woman roam through your whole house."

Leo had to admit it was unusual to allow someone she had only just met so deep into her personal space. But Claudia's fascination with the house was charming and an easy subject to talk about as they got acquainted. "It never occurred to me you might be crazy. I thought you just liked old houses."

Claudia smirked and leaned through the next doorway. "Guest room?"

"Correct, except that I haven't had any guests since my mother visited last Christmas. I hate to think how much dust is under that bed." She gestured across the hall. "The bathroom, which we all shared because it was the only one in the house until we added a powder room off the kitchen. Now for what used to be my parents' room."

They walked into her den, a circular room that comprised the second floor of the turret. The corner by the window was set up as a reading nook, with a Scandinavian recliner and gooseneck lamp. Across the room a tan leather couch faced a coffee table and entertainment center made of teak.

"This looks so homey. Except that I haven't seen your cat yet."

Leo nodded in the direction of her television cabinet where Madeline looked down on them with her usual curiosity. "Check out the highest point in the room."

"Aw, she's adorable."

"She knows. I have to keep the kitchen door closed or she'll come into the studio to try to get in everyone's picture." She picked up the packet on the coffee table. "Speaking of pictures…"

Claudia's face lit up as she thumbed through the three poses. "Damn, I look good. What was I so happy about?"

"Maybe it was twenty-five kids trying to get you to laugh."

She studied the photos again. "That was a fun day. It was my first full day in charge of the class and when the last bell rang Sandy said she never wanted them back."

Leo had decided to mention her friendship with Sandy and Maria over dinner, just in case Sandy hadn't made it clear. That way she could let Claudia know she too was gay. "You looked like you were enjoying yourself that day. I take a lot of school pictures. Most of the teachers I see look miserable."

"Yeah, maybe I haven't been there long enough to get cranky. My grandmother that I told you about, the one with the Victorian house…she was a teacher for forty-some years. I've always wanted

28

to be just like her."

That certainly explained why Claudia seemed like such a natural in front of her class. "I don't think I could be around kids that much, but I have a lot of respect for people that do."

"Grandma always said we were meant to do something worthwhile with our lives. But it's a battle I've had with my mom since junior high."

"What sort of career did she have in mind for you?"

"She wanted me to major in art history or romance languages, something I wouldn't actually use except to impress the women in my bridge club. That's her idea of a worthwhile life. Fortunately, my dad is more like my grandma. He's a pediatrician and he loves kids."

Leo was glad Claudia had taken after her father. She had seen her share of social climbers in the studio, both men and women who hired her services but couldn't be bothered to be friendly, as though she were only a minnow in society's food chain. In those cases it worked best to maintain an air of professional detachment, since she wouldn't get a word of praise for her work, just a check to cover her fee. From those kinds of people the check was enough.

"I think you made the right choice," Leo said. "Your students do too because they obviously love you."

Claudia grinned. "It's mutual. I just hope I can find a job for next spring. It's hard to get on board in the middle of the year, but I'm graduating in December."

"Maybe something will open up." Leo grabbed her wallet from the coffee table. "If you're finished rummaging through my house, why don't we go grab a bite? You like Isabella's?"

"Never been."

"Pasta and seafood."

"My two favorites at the same table. Who could ask for more than that?"

As they turned the corner at the top of the stairs they dodged the thin rope that hung from a door in the ceiling.

"You have an attic?"

"Yeah, it's where I hide all my junk. Don't tell me you want to go up there too."

"I do, but not today. Now that you mentioned food I'm ready to eat."

There was much to do in the attic to make it presentable, but Leo was already turning over her schedule for when she might start. Getting it cleaned out was a built-in excuse for having Claudia come back for another visit.

Chapter 5

Their table on the rail afforded a full view of the marina, which was bustling with activity on the docks as boaters cleaned and secured their craft after a beautiful day on the water. A crisp breeze rippled the tablecloth, but both of them were prepared for the cool California night. Leo had donned her brown leather bomber jacket and Claudia had plucked a tweed blazer from her car when she dropped off her packet of photos. A waiter brought their drinks, a chardonnay for Claudia and a Black Russian for Leo.

"This sure beats doing laundry," Claudia said, raising her glass in a toast. "I've been in Monterey since August and this is my first time at the wharf."

"So you aren't from around here?"

"My folks live in Cambria down the coast near San Simeon."

"Where the Hearst Castle is?"

"Right, and to hear my mother tell it, we're neighbors," she said, rolling her eyes. She was relieved that Leo had loosened up during the walk down to the wharf. The shyness that Sandy had described wasn't evident during the house tour, though she had indeed seemed a bit nervous. "I ended up here because I went to school at UC-Santa Cruz. They try to place all the teaching interns as close as possible so they can drop in unannounced and watch from the back of the room. Very unnerving."

"Melrose seems like a pretty good place to teach. You could have done a lot worse."

"You're telling me. And I couldn't have asked for a better supervising teacher than Sandy Irwin. I was so lucky to get someone who wasn't jaded and grouchy all the time. Can you imagine if I'd been paired with Betty Tyler? The kids would be schizophrenic, what with my positive reinforcement one minute and her harping at them the next." She wondered if Sandy had mentioned her invitation to the Halloween party. "How long have you known Sandy?"

Leo squinted as if counting in her head. "About four years. I ran into her at a party and recognized her from doing the school pictures at Melrose. I already knew her…uh, her friend Maria because she's a photographer too."

"Right, I've seen some of Maria's work. She's amazing." It was interesting that Leo had stumbled over how to describe Sandy's partner.

They put their conversation on hold to order dinner.

Once the waiter left Claudia continued, "By the way, Sandy invited me to their Halloween party next weekend. She said you'd probably be there. Is that right?"

"I…yeah, sure. I go every year."

The quake in Leo's voice suggested she was dancing around the topic of being gay, probably because Claudia hadn't yet made it clear she was cool with having lesbian friends. "She warned me I'd probably be the only straight person there but I told her it didn't matter. I just like to be around interesting people, and

I'm not the kind of person to go judging somebody or blabbing their secrets." ·

Leo nodded and offered a faint smile. "Good to know. Not everyone feels that way."

"That's ridiculous if you ask me. What people do with their personal lives is nobody's business." She waved a hand dismissively. "I had a gay roommate my freshman year. I even went with her a couple of times to a gay bar." In fact, she had danced with several of the women there when they asked, but not when the music was slow and romantic.

"Wow, I have lesbian friends who wouldn't dare go out to a gay bar. They're afraid of people finding out."

"Yeah, that's what Sandy said. She doesn't think she'd get fired after fifteen years in the classroom, but she'd still have to put up with parents getting bent out of shape about it. And then she'd end up with a big chip on her shoulder, worrying that every single criticism on her evaluation form was really about who she slept with, not what kind of teacher she was. Somebody who was open about being gay probably couldn't get hired at all."

"I'm sure you're right. I'd probably lose a few of my customers if they knew, maybe even the school contract. Can't have those deviants around little children, you know?"

Claudia swirled the last of her wine in her glass, noticing that Leo's green eyes had gone dark in the waning sunlight. With the black hair that flopped on her brow, it was an amazingly dramatic look that most women only got with makeup. "Did your folks know about you?"

"Good question. I never really talked to my dad, but I had started seeing Melissa when he first got sick. I told my mom about a year later and she said she wasn't surprised, so I figured Dad probably knew too." Leo drained her drink and sucked an ice cube into her cheek. "I wish I had talked to him, but I was just figuring things out for myself. I think he would have been okay with it though."

"I'm sure he would have been. It sounds like you two were really close." Based on what Sandy had said about Leo keeping her personal life to herself, she had a feeling she had just heard something few others knew. "Whatever happened to Melissa?"

Leo shrugged. "It ran its course. She didn't really want to be tied down, which is another way of saying she wanted to see other people too. I tried to be blasé about it, but I guess I'm not cut out for the casual romance thing. After I realized she'd been with somebody else…" She shuddered and shook her head. "It wasn't special anymore. I figure either it's serious, or why bother at all?"

"I hear you."

On Leo's signal, the waiter dropped off another round of drinks. When he disappeared, she pointed to Claudia's diamond ring. "It looks like you're serious. When's your wedding?"

"Who knows? We can't even figure out how to be in the same country for more than a week or two at a time."

"You lost me."

"My fiancé, Mike. His family owns this enormous international development corporation. And unlike my family, they really are neighbors of Hearst." She lapsed into an exaggerated haughty tone. "In fact, Mike's grandfather used to go to parties at the Hearst Castle with all the Hollywood stars. What my mother wouldn't give just to live in their guest house. They have this gigantic mansion right on the ocean in San Simeon."

"I didn't realize I was in the presence of such a celebrity."

Claudia swatted her hand playfully. "Believe me, there's nothing about my life that says celebrity. I'm about as plain as they get. Anyway, Mike's in Taiwan right now building a mall. I think this ring was his way of apologizing for being gone so long."

"It must be tough being so far apart."

Lots of people said that, and they probably found her response peculiar. "You know, it's really not so bad right now. I need to be concentrating on finishing my degree and that's a whole lot easier with him halfway around the world. And he needs to concentrate on finishing his project too, so he can come home for good. He's only been back to the states about six times in the last year and a half. And before Taiwan he was in Bangkok for two years."

"Wow, it's a wonder you ever met."

"I've known him forever. Our mothers play bridge together, and they're both on some committee for historic preservation." She leaned over and lowered her voice. "My dad says their main objective is keeping the so-called *wrong people* out of the county. It makes him nuts the way they go on about the Mexicans or the Vietnamese. Anyway, the first time I saw Mike was at a Christmas party at the country club when I was thirteen years old. He was an absolute dreamboat, home from college at Southern Cal, all suave and handsome. You know how it is when you're thirteen years old."

Leo scrunched her lips and tipped her head thoughtfully. "Does having a crush on Susan Saint James count?"

"Same thing," she said with a chuckle, appreciating that Leo trusted her enough to make a joke about her sexuality. "I liked her too, but I wanted to be like Lindsay Wagner."

"Didn't we all? But I interrupted your story. You met Mike when you were thirteen?"

"Right, and I fell in love at first sight, but I didn't see him again for six years. Same Christmas party, but then it was my turn to be coming home from college. The first thing he said was 'Let's get out of here,' and we did. We ended up spending the entire holiday together and then I went to Bangkok for spring break and again for the whole summer."

"Sounds like you got swept off your feet."

"That's what it felt like. Never in my life had anything hit me like that. Mike has this uncanny ability to focus. Not like you focus…because you *really* focus." They both chuckled. "When he's working, that's all he thinks about. But when he turns his attention to me…wow. It's like I'm the only person in the whole universe. It's such a powerful feeling."

"Sounds like love."

"I guess that's how I knew Mike was different from all the rest."

Leo raised her glass in another toast. "Good for you. How

35

long is he going to be overseas?"

Claudia smirked. "Believe me, we've had that conversation more than once and it hasn't been pretty. At first he said he just needed to get some on-site experience. It was only supposed to be that job in Bangkok, but then his father had a small stroke last year. That worries me because Mike and his dad are so much alike. They're both big and barrel-chested, and they have the exact same personality. Anyway, now he says he'll have to shoulder more of the load. In other words, he'll probably work abroad a couple more years. But I figure that gives me time to get settled into a job, and it gives my mother time to plan the most ostentatious wedding imaginable."

"Maybe you'll let me shoot it for you—at the friend's discount."

"Thanks, but don't count on it. If Mike has his way, we'll elope. In fact, if it were up to him we'd do it as soon as I got out of school."

"So soon?"

"If there's one thing he hates, it's a drawn-out spectacle. Once he makes up his mind, he's ready to do it. Married? Check. Kids? Three. He's the same way about everything."

The waiter returned with their pasta and the conversation turned to food. It was clear to Claudia they had crossed a threshold toward friendship when they sampled each other's entrée, even sharing a fork to polish off a piece of cheesecake. After a spirited protest she allowed Leo to pick up the check, but only after insisting they would go out again soon at her treat.

"If we walk to the end of the boat dock, we can catch the sunset," Leo suggested as she zipped her jacket against the stiff breeze.

Claudia looped the elastic headband around her hair and turned up her collar. "This is so beautiful. I was supposed to be doing my lesson plans today. I didn't know I was going to play hooky with you."

"So you're saying I'm a bad influence."

She followed Leo's gaze to a cluster of seagulls that seemed to hang in the air behind a sailboat. "I wouldn't call it bad at all. Gosh, if I lived as close to this wharf as you, I'd be out here all the time."

"It's one of my favorite places. When I was a teenager I used to walk this dock every day dreaming about my life and making all the plans in my head for how I would get there. I don't know why I stopped coming."

"Maybe because your dreams are coming true now."

Leo shrugged. "Or maybe because I know some of them won't ever come true. I used to walk out here and think about how I'd build the business with my dad. Instead I ended up having to scale back to just the jobs I could manage."

"Like school pictures?"

"And sports teams, weddings…studio work. A lot of it's pretty mundane. I always wanted to branch out into some of the high-art stuff like magazine work, but I don't have time to do that on my own because it means I'd have to go out there and sell myself to a whole new audience. I'm too busy just trying to pay the bills." She sighed. "Besides, that kind of work calls for skills and connections I don't really have. I was hoping for an apprenticeship or something, but I can't do that and leave my studio sitting empty."

"It sounds like your whole world was turned upside down when your dad died." She had nearly come undone when her beloved grandmother died, but that didn't compare to losing a parent.

"That's what it felt like, but at least he trained me well to do what I do, and he left the studio in good shape. It could have been a whole lot worse."

"Still, it says a lot about you that you held on." Claudia was beginning to wonder if Sandy was mistaken about Leo being shy. She had talked about her first girlfriend, her mother's feelings of exclusion from the family and now her father's death, all in what Claudia considered very personal terms. Maybe these were just surface emotions she shared with everyone, but Claudia felt privileged to see them.

37

It was fascinating that someone so young had taken on the burdens of a business while dealing with the loss of her father. She couldn't name a single friend from home or college who had proven so much—with the exception of Mike, who was only twenty-nine and already heading up a whole division of his family's company in Asia. Her recognition of the similarities between Mike and Leo made her realize how much she valued maturity and self-sufficiency. It was one of the main reasons she wanted to teach for a year or so before getting married—to prove she could stand on her own two feet.

They reached the end of the wharf, where Leo indicated a wooden staircase leading down to the marina. "I'd suggest walking out to the end, but with all these people spraying off their boats, we might get wet."

"This is far enough for me." They leaned over the rail to watch the activity below. "So tell me about this party. Do people go in costume?"

"Not me, but Sandy keeps a basket of masks by the door. Anyone not wearing a costume has to put one on when they come in."

"That sounds fair. I have a biker chick costume I wore to a party a couple of years ago. The only problem was that in Santa Cruz nobody realized it was a costume."

Leo laughed. "You in a biker outfit? That I've got to see."

"You want to ride together? I can swing by and pick you up."

"Sure."

Claudia caught herself grinning to realize she had just asked a lesbian for a date. That would have raised some eyebrows back in San Simeon, but no way was she going to tell Mike she was going to a lesbian party. He would surely disapprove.

They turned back after sunset, strolling silently across the wooden planks of the marina, then past the storefronts on the wharf. It was a comfortable quiet because Claudia felt satisfied she had wrung as much as possible from Leo in one day. They would see each other again in only a week and she might probe

38

to see how Leo balanced her professional life with her personal one. Of course, that would mean Leo would have to open up more about the personal side.

When they reached the old house, they stopped at the end of the sidewalk.

"Would you like to come in again? I can fix some tea…or I'm sure I have some coffee somewhere if that's what you like."

"Thanks, but I need to head home. Mike always calls on Sunday night. How about a rain check?"

"Absolutely. Stop by anytime you feel like walking back down to the wharf. If I'm not here, you can park around on the side and save a few quarters on the parking meters."

"Better be careful what you ask for. I could make a habit of this." She rounded the corner of the house and looked over her shoulder to find Leo still standing in the same spot watching her retreat. She smiled and waved goodbye. "Next Saturday for sure. Around seven."

Chapter 6

Present Day

Leo's gut tightened when the door to the bridal suite opened behind her, and she glanced quickly over her shoulder with anticipation. A thin woman bent low to drop a small prissy dog onto the carpeted floor.

Lon leaned into Eva and covered her mouth with her fingers. "What kind of idiot brings a dog to a wedding?"

"Aunt Deborah! How nice you look," the bride said animatedly, holding a hand over her brow as she peered from the bright terrace into the room.

Nice wouldn't have been the word Leo might have chosen. More like anorexic. Her gold silk gown was probably a size two, and its low-cut collar revealed razor-like collarbones and a prominent sternum.

"Has your grandmother been here?" the woman queried, not even acknowledging the compliment.

"Not yet, but she's supposed to come any minute for her sitting. Do you want to come be in our picture?"

"I'll just wait here." She poised primly on the sofa and scooped the dog into her lap.

Leo wanted badly to snap a candid photo just to preserve the incongruous scene. She had photographed a recording artist's wedding several years ago in Healdsburg in which four golden retrievers had run free, but that ceremony had been held at a family winery, not a five-star resort.

"Girls, I have all the formal poses I need. Let's take a few just for fun. What do you say?"

"Absolutely! Definitely!" they answered in unison.

She walked in front of them holding out a plastic nylon bag. "Reach in here and grab something."

One by one the girls donned frivolous disguises, including oversized sunglasses, a moustache and beard, animal ears, eye patches, a Toucan bird beak, and for the elegant bride, a pig snout. They could barely contain their giggles as Leo positioned them for the final shot.

Suddenly Eva's face broke into a broad smile. "Grandmother, what a beautiful dress!"

The bridesmaids murmured their agreement, and Leo stiffened to realize someone had slipped into the room without her noticing. She had the whole day scripted in her head and didn't want any surprises.

The new arrival was Marjorie Pettigrew, the matriarch of the family and the one who was footing the bill for the elaborate wedding. Without turning to acknowledge her, Leo forced herself back into work mode, peering through her viewfinder to frame the portrait. *Light and composition.* "All right, ladies. Show me some attitude."

On cue the women assumed looks of playful defiance behind their newly-donned masks.

Leo snapped the first shot from the camera on her tripod and the second from a squatting position that caused her forty-nine-year-old knees to scream in protest. "That one's a keeper," she announced.

Mrs. Pettigrew emerged onto the terrace, twenty minutes late for her photo session, and tugging uncomfortably on the seams of a deep blue dress that might have been one size too small. Her gray hair was teased high, accentuating an elaborate sapphire necklace and dangling earrings that Leo found gaudy. "Take off those silly faces and get to your positions in the Miramar Room," she barked. "It's time to order the processional and put an end to this childishness. A wedding is supposed to be a serious occasion."

"No, it isn't, Grandmother," the bride said with gentle reproach. "It's a celebration. Besides, Todd and I will have years to be serious. We want everyone to have fun today."

The elder woman harrumphed with undisguised condescension as the bridesmaids scooted from the suite like children being scolded for their foray into frivolity.

Every wedding had a Marjorie Pettigrew, Leo thought, someone for whom the event itself was far more important than the occasion. Her attention to the festivities likely had less to do with honoring the solemnity of her granddaughter's vows of loving commitment than with putting on the most ostentatious spectacle imaginable. From the looks of things, she had succeeded.

Chapter 7

October 1986

The elderly gentleman took his wife's hand and looped it through the crook of his elbow as he guided her into the studio. "Let's follow Miss Westcott so we can have our picture made. Won't that be nice?"

"Do I look all right?" Claire Compton anxiously looked first for her husband's approval and then for Leo's, as she had done twice already in the short time since they had arrived for their appointment. It wasn't vanity that prompted her to repeatedly seek assurance, Leo knew. Dementia had stolen Mrs. Compton's discretion.

"You look lovely, darling," Melvin Compton said patiently for the third time, patting her hand with unbridled affection.

Their oldest son, Randall, had called Leo a week earlier to schedule the portrait as a commemoration of his parents' fiftieth wedding anniversary. His voice had broken as he explained the

43

importance of capturing their devotion on film one last time before his mother's condition deteriorated further. Leo had promised a photo he and his brothers would cherish.

Since Melvin towered over his wife, Leo seated him on a padded stool and positioned Claire behind him with her hands on his shoulders. As she framed the shot through her lens, she recalled her parents' similar pose in their last portrait together, which she had taken just weeks before her father died. In that instant, she felt Randall's heartbreak acutely.

"How does this feel? Is it comfortable for both of you?" she asked.

Melvin gave her a wistful look. "I think it's fitting. Claire's been standing behind me all my life."

The woman's brow furrowed with confusion, a sure sign she hadn't understood her husband's metaphor.

Leo's usual approach to taking portraits was to build a rapport through casual conversation, whatever might distract from the formality of the session. Her goal was to elicit candid expressions that family and friends would recognize as genuine, and the only way to do that was to get her subjects past their instinct to pose for the camera. That proved difficult with the Comptons because of Claire's anxiety about the unfamiliar setting. Her uncertainty seemed to grow as Leo probed for information about her hobbies and interests, anything that might help her relax. After ten minutes, Leo had yet to coax an authentic expression.

"Bear with me while I make a few adjustments," she said, tilting one of the reflective umbrellas to cast more light onto the scene. If she increased her shutter speed and took multiple photos in a span of several seconds, she had a greater chance of capturing a fleeting smile. "I had a nice chat with Randall the other day. He's very excited about seeing this portrait."

At the mention of her son's name, Claire's face lit up and Leo realized she was onto something.

"He told me he had two brothers, but I don't remember their names."

Claire struggled for several seconds, her face contorting as her mind processed the question. Then she blurted her response. "Randall, Alan and Greg," she said by rote. "Randall's the oldest, then Alan. My Greg is the baby."

"Some baby," Melvin added with a chuckle. "He's taller than any of us."

"Goodness, he grew so fast. I couldn't keep that boy in shoes."

Leo held up a finger next to the camera, cueing Melvin to look her way. She already had Claire's attention. "I bet holidays are fun when they all come to visit." She snapped off two quick photos of the now-smiling couple.

"I always fix a big turkey, and to this day those boys fight over the drumsticks. Greg used to say I needed to buy a three-legged turkey."

That was the pose she wanted—both of her subjects looking directly into her lens, grinning broadly as they recalled their happiest of days. After a dozen rapid-fire shots they were finished.

Claire continued her stories of her boys as Leo walked them to their car. Melvin helped his wife into the passenger side and closed the door, and as he walked past Leo to the driver's side and extended his thanks, she noted a cheerful lilt in his voice that hadn't been there when they first arrived. She prided herself on the quality of her photographs, but it was the emotional response to her work that was most rewarding. The Comptons would treasure today's portrait forever.

No sooner had Melvin backed out of the parking space than a familiar car appeared to take its place. Patty Clemons, still in her work attire of dress slacks and pumps, emerged from her black Mustang hatchback with a mischievous grin. "I brought you something," she announced.

"I'm afraid to ask." Leo cast an uneasy look, but it was mostly for show. Patty was one of the few people who dropped by on a whim, and Leo had come to enjoy her company. She could do without the flirting, but her consistent approach to rebuffing Patty's romantic overtures—direct but playful—had paid off in friendship.

Tall and muscular, Patty effortlessly hoisted an enormous pumpkin from her trunk. "I hope you appreciate this because my car's going to smell like pumpkin for a month." She spun her creation around to reveal diamond-shaped eyes and a toothy snarl. "I don't get that many trick-or-treaters at my condo, so I thought this would look better on your front porch."

"Are you kidding? It's fantastic!" Leo hurried over to muss Patty's spiked red hair and take the jack-o'-lantern from her arms.

"Yeah, I know. I keep trying to convince you of my many talents but you still won't give me the time of day." She climbed the porch and took a seat on the wooden swing.

As usual, Leo ignored Patty's backhanded overture. She set the pumpkin on her top step and reached inside the front door to flip on the light switch. It was only half past five, but the recent change to daylight saving time made it seem later that that. "You want dinner? I made a big pot of chili last night."

"No, I'm on my way to my mother's for lasagna and I stopped by for some moral support." Patty and her mother tangled over everything, from politics to baseball.

"When are you going to learn to stop arguing with her?"

"I try to bite my tongue but you know how she pushes my buttons. Why don't you come with me? She likes you."

"No, thanks. The last time I went over there, you two ended up throwing food at each other."

"She started it," Patty said petulantly.

Leo chortled at the childish reply, which she recognized as Patty's sense of humor on display. If there was one thing she loved about Patty, it was that she always made her laugh. "You're just like her. That's why she bugs you so much." She plucked a broom from the corner and started pushing oak leaves off the porch.

"Am not." Patty lifted her feet so Leo could sweep under them.

Despite Patty's refusal to take no for an answer on the romantic front, Leo couldn't help but like her. Her relentless

46

flirtation had been annoying four years ago when it started, but when Leo overheard her making similar overtures to other single women, she realized the cocky manner was nothing but a false bravado that masked her insecurity. Patty was a hopeless romantic who wanted someone to take all the things she had to offer, and whoever stepped forward first would have her undying devotion. It was more than Leo could handle—the idea was almost suffocating—but she was sure the right woman was out there for Patty.

A horn tooted as a white sports car raced by. Leo's stomach fluttered when she recognized the driver, and then roiled in anticipation of Patty's curiosity.

"Who was that?"

"Just somebody I know."

"I figured that much. Does she have a name?"

Leo thought ahead to the Halloween party and realized there was no point in stonewalling. It wasn't as if she could keep her arrival with Claudia a secret. "Her name is Claudia Galloway. She's Sandy's intern. I met her last week when I was out at Melrose taking pictures."

"Glad you mentioned Sandy. I was meaning to ask you if you wanted to go with me to their party on Saturday. Then you can drink too much and maybe I'll get lucky."

Leo rolled her eyes, thinking she would never drink that much. "You're just so damned charming sometimes."

"I know. It's unbelievable that you manage to resist me."

Slumping into the rocker across from the swing, she took a playful swipe at Patty's swinging foot. "And yet I do. It so happens I've already made plans to ride with Claudia."

Patty's foot dropped and skidded across the floor as she brought the swing to a stop. "So you have a date with the woman that just drove by here?"

"It isn't a date. Claudia isn't even gay. She's just a nice—"

"If she isn't gay, why is she coming to Sandy's party? And why is she coming with you?"

"Sandy invited her because they're friends and she's cool with everything. And she's coming with me because she won't know anybody else there."

Patty eyed her skeptically. "And we're supposed to believe she's not gay?"

"She has a fiancé."

"Whoop-de-doo. I bet he's light in the loafers."

"I'd take that bet. He's off managing some gigantic construction project in Asia. That's why she's hanging out here by herself. Plus she's finishing school." Patty's conjectures were usually entertaining if not insightful, but not where Claudia was concerned. "She told me all about the fiancé on Sunday when she stopped by to pick up her photos. They'll probably get married when she finishes her internship and finds a job." She added the last part to bolster her point that Claudia wasn't a closet case, even though Claudia had intimated that she might want to teach for a couple of years before getting married.

Patty folded her arms across her chest indignantly and smirked. "He's probably just a beard. I'll ask her myself."

Leo gave her a scolding look. "You'd better behave yourself. She might think you're serious."

"Who says I'm not? You know how I feel about curious girls."

"She isn't curious. She's just nice."

"And you'd rather go with her than me?"

She hated it when Patty forced her into a blunt reply, and she refused to rise to the bait.

"You always shoot me down, Leo." It came out as a simple statement, neither angry nor whiny. "I was starting to take it personally, but then I realized that you don't ever date anybody. They fix you up, you go out one time and that's it. What's up with that? Don't you like girls?"

"You're kidding, right?" It unnerved her to have someone speculating on her sexual credentials, but it just so happened she had been thinking about the subject of dating since her dinner with Claudia. Besides, it wasn't as if she had rejected hoards of women. It had been only two blind dates, each as a favor to Sandy,

48

who wanted someone to make her new friends feel welcome. "I have a lot more important things on my plate right now than going out. I've finally gotten this business sorted out and I have to stay on top of it."

Patty rolled her eyes. "That was a good answer four years ago, but it's no excuse for putting your whole life on hold forever. We all have responsibilities at work. Hell, I'm responsible for computer systems worth millions of dollars but you don't see me holing up in my house."

"I don't hole up in my house. I go to parties. I go out with friends."

"Those are just little guarded pieces that you dole out to people. Let somebody in there," she said sternly. "Like me, for instance. If you keep blowing me off, I'm going to start going out with Joyce."

Leo nodded thoughtfully. "I like Joyce."

A thumping on the window behind her saved the day.

"Madeline's hungry and so am I. Sure you don't want something to eat?"

Patty slapped her knees and stood. "Damn cat. You trained her to rescue you from prickly conversations, didn't you?"

"I don't know what you're talking about."

She tapped the top of the jack-o'-lantern as she started down the steps. "If you put a candle in here, Claudia can see it from the street when she drives by your house and toots the horn because she isn't gay. I'll see you Saturday."

Leo chuckled as she went inside, where Madeline wound through her legs, meowing insistently. "Good timing, Madeline. Extra treats for you tonight."

Leo gave a yank on the rope and stepped aside as the attic staircase unfolded. She hadn't been up there since last spring when an antique dealer bought the handful of old cameras she had saved since childhood. She had resisted his bid a year earlier, but needed a few extra bucks when Maria offered a barely-used Mamiya medium-format camera for half the usual price. It was too good a deal to pass up.

Letting go of her collection had been easier than she thought. Her father had never been sentimental about the tools of his trade, always upgrading to the best camera he could afford. His favorite camera—if he had one—was whatever made the studio more efficient and competitive, as long as it produced top-quality portraits. Still, Leo had been unable to part with his Bronica EC-TL, the last camera he had used. It was solid, and it yielded reliable portraits.

Musty air wafted from above as she climbed the stairs. When she was fourteen she had asked to move her bedroom into the attic so she could have more space and privacy, but the unfinished floors and walls had been a deal breaker for her mother. Leo had since added insulation to keep her heating and cooling bills in check, and put down plywood sheets to the edges of the sloping walls. It needed a lot more work to be livable, but at least it was usable for storage.

Two boxes sat near the top of the steps, some of her father's files she no longer needed but couldn't bring herself to discard. Bit by bit, odds and ends from the studio that had belonged to him had found their way into the attic—outdated backdrops, a female mannequin, broken tripods, lights and reflector umbrellas, appointment books…even the worn out leather satchel he had carried for almost thirty years. It wasn't that she ever thought she would use these things. She just didn't want to be the one to throw them away.

"Get over it, Leo," she said, her voice rebounding off the bare walls and floor. She had promised Claudia a tour of the attic, so it was time to deal with this mess. Now that she had crossed the threshold of sentimentality by selling the cameras, it shouldn't be so hard to get rid of the other items.

The Christmas decorations were another matter entirely. Leo usually put up a tree for her customers, but she felt claustrophobic when holiday knick-knacks filled her house. She had tried to talk her mother into taking those with her to Modesto, but her mother hadn't wanted to impose more than necessary on her sister. At least she had taken all of her bedroom and dining room furniture, which had paved the way for Leo to move everything but her kitchen to the second floor. She liked having a den to herself now, though it didn't solve the problem of her tiny bedroom.

Madeline appeared through the opening and immediately set about exploring the new environs.

"How about it, Madeline? You want me to move your bed up here?"

The plywood wobbled under her feet as she walked the length of the room and peered out a small window onto the courtyard behind the kitchen. Her mother had grown herbs and spices back there, but Leo had let them go to weeds. She had no time to tend a garden, and besides, she couldn't tell one plant from another unless it was labeled in a package at the grocery store.

The other end of the long room was the main reason she had wanted to claim this space for her own years ago, and why she still toyed with the idea of finishing the room. From the third story of the turret she could see the ocean. Not only that, the attic was filled with natural light all afternoon, something she missed in her own bedroom because her small window faced south.

One of these days she would remodel the attic in grand style—hardwood floors, ceiling planks and a staircase from the hallway on the second floor. The window over the courtyard would shine into an enormous master bath, with a walk-in shower and cabinets to hide all her junk. But those dreams would have to wait until she could afford to put money into something besides her business.

Chapter 8

Present Day

Leo collected her props and stowed them in the corner of the terrace with her camera bag. Fun was wasted on the likes of Marjorie Pettigrew and her skeletal daughter Deborah. The sooner she wrapped up this round of photos, the better for everyone.

Deborah set her terrier aside and stood to brush her dress. Versace would be spinning in his grave to see his label decorated in animal fur, Leo thought.

"Mother, we need to talk about the wheelchair," Deborah said. "Chantal thinks we should put Daddy on the left side so he won't be in the way. I told her no, that he wouldn't be able to see from there."

"Nonsense. Your father can barely see as it is." Mrs. Pettigrew made a dramatic display of pulling on a pair of long white gloves. "You can sit on the end beside him."

"I don't mind if Grandfather sits in the center aisle," Eva ventured.

"No, it's settled. People will be watching you walk down the aisle. They don't want to see some old man drooling. Chantal's absolutely right."

So far, Leo had managed to avoid Chantal, the wedding director from LA whose actual name was probably Linda or Susan. The last thing she wanted was someone looking over her shoulder telling her what to do.

It was hard to believe Marjorie and Eva Pettigrew were related. There was no physical resemblance beyond their blue eyes and fair skin. Marjorie was tall and rotund, while Eva was petite and slender, with an angular chin and high cheekbones.

"Mrs. Pettigrew, why don't you join your granddaughter?" Leo suggested politely. "A photo of the two of you out here on the terrace would make a wonderful keepsake."

"She's right," Eva said. "The two of us in our beautiful dresses."

"I see not everyone got the memo that this was a formal affair," the woman grumbled.

Leo absorbed the snipe that was clearly meant for her, as she was the only woman present not decked out in a formal ball gown for the approaching ceremony. As a nod to today's occasion she had worn a black silk vest over her usual white shirt, which was tucked inside pressed wool slacks instead of tight black jeans. That passed for formal in her book. Mrs. Pettigrew could like it or lump it.

Though she wasn't privy to the story behind the elder woman's scowl, or that of her daughter, anyone with eyes could see they felt Eva was marrying beneath her class in Todd McCord. Leo's camera would capture that sentiment on their faces for posterity, where it would contrast starkly with the happiness on display from everyone else.

Chapter 9

Halloween 1986

The gravel crunched as Claudia pulled off the shoulder of the road at the back of a long line of cars. Butterflies welled up in her stomach. She was nervous about meeting a houseful of lesbians, but hoped her friendship with Sandy and Maria—and now Leo—would be enough to earn her a welcome. "Looks like a big crowd."

"It's always like this," Leo said. "No one wants to miss one of these parties."

Claudia felt a little silly in her leather pants and riveted jacket, especially since Leo wasn't in costume. But Leo had vowed to put on something from the bag by the door, and that would help with her self-consciousness.

With growing anticipation, she turned off the headlights and ignition. "I've never been to a lesbian party before. Is there a secret handshake or something?"

"Not that I know of." Making no move to exit the car, Leo added deadpan, "But don't take my word for it. Nobody ever tells me anything."

She was curious about whether Leo's famed shyness was only for new friends like her, or if it extended even to people she had known for a while. "Will a lot of your friends be here?"

Leo shrugged. "I suppose I'll know most of them, but not very well. The only ones I'd call friends are Sandy and Maria... oh, and Patty."

"Who's Patty?"

"The woman who brought me the jack-o'-lantern. She was on the porch the other night when you drove by."

Claudia had gotten only a glimpse of the tall redhead, and it hadn't occurred to her until that very moment that she might have been something more than a friend. "Is Patty someone special?"

"Oh, no! She's just a good friend."

By the rapid and emphatic denial Claudia surmised there was more to it than that, but when Leo didn't volunteer more, she gripped her door handle and drew a deep breath. "Shall we?"

They walked under the streetlight toward the house. Leo was dressed in dark jeans with a white shirt that seemed to swallow her, its sleeves rolled to her elbows and the collar turned up. It was a popular style, and Claudia thought it suited her perfectly— the flowing shirttails made it distinctly a woman's look, but not overly feminine for someone like Leo.

She tugged Leo's sleeve. "I like this look. I stole one of Mike's shirts once to wear around the house. It was so comfortable but then he stole it back."

Leo was enigmatic, a study in contrasts. She was attractive, intelligent and self-sufficient. Yet alone. The line of women wanting to date her should be wrapped around the corner. Perhaps it was, and Leo was holding them all at bay.

A printed sign by the door said friends didn't need to knock, so Leo led them in to find the party well underway, the stereo blaring a familiar Eurythmics tune. About three dozen women—

55

many of them in full costume—were crammed into the living room and spilling onto the deck.

"Here's the basket of masks. I have to pick out something."

"Let me," Claudia said, covering her eyes with one hand while she groped in the basket with the other. Her fingers brushed against a feathered mask and she pulled it out. "You aren't allergic to birds, are you?"

Leo smiled to see a simple black mask with white feathers sweeping upward over one eye, and brilliant blue feathers over the other. "That's probably the one I would have picked if I'd been looking." She slipped the elastic string over her head.

"That looks terrific." In fact, she looked dashing, especially with her broad white smile.

As they made their way into the living room, Claudia's eyes adjusted to the dim light and she spotted Sandy in the witch's costume she had worn to school the day before. She waved and grabbed Leo's sleeve to pull her past the crowd.

Sandy's eyes lit up with recognition and she set down her snack tray. "You made it! And look who you dragged in with you."

Leo shouted over the music. "I wouldn't miss one of these. You'd all talk about me."

"We talk about you anyway, sweetie." Sandy gathered up her long black skirt and stepped onto an ottoman to scream for quiet. Someone killed the music and the crowd went silent. "Everyone, I want you to meet my new personal slave. Actually, she's my intern this semester, Claudia Galloway."

Claudia felt herself redden under the attention, but she managed to smile and hold up a hand in greeting.

"I told her all of you were nice. Imagine that." She leaned over and tugged Claudia closer. "Now I hate to break your hearts, but she doesn't play for our team."

The news was greeted by hisses and boos. "We'll fix that," someone shouted.

"You're too late," Sandy continued above their laughter, lifting Claudia's hand to show off her ring. "Claudia here has a fiancé."

"Somebody better tell Leo that." Claudia followed Sandy's eyes to the red-haired woman she had seen on Leo's porch. Patty, who wore a San Francisco Giants baseball uniform, gave her what she hoped was only a playful sneer before shooting a lascivious grin at Leo.

"Let's go outside," Leo said, nudging her anxiously as the music started again and people turned back to their conversations. They passed through the sliding glass door and found a spot to themselves in the corner of the deck. "Sorry about that."

"What was that all about? I thought you said Patty was a friend of yours."

"She is. But she's also notorious for saying whatever's on her mind. Nobody takes her seriously."

"Was it my imagination, or was she shooting daggers at me?" Claudia was beginning to suspect Leo and Patty had a history.

Leo propped her elbows on the rail and pushed up her mask to rub her eyes, obviously flustered. "I'm pretty sure those were meant for me, not you. When Patty brought the jack-o'-lantern the other night, she asked me to come to the party with her. She sort of got her nose out of joint when I told her I was coming with you."

"You should have called me, Leo. You could have gone with her instead. I would have understood that."

"I didn't want to go with Patty. She has a...a different idea about her and me. Don't get me wrong. She's a nice person and I like her a lot. I just don't want to date her."

"Ah." That confirmed Claudia's earlier suspicions that it was Leo who wasn't interested in dating, or at least that she hadn't found the right woman yet. "Have you known each other long?"

"About four years. A bunch of us rode up to San Francisco for Pride. We went out a few times after we got back. No spark or anything, though, and after a while it started to feel forced. I quit going out with her but she never stopped asking. Now I think she just does it out of habit. She'd probably fall over if I ever said yes."

"So she's just playing, huh? I'm not going to walk out later

57

and find a key scratch down the side of my car, am I?"

"No, she'd never do anything like that." But an ambiguous expression crossed her face, which Claudia took to mean that it wasn't entirely out of the question.

"Any other spurned lovers I need to know about?" she teased.

"None, and just for the record, Patty and I weren't lovers. I wouldn't do that with just anybody. I'd have to feel something."

"That's a pretty good rule to live by." She wondered if that meant Leo hadn't had sex with anyone since Melissa. That was four or five years ago. "A lot of us like to think we're that way but we don't exactly live our values, especially when it comes to sex. Sometimes we even try to manufacture feelings after the fact so we can justify our behavior...not that I'm speaking from experience or anything." She looked away and whistled with exaggerated innocence.

"You did that?"

"It wasn't that bad. But you know what they say about men—they want their lovers to have a lot of experience in bed and their wives to be virgins. Mike wasn't too happy to find out someone else had gotten there before he did. He had to know all the details about my first time, and I didn't want to tell him it was just a typical case of teenage hormones gone wild, so I made up some tragic story about how I thought I was in love and it turned out I was just young and naïve." She couldn't quite read Leo's expression, but the upturned corner of her mouth suggested amusement. "I bet you're thinking it doesn't bode well that I'm not even married yet and already I'm concocting tales, but trust me. A man doesn't always want to hear the truth, especially if it means his future wife had horny sex for curiosity's sake. And I'm sure he wouldn't be too thrilled to know that he's not even the second. Definitely a case of what he doesn't know won't hurt him."

As several quiet seconds passed, Claudia got the sinking feeling she had said too much. She should have realized sooner that being friends with a lesbian didn't necessarily mean she should talk freely about her sexual exploits with men.

"And there you have it, more than you probably wanted to know about Claudia Galloway."

"No, no," Leo said. "I was just thinking you're probably right about how we pretend to be in love. We convince ourselves that's what it is because that's what we want it to be. Otherwise we have to admit we gave away something for nothing. Not just with sex, but with letting someone that close."

"Were you in love with Melissa?"

"I thought so at the time, but then I decided it wasn't really love unless both of you felt it." Her voice implied indignity rather than sadness.

"I don't know about that. Just because Melissa had other ideas, that didn't make your feelings any less real. It probably made it impossible for things to grow between you, but it doesn't mean you didn't feel love." She wondered how much Leo's experience with Melissa weighed on her apparent reluctance to date other women. "Sooner or later, you'll meet someone and have all those feelings again."

Leo looked over her shoulder, as if making sure there was no one within earshot. "I'm not too bothered about it, if you want to know the truth. If it happens, it happens. If it doesn't, I'm not going to pine my life away like some old brokenhearted spinster."

"I'm sorry, Leo. I didn't mean to sound so patronizing."

"No, it's not that. I just don't want people to worry about me. Even if I never fall in love again, I'm sure I'll be happy, because I'm not going to let that become the most important thing in my life. People like Patty are just the opposite. All she wants in the world is somebody to love. Every day that goes by that she isn't in a relationship is a day she isn't happy. I hate it for her because she needs that, and I don't ever want people to feel that way about me."

"I understand." Though Leo had explained it in terms of not wanting her friends to worry, Claudia couldn't help but feel admonished. "It's not like I'm some great sage when it comes to love anyway. I just got lucky with Mike. It would have been agonizing if I'd fallen in love with him and he hadn't fallen in love with me."

"I think that's what it's like for Patty. I feel bad for her, but not enough to date her. At least we're still friends."

Claudia spun at the rail to face the party and nudged Leo with her elbow. "Let's go back in so I can meet her. Maybe I can talk her out of keying my car."

Leo could barely contain her smile as Claudia poured on the charm with Patty, who was glowing with pride at the attention.

"Seriously, Patty. You must be very smart to have a job like that. My father has a computer in his study but I can't even figure out how to turn it on."

"It isn't hard. Get Leo to bring you over sometime and I'll show you all you need to know. I have an IBM AT with a twenty-meg hard drive. It runs on DOS—we're talking the future of the tech industry. I've loaded WordStar and Lotus so all I have to do is put in my floppy disk. That's just for personal stuff, though. At work I do most of my programming in dBASE on the mainframe."

"There's Maria. We should go say hi," Leo interjected after noticing Claudia's eyes had glazed over in confusion from Patty's technical jargon.

"I'm so happy I got to meet you," Claudia said, putting out her hand.

"Believe me, the pleasure was all mine." Patty leaned in and whispered mischievously, "And if things don't work out with that fiancé of yours, come on back and we'll show you a good time."

Leo steered Claudia toward the kitchen, where Maria had just taken a stack of empty cups. She was glad to have the confrontation behind her, especially since Claudia had shocked her by playfully telling Patty she had no idea how much fun lesbians could be, and she was glad she still had time to change her mind. Patty would never have expected such nonchalance from someone with real questions about her sexuality.

Maria, thirty-six years old and sculpted from hours in the gym, stood at the island of her gourmet kitchen arranging stuffed mushrooms on a tray. Her short blond hair looked almost golden under the tinted track lighting. "Hey, girls! Sorry I didn't say hello earlier. I was upstairs showing Joyce some of the photos I'm putting into a gallery in San Luis Obispo."

"You got into another gallery?" Leo exclaimed. "How many is that?"

"Eight. But that's not the big news." Maria motioned for them to come closer. "I haven't told Sandy this yet. She's going to flip out. You remember that black and white collection I showed last year in Santa Monica, the one with all the octogenarians? I asked an agent to shop it around and she called this afternoon—some publisher wants six of them for a coffee table book."

"That's fantastic!" Leo held up her hand for a slap. "That's my favorite collection of yours. I loved the way you lit the lines in their faces."

She gripped Leo's forearm and shook it emphatically. "That's the kind of thing we learned at the Santa Fe workshop. Why do you think I keep telling you to apply?"

Maria had been raving about the portrait workshop for two years and had offered half a dozen times to write a recommendation for Leo. "I don't think they'd take me," Leo argued again. "I haven't had enough practice with the fine art aspects of portraits."

"That's the whole point of the workshop, silly. And besides, you already know more about portraits than most of the people who were there when I was. You're just not getting credit for it." She turned to Claudia. "Have you been to her studio? Her work is so…" She frowned dramatically as she searched for the right word. "Solid. She's got the best fundamentals of anyone around when it comes to shooting people."

Claudia plucked a mushroom off the tray and nodded. "I don't know the first thing about photography, but even I can tell Leo's work is good."

"And that's exactly what it is—work," Leo said. "I can't afford the luxury of trying to turn everything I do into a work of art. My clients don't want to sit for two hours while I make a million adjustments to get it just right."

"But you don't have to choose one or the other," Maria said. "All you'd be doing is adding to your skill set. You know as well as I do that once you start using new techniques or equipment, it gets easier, and before you know it you're incorporating those things naturally. You've always wanted to take that next step, Leo. Magazine shoots and high-end clients don't hire out of the Yellow Pages. You're going to have to break out and distinguish yourself."

They'd had this conversation before, and Leo always agreed with each of Maria's assertions. Still, the impracticality of clearing her schedule for ten days so she could go to Santa Fe precluded actually following through. "Why do they always hold this workshop in June? That's my busiest month for weddings."

Maria put a hand on her hip and glared. "Look, kiddo. Everything worthwhile takes sacrifice. What's a few thousand dollars up front compared to how you're going to spend the rest of your life? Bite the bullet now so you can start doing what you want. It'll be worth it."

"I think Maria's right," Claudia offered. "Remember what we were talking about the other day on the wharf? Maybe it's time to make your dreams happen."

They were both right, of course. If Leo was ever to build her business into the kind of career she truly wanted, she needed to get off her butt and lay the groundwork. She mentally calculated the cost of the workshop along with the impact on her studio's bottom line. It was a major commitment, but she was emboldened by their encouragement. "What would I have to do to apply?"

"Now you're talking. Come upstairs. I'll give you the papers. They'll want a small body of work—I think it was only six portraits. You have to demonstrate mastery of the basics. You can do that with your eyes closed."

"Can I just send them samples?"

"No, they want to see everything with the same model so

they can compare. You need head shots, body shots, all kinds of different lighting...that sort of thing. I did it in three or four sessions."

The idea lost steam when Leo added the cost of a model to her estimate. "I'd have to hire a model. That's another thousand dollars. I may have to save up until next year."

"You don't have to use pretty people. Get Patty to do it." Maria slapped a hand over her mouth as Claudia and Leo burst out laughing. "I didn't mean it that way. What I meant is you can get a friend to do it as long as you have a release. It's only about technique."

Patty was probably the only friend she had who would sit for four sessions for free—except it wouldn't be free because she would probably want a date in return. "Maybe I could put up a sign at the college. I'm sure someone there could use a few extra bucks."

"What kind of modeling are we talking about?" Claudia asked as they climbed the plank staircase to Maria's office on the second-floor landing.

Maria stopped abruptly on the top floor and spun around. "There you go, Leo. Claudia can model for you."

Leo had taken Claudia's question as curiosity rather than an offer to pose. "Claudia has enough to do. Sandy's working her to death."

"No, seriously," Claudia said. "Is it something anybody can do, or do you need a certain kind of look?"

"I'm sure you'd be a great model," Leo said. "But three or four sessions in studio is way too much to ask of somebody who's trying to get through college and plan a wedding."

"I'm not planning a wedding. I told you that's my mom's obsession. All I have to do is pick a date and show up. If you're willing to do it after school or on the weekends, I can help. You're not talking nude, are you?"

Maria chuckled. "No, so don't believe Leo if she tries to talk you out of your clothes."

"I wouldn't do something like that." Leo was aghast until she saw Maria's impish grin.

"Don't believe her, Claudia. We all say that, but then we convince our subjects to do it in the name of art." Maria shuffled through some papers on her desk and located a brochure. "Yep, it's still the same—six portraits, all black and white. These are the specs." She handed it to Leo. "Due date is the end of January."

"I could probably put together a body of work by then." She turned to Claudia, still mildly embarrassed by Maria's joke. "She really is kidding about the nude part."

"Hey, ply me with tequila and there's no telling what I'd do. This could be fun…unless you don't think the pictures will turn out. I don't want to hurt your chances of getting into the workshop."

"No way," Maria said. "You're more interesting to look at than most of the models I've used. Isn't that right, Leo?"

Leo nodded her agreement. She had hired only a handful of models, mostly for industrial shoots. Since the goal had been to show off products and services, she had chosen ordinary-looking people who would disappear into the background. Claudia was anything but ordinary.

Chapter 10

Claudia picked up her pace to follow Leo through the studio to the back stairs. When Leo had called to ask about getting together to schedule their sessions, she had offered to stop by on her way home from school. As it turned out, this was Leo's busiest time of day and they had only an hour before her next appointment. "Are you sure we have enough time for this? I can try to stop by tomorrow."

"Tomorrow's worse. I'm jammed from three o'clock till nine."

In the den upstairs, papers were strewn all over the sofa with Madeline curled in the center like a paperweight. A large plastic bowl on the floor held popcorn remnants. It was a homey setting, not at all the formal and pristine atmosphere Claudia was accustomed to at her mother's home, where the most important thing was making the right impression on visitors. Heaven forbid a living room ever looked as if someone lived there.

"Come here, little girl," Leo said, scooping up the calico and boosting her atop the entertainment center. "Thanks for all your help. We'll take it from here."

"Your furry assistant is adorable. Looks like she's gotten over being bashful. She was hiding up there the last time I was here." Claudia thought Madeline was a lot like her mistress—shy at first, but more comfortable after she got used to people. She was mildly disappointed when it struck her that Leo seemed more relaxed today not because they were closer, but because she was in work mode.

Leo paged through her planner, which was dotted with appointments. "I do a lot of portrait appointments around five or six because that's when people get off work, so the only time I have during the week is probably too late for you. And it looks like I have weddings every Saturday between now and New Year's except the week after Thanksgiving."

"Wow, I thought you said June was your busy month."

"That's because in June people get married every day of the week instead of just Saturday. By the end of the month I'm whispering all the words before they do."

"Careful. You could accidentally get married that way." She grinned as Madeline descended from her perch to settle in Leo's lap. "Somebody loves her mom."

"More like somebody wants to be the center of attention."

"As she should be. Did she wander up to your back door one day and demand dinner?"

"No, she was a birthday gift from Patty. I never wanted a cat, but damned if I didn't get used to her. Took her about two days to wrap me around her paw. Now I get lonesome if she goes into the other room."

"Sounds like you're good for each other." Claudia couldn't resist reaching out to scratch Madeline under her chin. "I think this little project is going to give all three of us something to do."

Leo checked her watch and visibly relaxed, propping her feet on the coffee table. "That's the irony. I already have plenty to do, but Maria's right. I need to take things up a notch if I want to compete for the high-end work."

Claudia placed her feet alongside Leo's, noting the contrast between her size sixes and Leo's probable nines. "Tell me what high-end means. What would you like to see yourself doing... let's say five years from now?"

Madeline rippled with pleasure as Leo stroked her from head to tail. It was obvious the two adored one another.

"Five years? Not school photos, that's for sure. No offense, but I'd like to do something a little more creative. I suppose if I had my dream job, I'd still have my studio but I wouldn't have to say yes to everybody just to keep my head above water. The only way for that to happen is for my work to get noticed by the people who appreciate quality and are willing to pay for it. That means the pros, like media relations people, ad agencies and photo editors for magazines. I want my name at the top of their lists."

She envied how clearly Leo articulated her professional objectives. Compared to goals like that, her teaching career probably seemed amorphous. "How will going to Santa Fe help you get there?"

"I could see a difference in Maria's work right away. Most of her stuff was outdoors in natural light. Now she's just as comfortable doing studio lights."

"But you already know how to do that."

"There's always more to learn. Besides, this sort of workshop isn't only about technique. It's also about making the contacts I need in order to get the jobs I want. That's how this business works."

"Sounds like Mike's dad. He always hired people inside his network of cronies, so naturally Mike wants to do the same thing now that he's calling the shots in Taiwan. The only problem is that Mike has a different circle of friends, so all of Big Jim's buddies are on the outside looking in. You should hear them fight about it." She shuddered at the memory of their last confrontation when Big Jim had pulled rank on the Asia project. Mike had stewed quietly through dinner, but erupted in a rage once he and Claudia were alone. It had taken her two hours to calm him down.

Leo chuckled. "My dad and I had only one fight in all the time we worked together. When we shot Sheila Harrison's wedding. She was one of those snotty girls in high school I didn't like very much. I said something to my dad about how she probably had to get married and I was going to frame all my photos with her belly in the middle. He let me have it. He said people would know us by our worst job, and that we had no right to judge the people who trusted us with their business. It was a lesson I never forgot."

"You were lucky to have such a wise man for a father. I feel the same way about my dad."

"Be sure to cherish every day with him." Leo pressed her lips in a tight line and picked up her appointment book, her visage passing instantly from wistful to businesslike. "What do you think, Madeline? Can we get Claudia to come see us on Sundays?"

Claudia pulled out her leather Coach planner and scanned it. "Sundays are good, as long as I can get home by eight for Mike's call. That's our regular time because it's eight on Monday morning in Taiwan. Other than that, all I ever do are lesson plans, laundry and television. I'll probably go home for Thanksgiving, but I should be around every Sunday until my internship finishes the third week in December."

Leo tapped the pages in her planner to count off the weeks. "That gives us five Sundays, but I don't think I'll need more than three. Just don't get impatient with me when I start messing with lights and things. I wouldn't think twice about doing that with a model, but I don't like doing it to a friend."

Claudia smiled at hearing Leo call her a friend because Leo didn't strike her as someone who threw the word around casually. "At least I'll get to tell everyone I'm a former model."

"I don't think they'll be surprised." Leo handed her a document. "Speaking of which, this is kind of a formality, but

I need it in the file with the portfolio. It's a model's release. Basically it says I own the photos, but I've stipulated that I'll use them only for the workshop. So you won't have to worry about showing up one of these days in a gallery or one of Maria's coffee-table books."

"That's too bad. I was sort of hoping for something shocking that could get circulated through my mom's bridge club. Double bonus if my future mother-in-law sees it and faints."

Leo led the way up the ladder to the attic and pulled the chain at the top to turn on the lights. She was bursting with excitement, not only at showing off her space, but in sharing her plans for it. "I owe you big time for asking to see the attic. I spent about six hours up here on Sunday cleaning things out and it gave me a great idea."

"Wow, look at all this space." Claudia stepped onto the platform, where her eyes went immediately to the turret. "This is the room I can see from way down the street."

"That's right. It's the highest point in the house. And not only that"—she walked briskly across the plywood to the front window—"you can see the water from up here."

Claudia joined her and they looked out onto the lights at the wharf. "That's beautiful. If this were my house, I'd be up here all the time."

"I was thinking we'd work up here, as long as you don't mind climbing the ladder."

"Don't you need your studio? What about all the lights?"

"A couple of the shots call for natural light, which I don't have in the dining room, but I do from this window. For the rest of it I can set up my portable kit. That's what I use when I go out to shoot somewhere, like weddings or school pictures. Most of the time I leave those in the car, but I can just keep them up here instead. That way I can tweak things with Miss Murphy and be ready to go when you get here."

"Who's Miss Murphy?"

Leo took Claudia's shoulders and pointed her toward a life-sized mannequin, which was already clad in the long white shirt she had worn to the Halloween party. "Meet your stand-in."

"I like her shirt, but she needs a sandwich," Claudia said. "Why do you have a skinny mannequin in your attic?"

"My dad did a catalog spread for one of the women's apparel stores in Carmel. I was about twelve years old and my job was to dress Miss Murphy in all the outfits."

"The more you tell me about your dad, the more I think you two were quite a pair."

"We were. There's so much of him left around this place."

"I bet there's a lot of him left in you too."

Leo hadn't talked about her father this much since the few months after he died. She still missed him, but talking with Claudia about how she'd grown up in the photography business had made her remember happier times. She pulled a squeaky toy from a cardboard box. "He used this when people brought their dogs in for portraits because it got them to look at the camera. And he would call me in to make faces at the babies so they'd laugh. No matter who it was, he always tried to make the portrait process fun. What he liked most was making people feel good about saving that moment. That's what I try to do too."

"That is what you do," Claudia said. "I saw it over and over at school. And you did it with me too. Do you think I would have volunteered for more if I didn't expect it to be fun?"

"You say that now. Wait until your neck starts cramping because I've made you hold your head in the same position for thirty minutes. And these lights are going to be murder, so you might want to bring along shorts or something."

"Is this where you start talking me out of my clothes?"

Leo snorted and shook her head. "Were you always such a smart aleck?"

"That depends on who you ask. My father thought I was an angel…except for the time when I wrecked his Porsche. As soon as he made sure everyone was okay he hit the ceiling."

"Now I see where you got your appreciation for sports cars. Was he upset about his baby?"

"Not as much as he was about the fact that I had four of my friends in it. Apparently that's a no-no in a two-seater."

"No kidding. Maybe we should trade cars. You can pack everyone you ever met into the Volvo." She gestured toward the ladder and waited as Claudia descended backward. Then she pulled the light chain and followed to the landing below. "I take it your mother didn't notice your angelic qualities."

"Not once in twenty-two years. She wanted to make me into her own image and I turned into my father instead." Her tone was more serious, a marked departure from the light-hearted references to her father's ire over the car. "I always thought that was a good thing."

"Sounds like it was tense in your house while you were growing up."

"It was. My mom used to ride me all the time about not being ladylike. She had this image that we were rich just because my dad was a doctor, but what she really wanted was to be rich like Mike's family. I wasn't supposed to do things like wear jeans or lie around listening to rock music on my headphones. She thought I should spend all my time reading the classics and playing piano. It horrifies her that I want to be just an ordinary schoolteacher, but you know what? There comes a point where you have to screw what everyone else wants and follow your own gut. I did that when I picked Santa Cruz instead of some women's college back east. And believe me, my father was thrilled. In-state tuition versus a hundred thousand a year. Now you know why he gave me a sports car."

Leo nodded along. There were little things about Claudia that showed what she thought must be her mother's influence, like the cashmere sweaters and alligator boots, but it was just as easy to imagine her at home in sweatshirts and sneakers.

Claudia returned to the den for her purse and day planner. "I probably still sound like a spoiled brat, but that isn't who I want to be. I'm serious about teaching, and I want to prove I can stand on my own two feet and take care of myself just like you do. Unlike my mom, I don't need some fancy house or bridge club."

71

She gestured around her at the living room. "This is so much more comfortable to me than a mansion on a cliff."

"I'm glad you like it. Maybe you'll find a house like this of your own one of these days."

"If I could have a house like this in Cambria I'd snatch it up in a heartbeat."

Leo glanced at the clock as Claudia continued down the stairs. Three minutes before her next appointment. "Any more questions about the photo shoot?"

"Just one." Claudia stopped at the front door and grinned back at her. "How come Miss Murphy isn't wearing any pants?"

"Because she—"

Claudia guffawed and bounded off the porch toward her car. "See you Sunday at two. Save me some popcorn."

Chapter 11

Present Day

The McCords weren't exactly middle class, except perhaps by the Pettigrews' standards. Leo had met the young couple for the first time last weekend at a coffee shop in Palo Alto, where they had planned the wedding album. Both had recently graduated from Stanford, Eva in sociology and Todd in law. He had won a prestigious clerkship in the US District Court headquartered in San Francisco.

Mrs. Pettigrew flinched slightly as Leo gently touched her shoulder to angle her alongside her granddaughter. "Bear with me, please. I need to get the shadow just right." To say nothing of the fact that a full-on shot would highlight the woman's girth, especially in contrast to Eva's slender figure.

The bride mouthed a silent apology for her grandmother's condescension, but Leo merely shot her a wink. She didn't care what the old biddy thought.

"How much longer is this going to take?" Mrs. Pettigrew demanded.

"Do you have someplace else to be?" Eva asked playfully.

"One hundred of my friends are arriving downstairs after a long drive, young lady, and I don't have time to be out here on the terrace chatting with the help."

Eva flashed Leo yet another apologetic look. "Grandmother, this is Leonora Westcott. She's one of the most gifted and accomplished photographers in California, and we were very lucky to get her on such short notice when poor Maria got hurt."

From her emotionless look, Mrs. Pettigrew was unimpressed. She tugged at her dress yet again and started toward the door. "We'll be even luckier if we don't all starve to death before the ceremony gets underway. It's time to gather the wedding party in the Miramar Room. Come along."

"Not yet. Mom hasn't been up for her pictures."

"Why does your mother always have to be so obstinate? She should have had her sitting by now," the woman groused to no one in particular.

"I asked her to be last so she could walk down with me and Grandpa."

Mrs. Pettigrew huffed indignantly. "That isn't the way it's done at proper weddings, Eva. That's why we hired a wedding director."

"Why *you* hired a wedding director," Eva replied firmly. "Todd and I wanted to elope."

"Don't even say such a thing! It shames your father's memory."

Eva was obviously biting her tongue, as if knowing another word would send them all into a melodramatic downward spiral—not exactly the atmosphere one wanted on her wedding day. Clearly, one crossed Marjorie Pettigrew at her own peril.

When the door banged to punctuate Mrs. Pettigrew's departure, an ironic breeze rustled the light blue sheers, like the proverbial breath of fresh air.

Chapter 12

November 1986

"…I know she's ready, but she's not the one getting married," Claudia said, stretching the phone cord to its full length so she could reach her coffee cup on the kitchen bar of her tiny apartment. Talking with her father on Sunday mornings was one of the highlights of her week. "I don't want to live in Taiwan for a whole year while Mike wraps up this job. It makes more sense to wait until he's done so we can buy our own house and be settled in one place."

"You don't have to convince me," her father said. "I'm just the messenger here."

"I know. I just can't understand why Mom's in such a hurry. Sometimes I think her biggest fear is that Mike will change his mind and she'll miss out on the chance to throw an extravagant wedding."

He chuckled. "That's my little cynic. Have you considered

the possibility she's just excited? After all, she'll only get one shot to be the mother of the bride. At least that's what we all hope."

"Don't worry. Mike and I wouldn't have gotten engaged if we didn't think this was it for both of us. But there's no hurry. Besides, you always said you liked my independent streak."

"I do, and I think that's what drives your mother crazy about both of us."

Claudia laughed, imagining the hours of fretful harping her father had been subjected to. If only he hadn't let her do this or that. "It's perfectly healthy if you ask me. Just because people get married, it doesn't mean they shouldn't have their own lives." She didn't want to talk about her relationship with Mike anymore. Though her dad understood her desire for independence better than anyone and was her ally in taking things slowly, the conversation always left her feeling defensive. "What are you up to today?"

"Tennis at the club at three. Dinner with the Bradshaws. Just another typical Sunday. You?"

"I'm heading over to a friend's house this afternoon. We may walk down to the wharf for a bite." She had decided not to tell anyone about her modeling sessions so it wouldn't become a topic of scorn. Mike would think it was a frivolous waste of time, and her mother would think it beneath her class. But then her mother thought teaching was beneath her class too.

"I'd offer to drive up next weekend for a visit, but I signed up for that charity doubles tournament. You want me to send your mom to keep you company? I'm sure she'd love a couple of nights in Carmel."

She had committed already to a photo session with Leo, and there was no guarantee her mother would leave on Sunday morning in time for her to make it to Leo's by two. "I don't know, Dad. I hate to have her plan that when I can't say for sure I'll have time to be with her."

"Okay, but don't forget we won't be here for Thanksgiving. We're going to Vail with the Hanovers."

"Right." And she would be having another fun-filled dinner

with Mike's parents, she thought miserably. If only she could marry Mike and not his whole family. On the other hand, Mike was getting Rosemary Galloway for a mother-in-law, so she was in no position to complain. "Maybe I can drive down for a quick visit in a couple of weeks."

"We'd love that."

"Don't tell Mom, though. She'll plan the whole weekend with lunches and dinners and people coming over, and then I might not be able to come."

They said their goodbyes and promised to talk again same time next week. By the clock on the stove, she had plenty of time to shower and dry her hair before going to Leo's, and just enough to return the call on her answering machine that had come while she was out working on her car.

"Hey, Sandy. I got your message. What's up?"

"Nothing much. I was sitting here going through my Thanksgiving list and realized I hadn't said anything to you about it. Maria and I take in strays for turkey dinner if you're going to be stuck here for the holiday."

"Take in strays?"

"Yeah, we have a lot of friends who don't go home for Thanksgiving for one reason or another, and we've made sort of a tradition of getting together to celebrate on our own. It's usually about ten or twelve of us. You met them all at the Halloween party. Patty does a football pool for anyone who's interested."

"That sounds like a lot more fun than where I'm going, which is to my future in-laws' house. The good news is that Mike will be home for a few days."

"So you won't be a refugee?"

"No, but I appreciate the invitation. If your Thanksgiving is anything like your Halloween, I'm sure it's the hottest ticket in town."

"I don't know about that, but we always have a blast. And Maria makes a mean chestnut stuffing."

Claudia wasn't surprised. Maria was one of the most amazing women she had ever met—a gourmet cook, a brilliant

77

photographer, and rich as all get-out from her family's investments. "Is there anything Maria can't do?"

"She can't sit still," Sandy answered, not missing a beat. "She called Leo this morning and found out you guys were starting your photo shoot this afternoon. I'm really glad you two are hanging out. Leo's one of our favorite people."

"She's very sweet. Can you possibly tell me why someone like that doesn't have a girlfriend?"

"Believe me we've all wondered the same thing. She just doesn't seem to want one. I've set her up a couple of times and introduced her to people at our parties, but she never follows through after the first date. I keep hoping someone will turn her head."

"She's such a cool person. I've never met anyone like her." She had been thinking a lot about Leo since their talk the week before. It wasn't surprising that Leo hadn't clicked with Patty, but she couldn't put her finger on why. "Did you ever meet Melissa?"

"No, nobody did. That was over before any of us ever met Leo, and I think she moved to Atlanta. Patty saw a picture of her once, though. Nice looking woman."

Claudia had no idea what nice looking meant to someone like Sandy. She had considered Leo the most attractive woman at the Halloween party, though she wasn't what most people would call pretty. Pretty was a word for women who fussed with their hair and makeup, and dressed in the latest styles. Leo did none of those things, and yet there was something about her she found captivating. Maybe it was because she was already comfortable with who she was, utterly without pretense. It was true not only of her appearance, but with the rest of her life as well. "All I can say is somebody is going to get a nice prize one of these days if she ever decides she's ready."

"I know what you mean. Patty says she thinks Leo might be afraid of losing someone the way she lost her dad, but Maria thinks she's waiting for everything else in her life to fall into place. That's one of the reasons she pushed her into doing the

78

workshop, so she'll be a step closer to where she wants to be."

Given what Claudia knew about Leo so far, Maria's theory made more sense than Patty's. "She certainly seems focused on her work...no pun intended. But I think this workshop thing is going to be fun."

"You'll have to bring in your pictures."

"Leo says I can't see them until she's finished. She doesn't want me thinking about how I look."

"Yeah, Maria always says that too. Anyway, I hope you guys have fun. And if you change your mind about Thanksgiving, we'll save you a place."

Leo had spent every spare moment since Tuesday preparing her quasi-studio, tacking bolts of black cloth to the open rafters in front of the window on the south wall of the turret. That left her a natural light option from the front, which would be brilliant by mid-afternoon, but today's shoot called for artificial light.

She hoisted the long cardboard box onto the platform and climbed up through the opening to the attic. Her setup needed one final touch before the first photo session, the two new light stands she had purchased the day before from a supplier in San Francisco. She had tried in vain to adapt her father's old tripods, only to admit there was a reason she had junked them in the attic in the first place. They now sat alongside her curb awaiting trash pickup. She had salvaged one of the seascape backdrops, since its flip side was bright white and she could use it as a reflector wall.

Her father's Bronica was mounted on a tripod facing Miss Murphy, who still wore the long white shirt. The new Mamiya in her studio took sharper photos, but she didn't want to risk lugging it up and down the ladder several times a week while she framed the next set of shots. Though the Bronica was eight years old, it was still a reliable camera and it produced far better photos than the 35mm Nikon she used for candids.

Assembling one of the light stands took twenty minutes, much of that spent looking for a wing nut Madeline had batted around the room. "Would you mind not helping so much?" she

79

groused at the calico. "Claudia's going to be here any minute and I'm not ready." She twisted the rod to tighten it and locked the leg supports into place. Then she attached a reflector umbrella, a light softener she needed for the day's second photo.

The more she thought about the workshop, the more certain she was Maria was right. Now was the time to take her skills to the next level. Most studio professionals were using LCD light meters and integrated strobes that flashed from their tripods, but she was still using her analog Sekonic meter and continuous lighting. It wasn't just the technology that was leaving her behind. Ordinary portraiture had become fine art, with the cutting edge photographers mixing ratios for multiple fill lights and creating color and texture effects she had never imagined. Her father had kept current through seminars and workshops, but she no longer had the benefit of his training.

A car door slammed outside and she hurriedly peeked around the blackout shade. "There she is, Maddie."

She started backward down the ladder, giving her makeshift studio one last glance. With all the preparations in place, her excitement about competing for the workshop was growing at a fever pitch. This portfolio would be her best work ever.

Claudia grinned broadly through the screen door. She wore a long blue turtleneck over a black leotard and gray leggings. "I'm here for my close-up, Miss Westcott."

"Come on in. I meant to leave the door open but I got sidetracked upstairs. I have everything ready."

"Great T-shirt," she said.

Leo tugged the hem downward to display her design, the UC-Santa Cruz mascot. "I thought you'd appreciate my Banana Slug. You want something to drink?"

"Better not. You'll get me perfectly posed and I'll have to pee."

"Good point, but I'm more worried about things going wrong on my end, like when the camera jams or the lights go dead." She led Claudia into the downstairs studio and gestured toward the stylist chair. "Hope you don't mind a little pancake. You can wash it off before you leave."

"I already put makeup on," she protested. "I've hardly been outside since July, and I'd look like a ghost without it."

Leo looked closely at her eyes, which were lined with brown pencil and dusted with a soft taupe shadow. It was subtle, just the right amount to highlight her natural features. "Your eyes look fantastic, but I need to polish your cheekbones and flatten your forehead a little more."

"Excuse me?"

She chuckled at Claudia's feigned offense. "Makeup's good for covering up blemishes and blending in the skin tone but we need a little texture too so you won't look like you've been airbrushed. But first"—she spun the chair around to face the mirror and handed her a clip—"I'd like to see your hair up. It's gorgeous the way it is, but I think we'll get more contrast from the contours of your neck, especially with the low lights."

"What does that mean?"

Leo looked around the studio and found a black flag she used to create shadows. Holding it up behind Claudia's head, she asked, "See how the edges of your hair get lost against this background? If we pull it up"—she swept it upward—"the light skin of your neck makes a clear line. That's going to make it easier to achieve the different effects I need in these photos. I'd leave it down if we were using a light background because it would have the opposite effect."

"I get it." Claudia deftly spun her hair into a twist and clipped it in place.

"That's lovely." Striking, actually. With that simple sweep Claudia went from a girl next door to an elegant ingénue. Taken aback by the transformation, Leo suddenly realized she had been staring.

"Something wrong?"

She shook off her lapse in concentration along with Claudia's question. "No, let me just…" She brushed powder onto Claudia's forehead, then took a cotton puff and gently swabbed both cheeks. "I think that does it, but I'll take this stuff with us just in case. You ready?"

"Let's find out."

They wound up through the house to the attic, where Leo held out a hand to help Claudia off the ladder. She was pleased to see the wide-eyed reaction to her improvised studio. She hadn't realized until just that moment how important Claudia's approval was. "I've been busy."

"I'll say. Look at all of this."

When she pulled the chain to turn off the light above the stairs, the tidy set came clearly into view. A small lamp on the floor illuminated Miss Murphy, who was positioned before a black backdrop and side wall. The camera and light stands were silhouetted in the foreground.

"It's so dark."

"It won't be once we get started, but I'll keep the studio lights off until we need them because it gets hot up here in a hurry." She picked up Miss Murphy and set her off to one side. "The first two shots are as simple as it gets—one hard light, one soft light. Same pose if we can get it."

"Since I don't know what you're talking about, I'll just try to do whatever you tell me."

"First I'll set one of my studio lights a few feet back and shine it directly onto your face from the side so it casts shadows. That's hard light. But most of my studio portraits are soft light, which means I bring the spots closer and bounce them off something else to spread the light around. When I light both sides of the face it cuts down on the shadows. Normally I use more light on one side than I do on the other, or maybe I'll shine it from the top or bottom. What I'm trying to do is highlight certain features."

"That makes sense, but why would anyone ever want to use hard light?"

"It's more dramatic. Remember me talking about Maria's exhibit, the one with all the elderly people? She used hard lighting to emphasize their wrinkles. Every line looked as if it had been chiseled by a sculptor. Very vivid."

"Great, so you're going to highlight my wrinkles."

Leo rolled her eyes. "You're twenty-two years old. You don't have wrinkles. But what I want to do is try to cast a perfect shadow on one side of your face with the first photo, and then erase most of the shadow on the second by moving the light back and adding a fill light. This is an exercise in technique. I'm not trying to capture anything candid or personal, so when we take this I'd like you to show as little expression as possible. All I want to do is demonstrate that I understand the concepts of hard light and soft light."

Claudia shrugged. "I'm ready. Except that Miss Murphy is still wearing my shirt."

"These are just head shots, so I left a few tube tops over there in the changing room." She pointed to the opposite corner where she had hung a curtain diagonally. "They're all black. Just pick the one that fits best. Would you mind taking your jewelry off too? You can leave the ring. I won't be showing your hand."

"Help me with this." Claudia turned her back and pulled her collar from her neck, exposing the chain of the jade pendant.

"This is pretty."

"Burmese jade. I bought it when I was in Bangkok."

"I would have guessed it was a gift from Mike."

"Pfft. If Mike had picked it out, it would be as big as a cowbell. He isn't much on ceremony, but he likes to make a splash." Necklace in hand, Claudia disappeared behind the curtain to change.

Leo turned on the studio lights and oscillating fan, and busied herself with making sure her extension cords were secure. There was only one power outlet in the attic but it was enough for her immediate needs.

"This one fits as long as I don't sneeze."

She tried not to stare as Claudia walked into the light. The leotard and tube top drew a perfect outline of her petite figure, accentuated by pronounced collarbones that would cast elegant shadows across her chest. She forced herself to concentrate on the task at hand, setting the mannequin aside and scooting an adjustable stool into its place. "Hop up here and I'll get to work on the lights. It's going to get warm in a hurry, but this should only take a few minutes."

That proved to be an understatement, as the temptation to capture a Rembrandt triangle on Claudia's cheek proved irresistible. Perspiration rolled down her back as she made countless adjustments to the camera, the light and to Claudia, who patiently endured her quest for perfection.

"I get embarrassed about this ring sometimes. I didn't want a diamond this big, but Mike didn't want anyone thinking he was cheap."

"It's very beautiful."

"Yes, it is. But since I'm the one wearing it, I wish it said more about me than him. I don't care what the people in his office think of it."

Finally, Leo got the angle she wanted. She turned off the fan to still the strands of hair and stepped onto a wooden box to look down into her viewfinder, where Claudia's upside down image was centered inside the frame. Her expression was one of slight annoyance, probably because she was still thinking about her too-flashy ring.

"Now look directly at the Banana Slug and empty your mind of everything." She drew a deep breath and exhaled slowly, snapping off two photos. "Perfect. Now try not to move."

"My nose itches."

"Think about what you're going to order at Isabella's when we get finished." She adjusted the aperture higher then lower, taking four more shots to bracket what she thought would be the perfect exposure. "That was great, but I need you to sit still for just another minute." She swung the umbrella into place with its fill light and held her meter to the cheek that had been shadowed. After eight minor adjustments she got the ratio she wanted and stepped back onto her box. "I want six more shots just like the last ones. Look at Mr. Banana Slug."

Claudia stared back at her chest, her expression vacant.

Again, she clicked off two photos, adjusted the aperture twice, and clicked again. "That should do it. I don't think we

84

could have started off with two more perfect shots. I can't wait to see them."

"Me neither." Claudia immediately held up her hand. "Except I know you're not going to show them to me until we're all done."

"Just trust me. If they aren't fantastic, we'll shoot them again."

"That's a deal. Now let's get out of this oven."

Chapter 13

"…and our dog bit my brother right on the nose." Katie Theroux, standing at the front of the classroom, turned the page of her journal and continued, "We had to get rid of the dog, but I wanted to get rid of my brother instead."

Claudia stifled a laugh, thinking she couldn't wait to share that story with her family and friends. The escapades of her third-graders, told through their weekly entries in a journal, gave her valuable insight into their personalities and the support they received at home. "Okay, we have time for one more. Who wants to go next?"

A dozen hands shot up and she zeroed in on a boy who rarely volunteered. As he finished his reading, Sandy entered the room, clearly bursting with news. "What's up next? I'll get them started while you go talk to Larry," she whispered with a mischievous grin.

Larry Hirsch was their principal, and Claudia couldn't imagine why he would want to talk to her. "What about?"

"Just go."

"Orbiting the sun. Page forty-one." She handed over her lesson plan book and the teacher's science text. "I'll be right back," she told her class.

Walking down the deserted hallway, she chuckled nervously to recall the ominous feeling from her childhood when she had been sent to the principal's office. At least Sandy had been excited about this, whatever it was.

"Miss Galloway." The school secretary looked up over half-glasses and smiled. "Let me tell Mr. Hirsch you're here."

She waited nervously until she was directed to enter the paneled office, where Larry acknowledged her with a nod as he finished his call. A man of about forty, he was slightly overweight and balding. Pictures of his two sons, one of whom was in Claudia's class, stood in frames on the bookcase behind him, and it crossed her mind that Leo had likely taken those photos.

When he hung up, he jumped to his feet and rubbed his hands together as though preparing for a feast. "So how do you like teaching, Claudia?" he bellowed.

"What's not to like at a place like Melrose?"

"Lucky, aren't we? Smart kids, active parents, dedicated faculty...and the best cafeteria on the whole peninsula"—he patted his stomach—"as you can see. Anyway, that's neither here nor there. You know Joan Palmer?"

"Yes, of course. She teaches fourth grade out in the portable classroom." Sandy had made certain she knew everyone on the staff.

"That's right. She was in here this morning. Said her husband was getting transferred to New Jersey. You interested in teaching fourth grade next fall?"

Claudia was floored by the question. First-year teachers seldom won coveted assignments at schools like Melrose. "Are you kidding? I'd love it."

"Hold on, there's a catch. I can't promise anything now

because we have to advertise the opening and interview all the applicants. But it usually comes down to my recommendation and I'd love to get a little new blood in here. Sandy tells me you're getting a lot out of her students."

"I certainly can't take the credit for that. Miss Irwin did a super job getting her students ready to learn."

Her head was racing ahead to what might happen if his tentative offer actually came through. If she took a job in Monterey next year while Mike finished up his work in Taiwan, she would have a year's experience under her belt when she moved back to Cambria. They could even set a firm wedding date for the end of the school year.

"Sounds like you two make a great team," he said. "I'd love to have you on board."

"Absolutely. I love it here."

"Excellent. If you need something to do between now and then, you might consider going down to the district office and signing up as a substitute." He came around his desk to grasp her hand in both of his, beaming with satisfaction at their new pact. "I bet I could keep you busy until summer."

She walked out stunned, both thrilled at the opportunity and overwhelmed at what she would need to do over the summer to get up to speed on fourth grade curriculum. Now that she had made friends, it would be fun to stay another year in Monterey, and Mike would probably be relieved that she had something to keep her busy while he finished his project overseas.

Most photographers got their biggest thrill in the darkroom upon seeing the image for the first time, but not Leo. She didn't allow for such excitement until the final print. As far as she was concerned, everything before that was merely an extension of the studio process. According to the application guidelines, the additional lab steps—things like toning, burning and dodging—were moot, since post-development enhancements were prohibited. They expected her to get the lighting right the first time.

Her lips turned upward in a satisfied smile as she rinsed the last of the soft light images. Not only had she captured exactly the light she wanted in her very first shot, the minute differences in Claudia's pose rendered this one better than the others. In particular, her eyes were wider, such that a barely perceptible crease appeared above her eyebrows, a subtle sign she hadn't emptied her mind of her annoyance with Mike over the ring after all. No one else would notice it because they wouldn't have the others to compare.

She clipped the photo to one of the skirt hangers she had pinched from her mother's closet years ago, added it to the line to dry with the others and closed the door behind her. By her calculations the workshop project had taken almost twenty hours of her time already and still she had four photos to go, plus the written application. Fortunately she had been able to do most of her work after hours, but the pull of developing the first two images had been too strong to put off until evening. Now after spending most of her Monday morning in the darkroom, she needed to tackle the stack of paperwork that had accumulated on her desk in the past week. There would be no money coming in unless she got her bills out.

No sooner had she sat down behind her desk than footsteps sounded on her porch, followed by a man's voice calling her name. She hustled to the parlor to find two workmen, one of whom was holding a large cardboard box.

"Man, you guys got here quick." She had called the local appliance store as soon as it opened to order an air conditioner unit for one of the attic windows. The remaining photos were more complicated than those she had shot yesterday and two of them involved multiple lighting. It was too much to ask of Claudia to endure the blazing studio lights without some relief.

While the workmen installed the unit in her south window, she staged the preliminaries for the next weekend's setup, in which she would use natural light from the window that faced the street. By the shadows falling across the rooftops between her house and the wharf, she estimated direct sunlight would hit the attic around one thirty. If Claudia came at one instead of two, she could have the light streaming down from above instead of directly in her face. That would make it trickier to position the reflector, but worth it not to make Claudia suffer. It was undeniable that using a friend instead of a professional model was having an impact on her process—spending three hundred dollars on an air conditioner was proof of that. But she had to admit it made her care even more about the quality of her work.

The office phone rang from down below, but there was no chance she could cover two floors in time to catch it so she left it to her answering machine. Besides, whatever it was could wait until tomorrow. Her schedule today was open until four, when the eighteen-member Cox family was due for its annual Christmas card photo sitting.

As soon as the workmen left she brought her files into the attic and set Miss Murphy in front of the window. Every fifteen minutes she interrupted her paperwork to snap a Polaroid, writing the time on the back to document the sun's position. Yes, it was ridiculously more preparation than she put into most of her sessions, but this was her most important work ever.

Claudia felt a twinge in her neck when she slammed her car door and slung the heavy satchel over her shoulder. Leo had warned her that the long periods of holding perfectly still could make her stiff and sore, but she hadn't expected to be feeling the effect today. Granted, her workday had been considerably longer than usual since she had held two parent-teacher conferences on children who were struggling to keep up with their classmates.

She was bursting to share the news about her job possibility with someone, but the only person who might celebrate with her was Leo, and right now was her busiest time of day. Mike would be the first to hear about it when he called at eight. She had missed his call the night before because it had come two hours earlier than usual while she was still with Leo. His message said he had to go out to the job site and would try again tonight.

As she fumbled with the key to her front door, she heard her phone ring. She tossed her satchel onto the couch and made it to the kitchen just before the fourth ring engaged her answering machine.

"Hi, honey."

"Mike!" She was startled to hear his voice and spun to check the clock, thinking she must be late. "I just walked in. You don't usually call this early. It's only seven o'clock."

"I know, but I have to go back out to the work site today. I was there all day yesterday because the architects fucked up something. Now I'm going to have to kick some ass to get it fixed."

She recognized the ire in his voice and didn't envy the construction crew. He had his father's temper. "I certainly wouldn't want to be those guys on the job."

"No shit. So where were you yesterday?" His voice carried a slight edge, which wasn't unusual when he was distracted by work.

"I was with a friend of mine. We went to dinner down at the wharf here in Monterey."

"Somebody from school?"

"Yes." The word came out before she could check it. If Mike knew about Leo it would only fuel more questions about why they were friends, and she didn't want to tell him about the photo sessions. Besides, it wasn't technically a lie that she had met Leo at school. "I don't want to make you jealous, but I had clam chowder."

He groaned. "Stop, you're killing me. I'm so sick of rice I could puke. I was looking forward to Thanksgiving so I could eat some real food."

"What do you mean you were looking forward to it? Don't you dare tell me you aren't coming home."

"That's why I needed to talk to you, baby." He sighed heavily. "They don't exactly celebrate the Pilgrims over here. I've got two subcontractors coming in that week from Shanghai and if I'm not here to show them what's what, they'll fuck it up again and I'll end up having to stay an extra year to fix it. Which would

91

you rather have happen?"

She didn't like either choice, but the idea of him being gone an extra year was her least favorite. He would push her to join him in Taiwan, but she didn't want to postpone starting her teaching career. "I definitely want you to come home sooner."

"That's what I thought. I'm sure you'll have a good time with Mom and Dad. Sis will be there with Hardin."

Ugh. Mike's mother was bad enough, but his sister and her snooty husband were insufferable. Without Mike there to redirect the conversation, she would have to endure Hardin's unending advice on where to invest, what to drive and how to vote. At least the food would be delicious, since the whole feast would be catered. "It won't be same without you."

"I know, but I'll make it up to you. How would you like to meet me in Honolulu the week before Christmas?"

"That's the week I'm supposed to graduate. If you have the time off, why don't you come to Santa Cruz and cheer for me when I finally get my diploma?"

He hissed as he drew in a deep breath. "Please don't ask me to do that. You know how I hate to sit through things like that."

She was hurt that he didn't even consider her request, but it wasn't as if he attended some events and not others. He avoided all of them, including weddings, funerals and virtually all social gatherings. Even at their first meeting, he had whisked her out of the Christmas party.

"I know, I know. Forget about it." Winter commencement ceremonies were always small, but still they didn't acknowledge graduates by name, just degree. "I know you hate these things, so I won't make you come."

"So what do you say? Three nights on Waikiki Beach? I'll get Nissa to book it."

"Let me think about it."

He let out a short, faint sigh of frustration. "Okay, but I'll need to get it on my planner within the next few days or Nissa will start filling it up with meetings."

"Please don't be disappointed."

"How can I not be, Claudia? I haven't seen you in months. I just offered you a trip to Hawaii and all you can say is you'll get back to me."

Mike's impatience served him well on the job site, where subcontractors bent over backward to avoid his wrath, but it was sometimes a challenge when it came to negotiating their relationship. She had learned from experience that a calm and reasoned response worked best to cool him off, and he often came around if she just left him to think about it on his own. "I want to say yes, but I need to check with Mom and Dad first. I invited them to come already, and they might want to, since they shelled out for four years of college. And besides, it's important to me too."

He was quiet for a long moment, which was his usual reaction when she resisted being pushed. She liked to think it was because he recognized when he was being unreasonable. "Sure, check with them and let me know. I'll try to keep those days free a little longer."

Clearly the part about graduation being important to her too had sailed over his head, but he had already made it clear how he felt about the mass ceremony so it was no use to belabor the point. "If it doesn't work out, maybe I could come to Taiwan for Christmas and New Year's."

"Okay, but I'd rather have you all to myself in Hawaii," he said in a lecherous tone. "I've got to go. Nissa says my car's here."

"Wait, I have something important to tell you. My principal wants me to apply for an opening next year. That means I could teach in Monterey while you finish up over there."

"That's a horrible idea. Why would you want to do that?"

She was stung by his response. "What's wrong with it? I was honored to be asked."

"Claudia, you can't complain about me being gone and then say you want to teach in Monterey. You've been up there for four and a half years. I was hoping you'd come over here when you got finished."

"Mike, I got a degree so I could teach, not so I could lounge

93

around all day while you're at work. And I only said I'd come for a visit, not to live."

"I'm coming!" he shouted brusquely to someone in his office. Then to her, "Why do you have to drop this shit on me when I'm running out the door? We'll talk about it next week."

The connection crackled as he hung up, leaving her staring slack-jawed at the receiver.

Chapter 14

Leo gathered the abundant cloth between Claudia's shoulder blades and pinned it, effectively turning her large white shirt into a size medium. "Don't move too much or you'll feel the wrath of these pins. I'm not much of a seamstress."

"It's okay." Claudia smiled impassively and gazed out the open window from her stool.

A ray of sunlight crept onto the floor. In a couple of minutes it would be wide enough to bounce upward from the reflector screen into her face. That would set off a systematic frenzy for Leo as she took the first set of photos. She would have to juggle her light meter, reflector and camera to capture a dozen images with the ratio she needed. Then she would wait for the sun to descend further and shoot several more straight on through a white nylon diffuser.

"I'll be taking a few more photos today than last week because the sun will be moving while we shoot. But I promise you won't have to hold the same pose for longer than a minute, two at the most."

"Don't worry about it."

Claudia's words were reassuring, but her voice sounded troubled. Something was bothering her, and whatever it was had been there three nights ago when Leo had called to ask her to come an hour earlier. "Is there anything I can do to make this more comfortable? Would you rather have an armchair? I can grab the one from my bedroom and bring it up."

"I'm okay, honest." Claudia sighed and her face took on a grim look. "I'm just a little preoccupied because Mike's being a jerk."

"I'm sorry to hear that." Not that she cared anything about Mike. She was only sorry Claudia was unhappy. The line of light had reached her feet, which meant the window for the first shot was imminent.

"I've been in a shitty mood all week, and I haven't told anybody why, not even Sandy."

"If you want to talk, I'll listen…but I've got to be honest. We're going to lose this shot in about ten minutes." As soon as the words left her lips, she felt guilty for her selfishness. She weighed the imposition of pressing ahead with that of rescheduling and putting Claudia through the setup again. "But if you don't want to deal with this today, that's cool. We can do it next week."

"No, let's go ahead. We're ready." Claudia wriggled her shoulders and settled into the pose they had practiced.

Leo angled the reflector upward until it erased the shadows below Claudia's brow, nose and chin. Then she stepped onto her platform to look down into her viewfinder and took three photos at varied exposures. "Okay, relax. I need to do that again in about three or four minutes. That was probably the best one, but I want one more angle of light to make sure."

Claudia took the opportunity to stretch her arms out to the side. "My principal asked me to apply for a job next year at Melrose. He can't promise anything, but he hinted that he'd find

96

a way to pull it off."

"He offered you a job?"

"Basically."

This was terrific news for Leo, as she had begun to dread Claudia's departure in only a month. "That's fantastic. So why don't you sound happy?"

"Because I told Mike and he had a shit-fit. He said I've been gone longer than he has, and that four and a half years was long enough."

"That's ridiculous. He's been overseas the whole time." As they talked, she took continuous readings of Claudia's face with her light meter. When it reached the desired exposure, she tilted the reflector to match the shifting sun. "Bear with me one more time."

Claudia stared blankly out at the water while Leo repeated the earlier process.

"All right, the first one's done. Let's take a break." She pulled the pins from the back of the shirt and fluffed it around Claudia's shoulders. "Why don't you get up and walk around? I've got a few things to do to get ready for the next one." The next photo required a filter, in this case, a white nylon screen that she stretched flat and tacked onto the window frame.

"It's ridiculous that I'm not even allowed to make my own decisions. He thinks I should just pick up and move to Taiwan to be with him after I graduate, like actually using my degree for anything would be quaint. Big of him to indulge my little hobby. He sounds just like my mother." Claudia spun on her heel and began pacing, her voice escalating with agitation. "But you know what the worst part is? He practically hung up on me Monday night, and then he wouldn't take my call on Wednesday. I had to leave a message with his fucking secretary, which he didn't even bother to return."

Leo was taken aback by the harsh tone. It was hard to believe this was the same person who had quieted a roomful of third-graders with her gentle voice. On the other hand, Claudia didn't strike her as someone who let herself get pushed around either.

"Why does he think he gets to control my life all the way from Taiwan? He isn't even coming home for Thanksgiving, but I've got to sit there with his whole family—including his jerk of a brother-in-law—and smile through dinner like Doris Day. I hope he doesn't think getting engaged gives him the right to tell me what to do. Marriage is supposed to be a partnership." Her voice was rising along with the color in her face. "And what is this not taking my call? It's like some three-year-old throwing a temper tantrum because he doesn't get his way. It just makes me so goddamn furious."

"I can see that."

Claudia blinked and stared back at her, as if suddenly aware she had lost it completely. "I'm sorry. I didn't mean to turn into a lunatic. It's just that I've been keeping this bottled up all week. There wasn't anyone else I could tell."

"It's okay. You can talk to me all you want." Leo stopped tinkering with the screen so she could give Claudia her full attention. "I wish I could offer some sage advice, but the truth is I don't have much experience in the relationship department. When I was with Melissa, all I learned was that thinking you're in love makes you do stupid things."

"The stupidest thing I did was call him back. The next time he wants to act like a child, he can go right ahead, but I won't be the one trying to smooth things over. I'll talk to him when I'm damn good and ready." She slumped onto the stool again and groaned in frustration as she stomped her feet. Then she blew out a ragged breath, as if expelling the last of a demon. "God, I'm so glad I got that out. Now, where were we? You wanted photos?"

From her angry expression, Claudia was past her rant, but possibly on the verge of tears.

"We don't have to finish this today. If you want to just go for a walk and scream at the world, we can do that. Or we can just sit here and you can talk it out some more."

Claudia blinked several times and dabbed at the corners of her eyes. "No, this is ridiculous. I'm supposed to be modeling for you, not bitching about Mike."

From a purely selfish standpoint, Leo wanted her shot today. The rainy season could start any day and there might not be another opportunity before Claudia left for good. On top of that, she had planned to present the six photos in three neat pairs. Foregoing the second shot meant reshooting the first. From the sound of it, though, Claudia didn't need someone else pulling at her. No doubt that's what she expected from the people around her, or she wouldn't have held her feelings about Mike inside all week. "What really matters is how you feel right now. I always want people to have fun when we shoot, but if you're upset about something else, the camera won't hide it."

"No, you know what would really make me feel bad? Taking this out on you." She straightened up and lifted her chin as if to pose. "Right now, I feel like you, Sandy and Maria are the only friends I have. Did I tell you Sandy asked me to come to their house for Thanksgiving? I might just do that. Mike can stay in Taiwan if he wants to, but that doesn't mean I have to entertain his stuck-up family, or that they have to entertain me."

Leo smiled gently. "You'd like Thanksgiving at Sandy and Maria's. We always have a good time."

"God, it's tempting."

"Do it…do it…do it." Her chant grew louder each time. "You know you want to."

Finally Claudia laughed. "You're so right. You guys would be a million times more fun than his folks. But I'm not sure I'm actually brave enough to piss them all off." Her angry expression dissipated. "I'm sure this will all blow over tomorrow. Mike wouldn't dare skip our call tonight. If he does, we're in a lot more trouble than I think."

Leo stepped onto the platform to gauge the light on Claudia's face. "If you're ready to go ahead, the sun's coming in for the next one."

"How do I look? Did I mess up my eyes?"

"Not at all," she answered, giving herself permission to boldly study Claudia's face. She gently touched a smudge of mascara and wiped it on her jeans. Their eyes met, and in that moment a feeling crystallized inside her—envy so powerful it made her ache. Mike probably had no idea what a wonderful prize he had. If Claudia were hers, she would never make her cry.

Claudia peeled off the scenic seventeen-mile route and turned for home. The drive had been cathartic, a chance to let go of her irritation and summon her resolve.

Talking things out with Leo had been just the ticket she needed. It was nice knowing there was someone who would take her side no matter what. That's what Mike was supposed to do, but when he resorted to hardball negotiations to bring her around to his point of view, she felt more like one of his contractors than his wife-to-be. They never had this problem when they talked things out face to face. It was only when they tried to sort out important things over the phone, which made meeting in Hawaii after Christmas all the more important so they could get this settled.

In the meantime, with Leo's encouragement, she had decided to stand firm. Since Mike chose to work in Asia, she had every right to pursue a job wherever she wanted. It wasn't as if she was being stubborn. This was her dream as much as working in his family's company was his. Once they talked it out in person, he would understand.

The first thing she noticed when she entered her apartment was the flashing red light on her answering machine. The robotic voice announced two new messages, and her finger hovered over the playback button. It would be nice if one of these was an apology from Mike.

In fact, both messages were from Mike. The first had come at four, which was four a.m. on Monday in Taiwan, and it cheerfully promised good news. The second came two hours later and was tinged with a barely perceptible impatience that she hadn't already returned his call. Still, he reiterated that he had good news, but only if she called him back quickly.

The incredulous, demanding tone he had exhibited last week

was gone. Most likely, he had stewed on it and realized he was out of line, but was unable to admit it. She blamed his father for that, since Mike had been raised to conduct himself in all matters without ever showing weakness.

This time, Nissa put her straight through to his office.

"Claudia?"

"I'm glad you called, Mike. I was starting to think you didn't want to talk to me anymore."

"What do you mean? I was four hours early," he quipped, his voice carrying a hint of mischief, confirming her suspicion that he intended to move on and pretend the whole incident had never happened. "I was wondering if you had any plans for, say… Thursday night?"

"This Thursday?"

"I should get into the airport at San Luis Obispo about nine o'clock. Since I can't come for Thanksgiving…"

"You're coming home?"

"Just for three days. I have to meet with a couple of our architects so we can make a few modifications on this retail structure and move the project forward. Trying to clean up after them from over here just wasn't going to happen. Besides, it gives me a chance to see my girl."

Her mind raced ahead to the weekend. If she left school promptly at three she could be in San Simeon by six. "I can be there in time for dinner on Friday."

"That won't give us much time, honey. I have to fly back on Sunday afternoon. I know you're supposed to be at school on Friday, but if there's any way you can meet me in the middle on this one, it would be great. It's a long trip for us to barely see each other."

He was right, of course, and she was glad he was the one flying so far and not her. "I don't know if they'll let me have the day off, but I can ask first thing tomorrow morning. The problem is that this is my phase to have total responsibility for the class so I have to make sure it's okay with my supervisor."

"Don't they have sick days or something?"

101

"Not for interns." To say nothing of the fact that she wasn't sick. "But I'll do everything I can to get there on Thursday night. I'm so glad you're coming."

"Yeah, me too. I can't stand being away from you so long. Talking on the phone just isn't enough. I need to see your pretty face again."

She savored his sweet words. This was the Mike she had fallen in love with. "I feel the same way, honey. Do you want me to call the inn?" They both were wary of sleeping together under their parents' roofs, so they typically got away to a local bed-and-breakfast for privacy.

"I'll probably have to stay at home at least a night or two, or I'll never hear the end of it from Large Marge."

Claudia laughed, as she always did when Mike invoked his favorite nickname for his heavyset mother. "Tell you what…I'll call and make sure they have a room and we can slip out when nobody's watching."

"Sounds like a plan. Oh, and I should warn you that I'll probably have to be in the office part of the day on Friday. Shouldn't be long though."

"Then we'll be even, because I'll probably have to bring a stack of papers to grade." She caught herself smiling to realize the stress of the past week had evaporated. It was possible the whole thing had been triggered by Mike's frustrations with the architects, not with her. Things like that happened. She had done it herself this afternoon, nearly screwing up Leo's photo shoot with her bad mood.

Leo…their third session was scheduled for Sunday at two, and they had agreed to have dinner afterward at the wharf. "Mike, what time is your plane on Sunday?"

"About four. I have an overnight out of LA."

She would have to reschedule with Leo for after Thanksgiving, but that shouldn't be a problem, since they had only one more session. Leo would have plenty of time to get the workshop application together before the deadline. "Will you call me tomorrow? I should know about Friday."

"I can try to call if I get a minute, or you can call Nissa and leave a message. Oh, and she'll probably ask if you're meeting me in Honolulu. She's holding those tickets, but I looked at my schedule and I can change it to the week after Christmas if you want to go to your graduation."

A wave of warmth enveloped her at hearing he had changed his plans just for her. This was the Mike she knew and loved, the one who knew exactly how to make her feel special. "I'll tell her yes."

"That's my girl. Thanks for calling back."

"I'm really glad you're coming home. I can't wait to see you."

"Same here, babe."

Chapter 15

Claudia squatted precariously in her skirt to tighten the Velcro strap on Kimberly Patton's pink sneaker. The moment she dismissed her class they would empty into a crowded hallway, where a thrown shoe could get a third-grader trampled.

"Thank you all for your hard work today. I'm very proud of you, and I can't wait to hear you read from your journals again tomorrow. You're dismissed."

She followed the line as they walked swiftly to the bus ramp, noting proudly that her children conducted themselves in an orderly manner compared to those from other classes who raced pell-mell for the door.

Once outdoors her tidy line splintered as children picked up their steps toward the various buses that were parked in a line by the curb.

"'Bye, Miss Galloway!"

She smiled and waved in response, but noticed that one of her students, a cherubic boy with curly blond hair, had lagged behind. Usually cheerful and outgoing, Jeremy Erikson had been out of sorts today. "Are you feeling all right, Jeremy?" She felt his forehead and quickly ascertained that he had no fever.

His eyes darted anxiously between her and the bus, and he took a step backward.

She looked over her shoulder toward the ramp, but didn't see anything amiss. "Is something wrong?"

He dropped his books and started shaking his hands fretfully.

"Jeremy, look at me. What is it?" She squatted again and took him by the shoulders. Tears had welled up in his eyes.

"I don't want to go home."

"Are you afraid of something? Did you get in trouble at home?" That wasn't typical of Jeremy, but all children misbehaved from time to time.

The buses began to pull out, including his.

"Wait!" she yelled, lurching toward the curb.

The driver didn't look their way as he followed the line to the exit. That meant Claudia would have to take the boy back inside and call his parents to come pick him up.

She picked up his backpack and nudged him toward a bench by the door. A horrible thought struck her as they walked—that he was afraid because someone at home was hurting him. Part of her teaching training had focused on the signs of abuse, including bruising, soreness or sexual acting out. Jeremy had exhibited none of those, though he had been quiet today, keeping to himself at recess and lunch. "Can you tell me what's wrong?"

"My daddy won't be at home anymore." He was crying so hard she could barely understand his words. "He's getting a divorce."

Her eyes stung with tears to see him so obviously crushed. She had met the Eriksons two weeks earlier when they had come together for the parent-teacher conference. Andrew Erikson was a soldier at Fort Ord, the nearby army base. His wife Susan worked as a hairdresser. Both had shown interest in Jeremy's progress, and no outward signs of discord. "Are you sure, Jeremy? Did they tell you they were getting a divorce?"

He nodded. "I said I'd be good."

"Oh, sweetie." Her heart broke for his tragedy. "This isn't your fault, not at all. I'm sure your mom and dad love you very much. They told me so."

That calmed him a bit, but she could still see the sadness and confusion in his face.

"Let's go call somebody to come get you. I'll wait with you in the office."

She placed a somber call to his mother at her salon, explaining the situation. The woman promised to come as soon as she finished with her current customer. Claudia sat with Jeremy in the office, sprinkling their conversation with questions about his toys and pets in order to distract him from his heartache. When Susan Erikson finally arrived, he bubbled over again in tears and ran into her arms.

"Thank you for coming," Claudia said. "I'm really sorry he missed his bus."

"It's okay," she whispered, fighting back her own tears. Like Jeremy, she was somewhat overweight, and had the tired look of a woman who worked on her feet all day. "It's a hard day for everybody."

"I'm sure." She knelt to get Jeremy's attention again. "I need to talk with your mom for just a minute. Can you go out and wait by the door?"

He looked at his mother and then left without a word.

"I suppose he told you what's going on at home."

Claudia nodded, noting the mother's look of guilt.

"I'm sorry you got caught in the middle of this."

"I'm afraid Jeremy is the one in the middle, Mrs. Erikson. He seems to think all of this is his fault."

"That's ridiculous. It's between his father and me."

"I know. I just wanted you to know he's feeling that way. He might need a little bit of extra reassurance, especially over the next few weeks while he gets used to the changes."

"I'll make sure I do that."

"It's probably important that his father do it too."

Mrs. Erikson wiped her eyes and said bitterly, "I'll be sure to pass that on to Andrew if I hear from him."

"Would you like for me to call him? I know it isn't my business, but your husband"—she paused for a second, hoping Mrs. Erikson wouldn't react badly to her untimely word choice—"he seems to care a great deal about his son."

"He does. We both do."

"Maybe...I don't mean to be offering advice, but I really care about Jeremy too. Maybe this is a good chance for both of you to show him that his needs are still your priority, whether you're together or not. If you don't think Mr. Erikson will be calling soon, I'll be happy to call him at the base. I don't want to make things worse, though."

"That's okay. I'll get word to him."

"We'll all pitch in to get Jeremy through this. I'll be finishing up my internship in a couple of weeks, but I'll make sure Miss Irwin knows to be on the lookout for any problems." Claudia couldn't resist offering a gentle hug. "Good luck with all you're going through."

She watched from the office lobby as Mrs. Erikson joined her son and took his hand. Her smile, though obviously forced, noticeably cheered the boy.

Leo handed over the diaper bag to Sheila Barnhill, who had secured her toddler son in his car seat. Mrs. Barnhill had a standing appointment every four weeks for photos, which Leo suspected she sent to everyone she knew. At each session, she extolled her "miracle" child, who had finally been conceived after more than twenty years of trying to get pregnant. All parents were proud, Leo thought, but this one took the cake.

"Thank you. I'll call you when they come in and put you down for another appointment next month. Bye-bye Joshua." She made an exaggerated happy face and waved, a gesture he completely ignored. At least he had looked at her when it mattered.

When Mrs. Barnhill backed out, Leo turned to smile at Claudia's car, which occupied her other customer space. A folded note was wedged beneath the windshield wiper.

Saw you were busy, so I went for a walk. Hope I'll see you when I get back.

She returned to the house for a jacket and sat on the porch swing to wait. The only other person who ever dropped by unannounced was Patty, and Leo had to admit she appreciated the break from her routine. She hadn't heard from Patty since the Halloween party, and Maria confirmed she had hooked up with Joyce, a dental hygienist who had moved to the area from Chicago a couple of years ago. It was nice to think Patty had found someone to make happy with her kindness and attention.

Claudia appeared just as the sun was setting, her head hanging low, as if she were lost in concentration. She made it all the way to the top of the steps without seeing Leo on the swing.

"Hey, stranger."

"Leo!" Her face lit up in a smile. "Did you get my note?"

"Yeah, I was busy shooting baby pictures. I thought about walking down to meet you but I was afraid we might pass each other on different streets." She slid over on the swing to make room and Claudia joined her.

"It's okay. I needed to get out there and clear my head."

"Something wrong?"

"I had to deal with a tough incident at school today." As Claudia related the story of a boy in her class whose parents were getting a divorce, her voice quivered with sadness. It was moving to see her so profoundly affected. "In college we studied all about how to teach reading and math, and how to get the kids excited about history and science, but we didn't talk enough about how to handle kids like Jeremy. I just wanted to beat up his mother and father for hurting him like that."

"I see that sort of thing too. People come in for their family Christmas cards every year, and then one year they'll show up without the dad. A year later it's a stepdad and new siblings. It's very sad, especially for the kids." Leo's parents had rarely disagreed, let alone fought. The worst problem she could remember was her mother's discontent with the weekend schedule, which limited their family time. Still, they were closer than most families, especially since she worked with her father.

"I can't believe adults can be so selfish. If you're going to have kids, you have to honor your commitment to them. They should act like grownups and work out their differences. All that matters is what's best for the kid."

"Maybe for some people it's better if they split up."

Claudia shook her head vehemently. "I don't buy that. I think it's just a cop-out so they can dump their guilt."

"I'm not so sure about that. Like my friend Patty, the woman you met at the Halloween party. Her parents divorced when she was little. From some of the things she told me, her father was pure evil. She said it was the happiest day of her life when he moved out."

"Okay, so once in a while it's better to split up, but Patty's the exception. Besides, I don't think that's what's happening with the Eriksons. Andrew Erikson seems like a very nice guy who cares about his son. And Jeremy isn't relieved about him leaving. He's frantic. If a mom and dad don't want to live together they should move into separate rooms, but nobody should get to just walk away."

Despite how much she wanted to take Claudia's side, Leo didn't agree with her on this subject. She knew too many women who had left their husbands and taken the kids because they couldn't live a lie anymore. It was just as big a lie to pretend you loved someone. The way she saw it, it was perfectly understandable to sacrifice for your children, but not at the expense of your own sanity. That wasn't good for anyone.

"This is personal to me," Claudia said heavily, kicking the floor to start the swing. "From the time I was little, I was Daddy's little girl. My mom and I just rubbed each other the wrong way. We still do, but I don't let it bother me anymore. When I was about eight or nine I heard them arguing and my dad told her he wanted a divorce. She said fine, but that she and I would stay in the house and he would move out. Dad came to my room that night and told me he was going, but he promised to come and get me every weekend and he said I could stay with him in the summer. I thought my whole world was falling apart. I couldn't bear the thought of living with just my mother, and I acted exactly like Jeremy Erikson did."

Leo listened with growing sympathy. No wonder this had hit Claudia so hard.

"I begged him not to go, but he said he had to, that he couldn't live with my mom anymore. So I pulled out the only weapon I had—I ran away."

Leo dropped her foot to stop the swing, nearly throwing Claudia onto the porch. "You actually ran away?"

"Yeah, I went about a half mile to my grandmother's and hid in the crawl space under her house. I came out late that night when I got hungry and rang the doorbell." She rolled her eyes and smirked. "If I ever got shipwrecked I'd be dead in two days."

"Your parents must have been worried sick."

"They were, and after a couple of days my dad said he'd changed his mind about the divorce, and that he wouldn't ever leave me."

Leo started their swing again. "That's an amazing story."

"I've never told anybody before. It's sort of the family secret, not just that I ran away but that my parents almost got divorced. I used to feel really guilty about it, because I knew I was forcing my dad to stay there when he wasn't happy. But when I got my driver's license I told him he could do whatever he wanted to do, that I'd be okay with it. He said he'd made his peace with my mom, and he was glad he stuck around."

"And you want Jeremy's father to do the same thing."

She nodded. "Maybe some kids can handle it, but I don't think Jeremy can. This is going to break his heart. I just don't see how his parents can do that to him."

"I understand where you're coming from." They rocked silently for several minutes. With this new perspective, Leo saw

110

clearly why Claudia was taking the whole incident so hard.

"I should have known today was going to suck. I dropped my necklace in the bathroom this morning and shattered the jade."

Her bottom lip stuck out in a pout, prompting Leo to drape an arm around her shoulder in a supportive hug. The urge to plant a kiss on her temple was almost overwhelming, but she touched her fingertips to that spot instead. "I'm sorry you've had such a bad day."

She felt Claudia relax into her shoulder, but it lasted only an instant. Then Claudia abruptly patted her knee and stood. "Thanks for letting me drop in like this. I hope I didn't interrupt your session."

"Not a problem at all. You can come by whenever you want." Leo was mortified that her physical gesture had gone past Claudia's comfort zone. She had only meant it as a friendly hug.

"I should go." Claudia started for the steps and stopped. "Oh, I almost forgot. Mike called last night and he's coming home to San Simeon this weekend. I'm going to have to miss our shoot on Sunday."

Leo's heart sank, not because Claudia would miss their session, or even because she was going home to see Mike. What worried her more was the tremor in Claudia's voice, and the possibility this was a permanent brush-off.

She was shocked when Claudia suddenly closed the distance between them and wrapped her arms around her neck. "Thanks for listening, Leo. I really needed a shoulder today."

Her arms went around Claudia's waist and she released a breath of relief. "You've always got one here."

"I'll call you when I get back. We'll pick another time to do the photo shoot."

Leo slumped back into the swing as Claudia disappeared around the corner to her car. What could have been a very awkward parting had instead become more evidence of their genuine friendship. Now that she didn't have to worry she had crossed a line, she could focus her anxiety on Claudia spending the weekend with Mike.

Claudia accelerated past the entrance to her apartment complex and merged onto the Pacific Coast Highway. The last thing she wanted was to be closed up with her emotions inside her small apartment. Her head was spinning from the events of the day, the most unsettling of which was the feeling that had come over her when Leo's arm went around her shoulder. It wasn't that she had never been physically comforted by her girlfriends or college chums, but none of them had made her feel so precious and protected. She had wanted to nestle into Leo's embrace and stay there. Instead, she had panicked and jumped to her feet.

The sensation had overtaken her, triggering something far more personal than just a feeling of support. There was no way Leo had meant to convey anything other than sympathy and friendship, and would probably be shocked to realize where her head had gone. At least she had realized her reaction and pulled away before making a fool of herself.

How on earth had Leo aroused such an intensive response? She had never felt a rush of warmth that strong, not even from Mike. Then again, she had never felt comfortable talking with Mike about such deeply personal things. It wasn't that she kept secrets, but he didn't believe in airing dirty laundry because it only gave people ammunition to tear him down. That was more of his father's business influence, but until now it hadn't occurred to her how much it stifled their communication, along with her freedom to share her emotions.

"Maybe I'm really a lesbian," she said aloud, chuckling uncomfortably. Or maybe she just needed to accept that her relationship with Mike was only a sliver of who she was. Her parents had one another, but they also had full lives with friends and interests outside of their marriage. It was silly to expect Mike to meet all of her needs, and perfectly normal to have a friend with whom she connected on an emotional level, even if that friend just happened to be a lesbian.

The thing with Leo bothered her for another reason though, one she was only now beginning to confront. Why had she been drawn to her in the first place, and why had it been so important to gain her confidence and friendship? Sandy said Leo didn't let many people close, so perhaps she felt special to be the exception. Right from the start, she felt privileged because Leo had let her inside a gate where few others had been, showing her through the house, talking about her plans and dreams, even sharing personal details about her past relationships.

So why had Leo singled her out? Was there something behind her friendly overtures? No, Claudia knew the answer to that. Leo had done nothing out of line. Claudia was the one who was fluttering because of a friendly embrace. She needed to get a grip before she did something that sent out the wrong message.

Chapter 16

Present Day

Eva's shoulders sagged. "You must think we're all pompous boors."

Leo chortled. "Not all of you."

"Fair enough."

"Don't worry about it. It comes with the territory. Weddings are stressful. Believe me, I've seen it all."

Eva looked longingly at a marble bench, fluffed her ivory gown and leaned delicately against the balcony rail instead. "What was the worst thing you've ever seen?"

Leo mentally sifted through thirty years of memories. "I've seen fistfights, no-shows…even one wedding that stopped right in the middle when the bride changed her mind. The pictures of that one were incredible." She laughed and shook her head to recall how she had been so absorbed in taking photos that she hadn't realized what was happening. "The strangest was one time when the groom was so frazzled he forgot his vows. The bride was so obsessed with having the perfect wedding that she made the whole wedding party leave the church so they could start over from the beginning."

"Now that's what I call obsessive."

The stepstool looked inviting to take a load off, but Leo resisted out of empathy for Eva. "A lot of little girls grow up thinking this is going to be the most important day of their lives. That turns everything into high stakes. If your most important day gets screwed up, what does that say about your life?"

"I see what you mean, but I don't think about it that way. Don't get me wrong—marrying Todd is the biggest thing I've ever done, but that has nothing to do with this circus. This is all Grandmother's doing. She's the one that's stressed."

"I can see that."

Eva laughed softly. "I'll let you in on a little secret, but whatever you do, you can't ever tell her."

Leo crossed her heart with her fingers, already smiling in anticipation of Eva's news.

"Todd and I got married for real on Wednesday afternoon at the courthouse in San Francisco. The judge he's going to clerk for performed the ceremony in his chambers, and the only people there were his parents, and my mom and grandpa. It was perfect, so no matter what happens today, that's how I'm going to remember my wedding."

"Now there's a terrific story if I ever heard one. Congratulations."

"Thanks. We sort of did it on a whim because Grandmother was getting worse by the minute. She kept calling to tell me about all these important friends of hers, and why it was *absolutely imperative* they be present, so I said fine, invite whoever you want. I don't even know most of these people."

"These things sometimes take on a life of their own."

"And then there's Aunt Deborah and her poor little dog. If you ask me, I think they both need to be on tranquilizers. Oh, and this Chantal person! She refused the orchid shipments because they were lavender and she had ordered purple. I felt so sorry for the poor delivery guy that I insisted on keeping the ones he brought, and I think Mom slipped him three hundred dollars for having to put up with that abuse."

The more Leo heard from Eva Pettigrew, the more she liked her. "If it's any comfort to you, a lot of hardworking people are getting paid today thanks to your wedding."

"That's what Todd said…Grandmother's money raining down on all the little people. Now if we could just get through the day without insulting all of them."

"Don't sweat it too much. The only person you have to look at in the mirror is you."

"Thanks, Leo. And thanks for jumping in at the last minute and saving our butts."

"It's my pleasure, really. There's no way I would have missed this."

Chapter 17

Thanksgiving 1986

Leo peered into the distance as three deer sauntered into the expansive open space behind Maria and Sandy's house. She envied the pristine view from their deck, especially in the late afternoon when the sun turned the hillside golden. It was a nice change from what she was used to, though looking onto a row of tidy homes on Van Buren wasn't bad if you didn't mind the power poles. At least she had the unobstructed water view from the attic, which her sessions with Claudia had allowed her to enjoy.

The eight days that had passed since Claudia dropped by to talk about the boy in her class had seemed like an eternity already, and the next three days would crawl by before she returned to shoot on Sunday. Since that day on the porch swing, Leo had dreamily played back the moment when Claudia walked back to give her a hug. Something had shifted inside her, and no amount of rational introspection could put it back in its place. Her head was bombarded by dozens of warnings to rein in the attraction, the loudest being that Claudia wasn't gay. There was also the matter of that rather large diamond on her hand, and while Leo didn't think an overbearing jerk like Mike deserved someone like Claudia, there was no denying that she wanted him. Otherwise, she wouldn't have raced home to see him after the way he had treated her on the phone.

She had convinced herself that a couple of weeks away from Claudia would help sharpen her perspective, at least enough to let reality set in. But what she had hoped would be "out of sight, out of mind" had instead become the opposite.

The glass door slid behind her and she turned to see Maria acrobatically juggling two steaming mugs as she pushed the handle with her elbow.

"Have you tasted Sandy's cider? No alcohol, but the cloves pack a wallop."

"Let me get that." Leo jumped to close the door behind her and took the offered mug. "Need any help in there?"

"You any good at crowd control? Patty and Joyce are fighting over the TV remote."

Leo sipped the spicy drink, which numbed her throat as it trickled down. "This is good stuff."

"Don't fill up on it. I've got enough food to feed Ethiopia. You getting hungry?"

"Whenever. We had a huge breakfast at IHOP." She had spent the night in Modesto with her mother and Aunt Ellie, a deed that had released her from the duty of accompanying them to Thanksgiving dinner at the home of cousins she didn't know very well.

"How's your mom?"

"She's doing great. A lot happier in Modesto than she was here after my father died. She just couldn't stand to face the loss every day."

Maria nodded and propped her elbows on the rail. "It's amazing the lengths we go to so we can cope. Look at Joyce. She moved all the way out here from Chicago after her parents found out she was gay."

Leo had coped with her father's death by throwing herself into her work, largely because she'd had little choice. The commitments on their studio calendar had to be honored, and she was fortunate most of those customers had trusted her to step into her father's shoes. The first year was a blur of school and recreation league pictures, weekend weddings, mornings at the mall taking hundreds of baby photos, and then a steady stream of evening studio portraits. She remembered feeling relief when her mother moved to Modesto because her home life became one less obligation to juggle.

Things had settled quite a bit since then, enough that she no longer felt guilty when she made time for her friends. Little by little, she had given herself over to parties and casual outings with Maria and Sandy as her main conduits. There was no denying how important their friendship had become. "It's nice you and Sandy host this every year. You guys feel like family."

"That's because we are." Maria looked back over her shoulder and lowered her voice. "I want to tell you about something so it won't come out of the blue. We'll be making an official announcement at dinner."

From Maria's upturned mouth, Leo suspected good news and she leaned closer to hear it.

"You remember that gallery in San Luis Obispo I told you about? I'm buying it. Sandy and I are moving down there next summer after the school year ends."

"You're kidding."

"We went down last weekend and bought some land in Morro Bay overlooking the water. If we're lucky, we'll break ground on our dream house by February."

Leo wanted to be happy for them, but her selfish side felt the loss instantly. If Maria and Sandy left—and with Claudia wrapping up her internship and heading home—that would leave only Patty among her close friends. She liked the other women in their group, but none were likely to convene the group for

119

parties or holidays and neither would she. Few people had Maria and Sandy's flair for bringing women together. "That's pretty big news. How come you haven't told anybody?"

"You know how fast things get around. Sandy hasn't had a chance to talk to her boss."

"Don't go," she said plaintively. "Who's going to cook Thanksgiving dinner for us?"

Maria laughed and chucked her arm. "I'm still going to cook, but you'll have to drive a little farther to eat."

In the distance, a car started up the hill toward the house—a white 300ZX—and Leo felt her pulse quicken.

"There's Claudia," Maria said.

"I thought she was having Thanksgiving with her fiancé's family." Leo cringed at how her voice suddenly squeaked, the result of both surprise and excitement. The last thing she wanted was for someone to see her getting weird about Claudia. "I talked to her just last week."

"She called Sandy this morning and said she decided not to go. Something about how she'd seen enough of them last weekend to last a while."

"Right, she went home to see her fiancé."

"I got the impression that didn't go well."

Leo looked blankly at Maria and back at the approaching vehicle. "What do you mean didn't go well? What happened?"

"I'm not sure, but apparently she was in a bad mood all week."

"That's because her fiancé's an asshole," Leo snarled, making no attempt to keep the venom from her voice. Maybe Claudia had dumped him.

Claudia fluttered with excitement when she spotted Leo by the sliding glass door. The bright smile that greeted her triggered one of her own, along with fresh regret for skipping their last session. Given the events of the past weekend, she would much rather have been with Leo than at home with Mike.

Sandy met her with a cheerful hug in the foyer. "Glad you

could make it. We're so much more fun than the in-laws."

"So is getting a root canal," she said, shrugging out of her blazer. "Thanks for letting me come empty-handed at the last minute. I promise to clean up the kitchen afterward."

"Oh, no," Sandy said, her voice booming across the room, where four women and a teenage boy lounged in front of the TV on the expansive sectional sofa. "Cleaning up is Patty's job. We gave it to her permanently after she brought a casserole nobody could eat."

Patty stuck out her tongue as Joyce mussed her hair playfully. "You guys better be nice to me, or I'll start bringing food again."

Claudia started her welcome tour at the sofa, stepping over outstretched legs to shake hands with Sharon and Lydia, whom she remembered from the Halloween party.

"This is my son, Zack," Lydia said, jabbing her elbow into the boy's ribs.

The lanky youth, dressed in jeans and a black Metallica T-shirt, jumped to his feet and smiled. "Hello, ma'am."

"Call me Claudia. Now sit back down and enjoy the game." When she reached Patty and Joyce, the two were standing for a greeting. She brushed her lips on Joyce's cheek and turned to do the same with Patty.

"Oh no, you don't," Patty said, enveloping her in a rib-crunching hug. "Get with the program. Dykes don't do air kisses."

As they turned their attention back to the football game on TV, she worked her way to Leo, who wore her trademark black jeans with a long-sleeved green and white rugby shirt. After Patty had set the stage for familiarity, she held out her arms. "I take it air kisses are out for you too."

Leo wrapped her in a hug, not as powerful as Patty's, but longer and undoubtedly affectionate. "This is a nice surprise. I didn't know you were going to be here."

Claudia followed her out onto the deck and to the rail, the same spot where they had talked at the Halloween party. "I tried to call you last night but I got your machine." It hadn't occurred to her until just now to wonder about where Leo had spent the night…or with whom.

"I was at my mom's in Modesto. We always go out for breakfast on Thanksgiving, since that gets me off the hook for going to my cousin's for dinner."

"Nice how that works, huh? My mom and dad went to Vail with some friends of theirs, so it wasn't even an option to spend the holiday with them."

"I thought you were having dinner with Mike's family."

She groaned. "I've had my fill of them for a while. I spent all day Saturday listening to his mother talk about how a supportive wife would keep house while her husband went out there to earn a living. It sounded just like my mother, only Large Marge takes it up a couple of notches because she doesn't understand why I'd care more about the children of 'lettuce pickers' than I would about staying at home with my own."

"You call your future mother-in-law Large Marge?"

"That's what Mike calls her. So there I sat with her while Mike was supposedly meeting with the architects. Turns out his meeting lasted only two hours, after which he and his father spent the rest of the afternoon playing golf."

"Ouch."

"The whole weekend was like that." She pushed her hair out of her eyes and turned into the breeze, remembering the last time she had talked with Leo about Mike. She had ended up in tears, something she wasn't going to do again no matter how frustrated she was. "I don't need to be going on about Mike again. As my mother pointed out, no one wants to hear it."

"Your mother doesn't know what kind of friend I am."

Claudia was touched by the words, but she suspected her mother was right for once. Either way, she didn't want to grumble about it today. People like Leo, Sandy and Maria deserved better than to have their holiday dinner spoiled by a pouting guest, and that's all she seemed to do lately. "I'm just glad to be with pleasant people for a change. Are we still on for Sunday?"

"You bet." Leo held up her hands as if framing her in a photo. "We're going to do a couple of tricky profile shots."

"Here we go again. Make sure you get my pointy chin."

The sliding door rumbled behind them and Sandy appeared. "Come on, ladies. Zack's already loading his plate and there won't be much left."

Claudia followed Leo into the rustic dining room, a sharp contrast to last year's holiday dinner at the majestic home of Mike's parents. That one had been catered by a small wait staff and served on china bearing the family crest. Here, in a room filled with sun from the skylights in the cathedral ceiling, the table was set with brown and burgundy stoneware. Gold napkins were folded in the shape of turkey fans, and food was piled high on steaming serving dishes in the center of the table.

Everyone held hands around the perimeter, so Claudia entwined her fingers with Leo's and joined the circle. Joyce began what appeared to be a ritual, expressing her gratitude for how the others in the group had rescued her when her family broke ties upon learning she was gay. Without her friends, she said, she hated to imagine where she might have ended up.

As they took turns saying a few words of thanks, Claudia was fascinated to realize the common thread—the people here regarded one another as family, even young Zack, who seemed as comfortable in a roomful of lesbians as anyone. Easy to see why. The table was surrounded by genuine love and a strong sense of unconditional support. What struck her even more was that she felt a part of it, far more at ease among them than she was even with her own parents, to say nothing of Mike's upper-crust family.

When she had come to the Halloween party here less than four weeks ago, it had felt like a novelty, a chance to demonstrate to her new lesbian friends that she was open-minded and accepting of their lifestyles. Today's gathering held none of that outsider feel. She was the one being embraced, and it wasn't only with hospitality. These women, whether they knew it or not, were giving her shelter from the parts of her life that had begun to unravel last weekend.

"This is such a beautiful family," Claudia said when her turn came. "I can't even express how grateful I am that you've made me feel so welcome. Thank you for that."

Leo was up next, and she glanced nervously around the circle. "You probably all know that I have trouble sometimes putting my feelings into words, so I tend to keep quiet. I hope you haven't thought it was because I didn't feel things, because I do." She cleared her throat and fixed her gaze on Maria and Sandy. "It's really easy to take things for granted, as if they're going to be there all the time. I just want you all to know that you can take me for granted, because no matter what happens you'll have my friendship forever. I love all of you."

Maria sniffed loudly. "Damn you, Leo!"

When Leo dropped her hand and met Maria in a long hug, Claudia felt a surprising wave of envy at their emotional embrace. It was possessive and silly to feel that way, but she was closer to Leo than she was to anyone else in the room, even Sandy, and she jealously wanted Leo to feel the same way about her. When Leo returned to her side, she staked her claim by snagging her hand again, squeezing firmly.

They turned their attention to Sandy and Maria, who then shared stunning news of their upcoming move to San Luis Obispo. Despite their obvious excitement about their new gallery and dream home, the announcement received mixed reactions from around the room, since none of their friends liked the idea of them moving away.

As they were sitting down, Maria suddenly clapped her hands. "Oh, I forgot the bread."

"I'll help," Claudia offered, following her into the kitchen and out of earshot of the others. "I didn't want to say this in front of everybody, but I'll let you in on a little secret. I think it's terrific you're moving down the coast. It's only a half hour from Cambria."

Maria's eyes twinkled as she leaned her head close and lowered her voice. "That's not the only secret around here. I think Leo might be falling in love with you."

She felt her face grow heated under Maria's teasing gaze. "Why do you say that? What did she say?"

"It's just a feeling I got. Nothing specific." She glanced over her shoulder to make sure they were still alone. "We were out on the deck when you started up the road, and she practically knocked me down to get into the house."

"She was probably just surprised to see me. We're friends, that's all."

Maria chuckled. "She's our friend too, but she doesn't light up like that when Sandy or I come into the room. And from the look on your face, I'd say you don't mind one bit that she feels that way."

Claudia hadn't realized she was smiling, and to her consternation, she couldn't seem to stop. "Who wouldn't be flattered by that?"

"Flattered, huh? Sure you don't want to ditch that fiancé of yours? I bet Leo would make it worth your while." Maria arranged the rolls in a basket and covered them with a cloth. "Especially since it looks like Sandy's job is going to be open next year."

Chapter 18

Claudia heard the shutter click for the sixth time as Leo exhaled, a signal the shot was complete. She had been studying Leo intently all day, looking for proof of what Maria had seen. She had watched her all afternoon on Thanksgiving Day, and there was no mistaking that Leo had shown little interest in anyone else. The problem today was that Leo was hard to read in the studio, where the task at hand commanded nearly all of her attention. "Did you get what you wanted?"

"Absolutely." Leo stepped down from her platform and turned off the spotlight, leaving the studio bathed only in light from the small lamp at her feet. "We have one more to go, but it's the most complicated."

"It's hard to believe this is our last day. Not only that, the semester's nearly over. It's time for Claudia Galloway to face the real world."

"I have news for you. You're already in the real world." Leo flipped another switch, turning on a spotlight mounted by a C-clamp to a beam overhead. "What could be more real than working every day and then trying to do what everyone else needs?"

"Some people might say I haven't done too well on that last part."

"I wouldn't be one of those people." Leo climbed a ladder to adjust the light above. "I couldn't have done any of this without your help."

"I hardly did anything but show up." She squinted upward, curious about the objective of the final photo. "What are you doing?"

"Lighting from the top is tricky, and I didn't get it set up quite right because you're a little taller than Miss Murphy. That wasn't a problem when it was just a head shot because I could adjust the height of the stool. But this photo is supposed to be three-quarter length so you'll have to stand."

"Why would they want you to light from up there? Won't my face be in the shadows?"

"Part of it will, but I'll also have a fill light off to the side behind you. It's going to hit your face with a little less intensity than what we've used before. It definitely won't be as bright as this one up here."

Claudia stood as still as possible, moving only when Leo reached down to guide her pose. For the first time, she noticed the softness of Leo's hands, that her touch was light and delicate...more feminine than anything else about her. It struck her that Leo seemed to keep her sexual side hidden. She never flirted with anyone, and in fact, seemed almost flustered by the sexual humor that had been bandied about by Patty and Joyce over Thanksgiving dinner. Yet she exuded sensuality, both in her soft-spoken manner and in the self-confidence on display right now. Claudia wondered which side of her would prevail in the bedroom.

She shook off the reckless thought, which she blamed on

127

Maria's power of suggestion. A shudder passed through her, leaving a trail of cool sweat across her chest.

"Okay, the light's ready. Now we have to get you into your final pose." Leo stepped down from the ladder and gently brushed Claudia's shoulders to straighten the fabric of the white shirt.

Since the attic was so warm, she had opted not to wear the tights, so the shirt hung loosely over her white bikini briefs to the middle of her bare thighs.

"Are you going to pin the back of my shirt again?"

"No...might have to pin the front though. I want to shoot this one over your shoulder. That means your body will be facing the back wall"—she spun Claudia in place—"but you'll be looking to the side again so I can get your profile. This is a tough angle because I want the shadows to fall off fast."

"What does that even mean?"

"You remember how we used the umbrella that first time to light up both sides of your face? I don't want to do that for this one." Leo touched her fingers to Claudia's cheek. "I only want to light the short side, which means I'll get a sliver of your face in the light. The rest will be shadowed. And the light overhead is going to splash on your hair and shoulder, but not down your back."

Claudia allowed herself to be bent, tilted and turned for several minutes while Leo checked her light meter and viewfinder. By the knit of Leo's brow, she still wasn't happy. "What's the problem?"

"It's your shoulder. The collar's catching all the light in the wrong place and it's making a shadow I don't like. I think we're going to need the tube top instead...which means you have to change and we have to start all over with the lights because the tube top is black."

With the sweat already gathering on her skin, Claudia didn't relish the idea of changing into something clingy. "What if I pull this down?" With her back to Leo, she unfastened the rest of the buttons on the shirt and pushed it off her shoulders, along with her bra strap. "How's that?"

"That could work. Let me see." Leo stomped onto her

platform to check her viewfinder. "Nope, that's not enough. I'm still catching the collar."

"Hold on." Claudia reached under the shirt to unfasten the clasp on her bra and snaked it off through a sleeve. Still facing the backdrop, she dropped her shirt to her waist, but brought the front up to cover up her breasts.

Leo hesitated for a moment before stepping back onto the set. "That's…it could work if we…" She tipped her shoulder, chin and crown to pose her just right, systematically metering the light. "Can you…would you drop your arms a little bit more? Don't worry. I can't see anything from back here."

Claudia did as she was asked, baring her breasts toward the black wall. Even with Leo well behind her and out of view, it was impossible not to feel exposed. What surprised her was the thrill that came with doing something so bold.

"That's going to be perfect. Now just look into the corner and try not to move."

A trickle of sweat started down her neck but she didn't dare wipe it. This was the critical moment, when Leo got the light and look she wanted and lapsed into a zone of intense concentration that rendered any last-minute adjustments moot. Claudia heard the familiar deep breath and held her pose firmly as Leo made adjustments on her camera and clicked off the photos.

"You can relax now." Leo stepped off her platform and pulled the plug on the overhead light, cooling the room instantly.

Claudia spun around and pulled her shirt back in place as she buttoned up. "For the record, this was my idea, so we don't have to tell Maria that you talked me out of my clothes."

Leo chuckled as she looked away quickly. "From where I was standing, it wasn't any more revealing than the tube top. Besides, no one's going to see these but the judges."

"Have you ever shot nude photos?"

"Once in a while."

"Models?"

Leo shook her head as she dragged the ladder back beneath the mounted light. "Women call me sometimes to see if I can do something special for their husbands or boyfriends. Most of them are pretty coy about it, but after a few minutes I can usually tell when they're talking about nude versus just an ordinary glamour shot."

"What's the difference?"

"The whole idea of a glamour shot is to bring out a woman's most beautiful public side. I usually go extra on the makeup and the hair, and then encourage her to wear something that might be a lot more elegant than she's used to, maybe something with satin and lace. A nude is obviously more intimate, something probably only the man in her life will see. We don't do much makeup for that, since it's not a close-up."

"Right, and no one's going to be looking at her face anyway."

"That's probably true. But sometimes all we do is create the appearance of being nude. We'll draw a sheet or something over the strategic places and try to go for a sexy expression. Or maybe I'll pose them so it's obvious they're nude, but they're angled so you can't really see anything. Magazines do that a lot."

Claudia found herself titillated at the thought of posing nude for Leo. In fact, it made her jealous to know Leo had done that with other women in her studio, but not with her. "Did you ever consider doing that for any of these photos?"

"I might have if I'd used a professional model, because the human body casts some beautiful shadows. But I got six great shots anyway, so I'm not complaining."

"I'm not sure I would have had the nerve, but maybe." It would have been interesting to see Leo's reaction if she had. "I bet if someone was really modest about taking off her clothes, she wouldn't be here in the first place."

Though Claudia was thinking more in personal terms, Leo maintained her professional demeanor. "The hardest part is always right at first, but I do things to make them feel secure about it. It's not all that different from what women go through at a doctor's office. I usually go through a big show of locking all the doors and taking the phone off the hook so they don't have to worry about someone else interrupting. And they understand before we ever start that this is extremely private, and that I'll be delivering both the photos and the negatives. I make it very clear that I don't keep copies, so if they ever want prints they have to bring them back."

"But what about when you're actually shooting? Is it really just another job, or do you get excited about seeing these women naked?"

She watched intently for an unguarded reaction to her increasingly sexual questions, but Leo persisted with formality. "It isn't as erotic as you might think, at least not for me. In my opinion the very best portraits—not just nudes, but anything— are the ones people want for themselves, because there's only one relationship in the room—the one between the subject and the photographer. But most portraits are intended for someone else, so I'm just a proxy on the other side of the camera. My job is to coax the expressions my subjects want to convey to the people who are going to receive the photos. Those aren't necessarily the expressions I think make the most interesting portraits."

"So you've never actually shot a nude just for art's sake?"

Leo shook her head. "No, I hardly ever do anything for art's sake, but that doesn't mean I wouldn't love to. One of the reasons these photos we've done are so special is because I'm shooting them the way I want."

Claudia was still fixated on the idea of posing nude, and wondering if she would ever have the nerve to do something so provocative. No way would she give photos like that to Mike, or for that matter, even a less revealing glamour shot. His first reaction would be irritation that she had posed like that, and his second would be to stuff it in a drawer or tear it up so no one else would see it. "Do you ever wonder what the boyfriends do with them? It's not like you can set a nude photo on the mantle beside Aunt Bess."

Leo released the light fixture and coiled the light cord in her hand as she descended the ladder. "I wouldn't be surprised if some people did."

"More power to them. I wouldn't have the guts to show off something like that. I'm not even sure I could handle the posing part, except maybe if you were the photographer. I'm sure I couldn't do it if it was a man."

"My dad did them all the time, but he never showed them to anyone, not even to me. I think it all comes down to whether or not you trust the person taking the picture, just like you have to trust the person you give it to. I worry sometimes about these women who want something for a boyfriend they've just met. There's always a chance those pictures are going to be circulated through all his friends, especially if things don't work out. I always try to make sure she's considered that before we ever shoot."

"That would be so humiliating."

"The Native Americans used to believe the camera stole their soul, and I think there's a little truth to that, no matter what kind of photo it is. But your soul isn't shared with the photographer. It's shared with the one who sees your portrait."

Claudia hadn't really considered until now that she was posing for the judges. As far as she was concerned, she was modeling strictly for Leo. "What about these we've done for the workshop? It never occurred to me I was sharing my soul with anybody but you."

Leo shrugged, and then nodded, as if conceding the point. "These are different. If I'd hired a model this would have been just an exercise in all the mechanical aspects. But I have a relationship with you so I don't see just the lights and shadows in these photos. I think of them as ours, but they'll also belong to anyone you share them with."

"Nobody. I don't need a set for myself. You didn't take them for me to show to someone else. It's fine if strangers look at them to see if you got the light right, but they won't mean anything to anyone but us." The time she had spent in the attic was too personal to share with anyone else, not even Mike. Especially not Mike.

Leo looked taken aback. "You don't even want copies?"

It suddenly occurred to her that presenting the completed

portfolio was the ultimate finale for Leo. Of course she would want to share it. "I hope I didn't just insult you. I'm dying to see these pictures when they're finished. It's just that I don't want them lying around for somebody else to find. They're ours, you know? That's what made this so special."

"I see what you mean."

Special wasn't even a strong enough word. Private…intimate. And to top it off, she had even toyed with the possibility of letting Leo photograph her in the nude. It would almost be worth it just to see her reaction.

Leo stepped onto the porch and drew in a lungful of unseasonably cold air. Claudia Galloway would be the death of her. Talking about shooting nudes had sent her heart pounding at twice its normal pace.

And if that wasn't enough, she now had a vivid image burned into the space behind her eyes. That came when Claudia had turned to fluff her shirt back into place, revealing one of her breasts for the longest millisecond in the history of womankind. A nipple…light pink, sitting high on a round, fleshy—

"I'm ready. Will you be warm enough in that?" Claudia joined her, now wearing her own clothes, a heavy brown corduroy blazer over a dark green turtleneck with khaki slacks.

Leo shook off her carnal thoughts and zipped her bomber jacket to the neck. She needed this walk more than Claudia did, and was plenty warm. "Three layers ought to be plenty."

"I'm sorry I don't have time to stay for dinner. I love it when we go down to the wharf."

"We can have dinner next week, my treat. We have to celebrate the end of your internship."

"You think I'll get to see your portfolio then?"

"I guess I can show you what I've got, but I won't make my final choices until I've finished the written application. I have to describe in detail what I did for each one."

"Don't rush on my account. I can always come back sometime after you get it ready. It's just three hours up here. At least that's

133

what I keep telling myself." She shook her head and mumbled, "Who knows? After last weekend, I might even be closer than that."

Until that confirming remark, Leo had wondered whether Claudia was still bothered about her weekend at home. "Want to talk about it?"

"I've been thinking I might apply for that position at Melrose after all, especially now that Sandy's job will be open too. If I go back to Cambria, my mother will pressure me to get married. I should never have told her what Mike said about wanting me to come to Taiwan." She had slowed to barely a stroll, as though she wanted to make their walk last longer. "He was impossible. I swear if I had spent one more day with him, I would have given his ring back."

Leo's heart leapt at the news, until she scolded herself for feeling good about something that was clearly upsetting for Claudia. Besides, breaking up with Mike didn't make her any less straight. "I figured you would have used the time to work things out."

"I thought so too, but we barely saw each other. That was part of the problem."

They waited for traffic to clear on Lighthouse Avenue and hurried across to the wharf. The cold weather was keeping tourists inside, unusual for a Sunday afternoon.

"First he asked me to take Friday off because he was getting in on Thursday night, so I did. I should have realized he wasn't thinking about us when he told me not to book a room at the guest house. That's where we usually stay when we want privacy."

Leo didn't want to think about their privacy. From a purely selfish standpoint, she wanted to hear more about their problems.

"So I picked him up at the airport and all he wanted to do was to go to his parents' house and sack out. We barely got a half hour together before he went upstairs to bed and I went home by myself. Then he worked until seven o'clock on Friday night— which meant I could have been at school all day and still gotten down there in time to see him." Claudia's pace quickened as the ire peaked in her voice. "We didn't even get a whole night alone. We got twenty minutes in his bedroom, going at it like teenagers while his mother talked on the phone. Pretty romantic, huh?"

Her stomach clenched at the mental image of Claudia having heated sex with Mike.

"I shouldn't be bothering you with this. I feel like all I ever do is complain about him."

"You aren't bothering me, Claudia. Friends listen to each other." They reached the end of the marina's public access and draped their arms over the rail. The sun had begun to disappear behind the bare masts of sailboats in the harbor. "But I don't like hearing that you're not happy."

"I was so mad at him by Sunday morning I wanted to scream, but before he left he asked me to sit down and talk." Claudia wiped her eyes with the back of her hand. "He really believes the answer to everything is for me to move to Taiwan and stay there until he finishes this job. He said we could either get married this spring or wait until we get back, whichever I want."

"And what do you want to do?"

"I don't want to just set my diploma on the shelf. I worked hard for it and now I want to use it."

"Did you explain that to him?"

"I've told him before, but he promises it'll only be a year. He even said if it took longer than that I could come back and go to work, and that we'd buy a house and he'd join me as soon as he finished. He says he loves me and he can't stand being separated for so long."

Leo's natural inclination was to offer a shoulder, but she didn't want a repeat of two weeks ago when Claudia had bolted from her embrace.

"I don't want to move, but it's more than that. Ever since we talked about it, I've been trying to imagine actually getting married...and I'm not so sure I want to do it anymore."

"You mean now? Or ever?"

"I don't know," Claudia said, and buried her face in her hands.

Her diamond ring glinted in the sun. "When we were at Sandy and Maria's the other day...that's what families ought to feel like. It felt so natural to be there with all those women. It made me ask myself if it was because I was...you know, gay."

Her heart hammered as she weighed the significance of what Claudia had said. "Are you saying you have doubts?"

"I don't know what the hell I'm saying." Claudia shook her head, staring out onto the water as if too embarrassed to make eye contact. "Don't take me seriously. It's probably just one of those moments where the grass looks greener on the other side. You guys know how to relax and have fun, and of course that's going to feel better than holding my hands in my lap while a servant in a white coat pours my soup."

Leo dug her fists into her jacket pockets and turned her face into the cool wind. With Claudia under such pressure, it was impossible to tell if she was genuinely having doubts about her sexuality, or just doubts about Mike. "Whatever you're feeling, I'm here if you need to talk about it. And I don't care what anyone else thinks you ought to do, I'm on your side."

"I appreciate that." Claudia turned and signaled her readiness to head back to the studio. "Mike wants me to meet him in Honolulu the week after Christmas. Maybe we'll get things sorted out once we get away from all the distractions."

Leo's heart sank to hear Claudia back away from her words so fast. As far as she was concerned, it was Mike who was the real distraction.

Chapter 19

Leo arranged the photos on her bed, enormously satisfied with the array. She couldn't have hired a better model than Claudia, whose angular face accentuated the shadows and light, the perfect display of contrast for the workshop judges. All she needed now was the application, and with it her final selection. These were gorgeous photos, possibly her best work ever.

The simple ones evoked memories of their first session when they had barely known each other. As she played back their conversation that day, it dawned on her what had triggered the worried wrinkle in Claudia's forehead. It was when Claudia had bemoaned the size of her engagement ring as ostentatious, saying it was more about Mike than her.

The natural light photos also confirmed her displeasure with Mike, as those had been taken on the heels of his childish behavior over the phone. The second of those, the one taken through the nylon filter, still bore traces of the tears she had wiped away and Leo was glad to have them. Though it recalled Claudia's sadness, it made for dramatic photography, exactly what she had meant when she described it as soul-stealing.

Her favorite by far was the three-quarter body shot she had taken with the spotlight above. Claudia's bare back stirred a wave of lust like she hadn't felt in years. If that weren't enough, the brief allusion to the lesbian grass being greener had set off a fantasy that ended that night in a self-pleasuring session in her bed, something she rarely did, and never with such a specific vision in her head. Her dream, in fact, went further than her sexual climax, with Claudia breaking her engagement and moving into her house in Monterey. Of course it was unrealistic, but wasn't that what made it a fantasy?

She was miserable to be facing their last day together. Her only solace, ironically, was that Maria and Sandy were moving away also, because it meant she would have a built-in excuse to show up in San Luis Obispo and keep their friendship alive—provided Claudia moved back to Cambria and not Taiwan. It wouldn't be enough to ease her longing, though. Claudia's plan to meet Mike in Hawaii was proof she wasn't seriously considering breaking up. It was more likely they would work things out and solidify their wedding plans once and for all. Once Claudia married and started a family, the fantasy would be lost forever.

One by one she slid the photos into plastic covers for preservation and display. Another set was already tucked inside a manila envelope awaiting her application to the workshop, and the negatives were wrapped safely in a cellophane sleeve and stored in the cedar chest at the foot of her bed. These photographs signaled a new phase in her life and career, the beginning of what she expected to be the intense pursuit of her professional dreams. It saddened her to think Claudia wouldn't have copies, though she was glad there was no chance Mike would ever see them.

She was bursting with pride to share the photos, but liked the idea of having Claudia come back for a visit once she had the whole package ready. Instead of the portfolio, she had chosen a simple gift to commemorate their friendship, and it was tucked inside the pocket of her bomber jacket.

Claudia held the phone underneath her chin so she could pull on her boots.

"...and Bill Hanover has a Ford Bronco. I'm sure he'd let me borrow it to bring your things back next weekend."

"It's okay, Dad. I brought a lot of it home before Thanksgiving. I bet I can get the rest in my car. It's mostly just some clothes and books." She wasn't emotionally ready to return to Cambria, but there was no way to justify staying longer. Her degree was finished and since her parents had declined her tepid invitation to attend the small commencement ceremony, she had decided to skip it too.

"You deserve some time off. Think you'll head over to Taiwan?"

"I don't know." Actually she did know, but she wasn't ready yet to have that debate. Up until recently, the plan had been for her to move back into her parents' house and work while Mike finished up his job overseas. Now that Mike was pressuring her to join him, both mothers would probably join the chorus. "I have my application in at all the school districts in San Luis Obispo County. If I can get something to fill out the school year, I'd like to find an apartment."

"I know you're not looking forward to coming back home after being on your own for so long. I can slip you some rent money if you want your own place."

"I appreciate it, Dad. Believe me, I'd take you up on it if I knew for sure I'd be going to work somewhere in the fall, but it doesn't make sense to do that if it's only for a few months. If you can stand having me around again, I can stand it too."

Having things up in the air with Mike made it impossible to plan, even for the short term. It would be so easy if she could just stay put in Monterey for the next year and a half and table all the marriage talk until Mike was ready to commit to coming back to the States for good. But she couldn't bring herself to ask her father to subsidize something that might not pan out.

"I promise I won't make you support me until I'm thirty."

He laughed. "I'll always support you, honey, no matter where you live."

"You always know the perfect thing to say." It was almost verbatim what Leo had said a week earlier when they were walking on the wharf. At the thought of Leo, she checked the clock. "On that note, I need to run. I'm meeting a friend for lunch today. We're supposed to be celebrating, but I guess we'll be saying goodbye too, at least until I can get back up here for a visit."

"Make sure all your friends know they're welcome here too."

She smiled to think of Leo meeting her mother, who would make her as a lesbian the second she walked through the door. That was another reason to get her own apartment, for privacy. She was sure to see Leo at Maria and Sandy's new house, but that meant sharing her with everyone else and being alone together had become one of her favorite ways to pass the time.

The December sky was brilliant blue, and in a moment of whimsy she popped the T-tops on her car and stowed them in the hatchback. "One last hurrah," she said aloud, twisting a knitted scarf around her neck and tucking it into her blazer. With the heater on full blast, she set out for the familiar Victorian on Van Buren. Leo had mentioned another walk to the wharf again, but today's weather was perfect for a coastal drive, and Claudia had just the place in mind for lunch—Nepenthe in Big Sur.

She had ruminated all week over her comments to Leo about feeling at home with the women on Thanksgiving Day and alluding to the fact that she might actually be a lesbian. As soon as the words had left her lips, she had felt a small surge of panic. It was perfectly natural to prefer the relaxed company of friends to her stiff in-laws or neurotic mother, but the idea that she might actually be gay was absurd. Women didn't interest her, at least not in general. It was only Leo, who just happened to be a woman. "The fact that I find Leo attractive does not make

140

me a lesbian," she said, nodding to an imaginary therapist in the passenger seat.

Whatever it made her, her relationship with Leo was unlike any she had ever known. She felt special to have broken down some of the boundaries Sandy had described, such as being one of the few people Leo welcomed into her home. Hearing Leo talk about her father, her dreams for the studio, and even a handful of snippets from what sounded like a disastrous first experience with love, gave her glimpses into a person probably no one else saw. Each time she had sensed Leo's shyness, she had pressed to overcome it with probing questions, reveling in the reward of seeing her open up. All of it had stoked her growing affection and interest.

If Mike hadn't been in the picture—she gulped at the admission—she almost certainly would have experimented with Leo, if only to find a way to express her feelings. There was no denying she was the whole package—kind, caring, independent... and alluring. Saying goodbye was out of the question today or any day. They had too much invested in one another to surrender their friendship just because they lived three hours away from each other. That was only a day trip on any Sunday for a walk down the wharf, or even a weekend if Leo didn't mind the overnight company.

She should have picked up a gift, something for Leo to remember her by. It was too late now. There were always the photos, but no matter what Leo said, those belonged as much to the workshop judges as they did to her. They would be studied and passed around, discussed by total strangers more interested in lights and angles than in her. Besides, once the application was finished, Leo might not even care about them. If Maria's experience was any indication, Leo's best work was ahead of her after the workshop and these photos would be only a reminder of her novice days.

Leo reached across the table and poured the last of their wine split into Claudia's glass. The afternoon so far had been idyllic, a mixture of laughing over shivering in the sports car and reminiscing about the fun they'd had over the past few weeks. Not far from the surface was a palpable sadness that their time together was coming to an end.

"This was a great idea, Claudia. I haven't been down here in years."

"It's pathetic to think we live so close to places like this and don't take the time to appreciate them."

Their outdoor table overlooked one of the most beautiful scenes in California, the mighty Pacific rising up to meet the rugged coastline. Scores of diners shared their space on the veranda of the famed restaurant, yet the atmosphere was private, since the view commanded everyone's attention.

Leo was captivated by another view, the pretty woman before her. With her long hair dancing in the breeze, Claudia looked every bit the girl next door she had watched that first day on the bus ramp. There had been a charming innocence about her that day, as if life had not yet challenged her. In fact it had, and the Claudia she had come to know was introspective and far more complex.

She raised her glass in a final toast. "I won't ever come back here without remembering today."

Claudia smiled and blinked back tears. "I'm going to miss you."

"So don't go," she said boldly. "Stick around and see what happens...with your job, I mean."

"Leo, what I said the other day, that bit about the grass being greener..."

The words had echoed in her head all week, but she didn't dare let herself believe them. "I didn't take it seriously. You were upset with Mike."

"But I wasn't just being flippant. I admit I was a little surprised I said it, but one of my friends used to say if it came out of your mouth, it was in your head. I've never thought of myself that way before, but the idea wasn't as far-fetched as I thought it would be. If it weren't for Mike, who knows what might have happened?"

If only she could convince Claudia to take the chance. "It was that way for a lot of us. We had feelings we couldn't fight. I'm not saying that's what you're doing, just that we all have things that make us stop and think."

Claudia blew out a ragged breath. Her cheeks were flushed, but there was no way to tell if it was from the wine or the conversation. "Thinking is all I've done for the last month, ever since that weekend when I got so mad at Mike for not calling me back. I know he's under a lot of stress to bring this job in on time and on budget, and that sort of thing always makes him try harder to control things, including me. The problem is I don't care much for being controlled."

"Nobody does."

"Maybe that's all I was reacting to. I have to make him understand how I feel. If he can't, then we don't have a future."

"I'm sure you'll work it out." With every dalliance toward the possibility of opening her heart to a woman, Claudia seemed to retreat with a new plan for dealing with Mike, as if it was the only choice she would allow herself to make. Leo couldn't ask her to try something that would throw her whole future in doubt, not when she seemed so certain of what she wanted.

"I don't want to think about Mike anymore. Today's about us."

"I'll drink to that." Leo tipped her glass again and pulled the box from inside her jacket. "I have present for you."

Claudia's eyes grew wide with surprise. "What's this for?"

She shrugged coyly. "Lots of things, like thank you for helping me with the photos, congratulations on graduating from college…good luck with finding a job." She grinned with delight as Claudia tore the paper away and removed a small pendant on a gold chain, dark green with streaks of amber.

"Leo, it's beautiful."

"It's called Vulcan jade. It's found in the rocks around here. It's thousands of years old, and best of all, it won't shatter if you drop it."

"It's perfect." She held the chain to her neck. "I've missed my other necklace, but I love this one even more. Put it on me."

Leo leaned over to fasten the clasp around her neck. "I know it isn't as dainty as most of the things you wear, but I hope it makes you think of me."

Claudia surprised her with a sudden kiss on the cheek as she rubbed the smooth stone. "I bet I wear it all the time. Now I feel bad because I should have gotten something for you."

"I have the photos, which are fantastic, by the way."

"Do I get to see them?"

"I still haven't decided on the final six, but I'm narrowing it down. If you can stand to wait, I'll show you everything the next time you come back."

"I don't know when that'll be."

"But that's part of my sneaky plan. You have to come back up here if you want to see them. And maybe I'll only show them one at a time."

"I promise I'll be back, Leo." Claudia's fingers crept across the table and intertwined with hers. "And when you get to be some rich and famous photographer, I'll be able to tell people you stole a part of my soul."

"I suppose I did," Leo said softly, studying their hands. Such an innocent show of affection, but one that made her heart ache with longing. "That last picture we took, the one with the overhead light…I was looking at it this morning. I've never shot anything so lovely in my life, and it didn't have anything to do with where the lights were or how I had the camera set. It was just you."

Claudia opened her mouth as if to speak, but closed it suddenly. Then she glanced at the nearby diners and leaned her head toward Leo's. "You want to do one more?"

"What do you mean?"

"You're not going to show these photos to anyone, right?"

"No, I've already locked the prints and the negatives away."

"I want you to do a nude photo of me…something beautiful and artistic that nobody else will ever see."

Leo was stunned, especially as the seconds passed in silence

144

and Claudia's serious expression never changed. She, not Claudia, would be the one exposed by such an intimate act. "I can't…I can't do that. It wouldn't be right."

"Why not? Because you have feelings for me? That's all the more reason to do it."

The impulse to withdraw was overwhelming, but Claudia had tightened her grip to hold her in place.

"It's okay, Leo. I need to feel close to you too, and this is the only way I can."

She lifted their hands so that Claudia's ring was on top. "This makes it not okay."

Claudia stared back at her, a gaze so intense it was unnerving. "It has nothing to do with anyone else. Just you and me. If you really don't want to, I understand. But you told me you'd like to do one just for art's sake. Let me give you this."

Leo's head was spinning from all that had come to light in only the last few seconds. Not only did Claudia know how she felt, she obviously had feelings of her own, feelings that craved intimate expression.

Chapter 20

On the drive back from Big Sur, Leo did her best to keep the conversation light and casual, though her stomach was in knots. Obviously her attempts to mask her attraction had failed, and she was dying to know what Claudia had meant when she said it was okay. Perhaps this was her foray into the "greener grass." What mattered most to Leo was having Claudia's trust, and that hardened her resolve to handle this in the most professional way possible.

When they reached her house, she half expected Claudia to lose her nerve, which would have been both a welcome reprieve and a colossal letdown. Instead, she had marched purposefully to the attic and was now behind the curtain shedding her clothes, set to emerge any minute in a dressing gown.

Leo looked around at her makeshift studio, thinking it had been a repository for junk only weeks ago. Now it was a sanctuary, an almost holy place where she had peeled back the layers of a kind and lovely friend to find and steal a piece of her soul.

Once she had agreed to accept Claudia's exquisite gift, her mind's eye formed the portrait. She wanted the softest light possible for today's sitting, something from the side so she could hide the detail in the shadows. An erotic photo didn't have to be revealing.

The Bronica was still in place on the tripod, which she lowered so she could shoot Claudia in a sitting position. With the camera waist-high she wouldn't need to stand on the platform, so she dragged it to the center of the set.

"Be right back," she called. From her linen closet she retrieved a dark blue blanket and returned to drape it elegantly over the platform. Claudia had not yet come out from the corner. "Is everything okay back there?"

"Do you mind if I put on the shirt again instead of the robe?"

"No problem."

Claudia emerged slowly looking exactly as she had for their last photo session, in the long white shirt with her hair swept high in a twist. She haltingly eyed the setup. "I thought this was going to be easy, but I seem to be freaking out a little."

"We don't have to do it," Leo said calmly. "We can fold it all away and still have time for a walk before sunset."

"No, I want to. I just have to get up my nerve."

Leo gestured toward the platform. "Why don't we sit and talk for a while? If you change your mind, that's fine."

Claudia lowered herself to the padded platform, holding the shirt in place around her thighs. "How do you usually do this?"

"I don't really have a set routine. The women are usually nervous at first, so I try to get to know them a little bit. Then we talk about what kind of attitude we want…you know, whether they want be alluring or coy." Her anxiety dissipated as she adopted a more professional tone.

"What usually makes the best one?"

"They're all individual. Like I was saying the other day, the most important thing is the relationship between the subject and the person who gets the photo. What does she want it to say?" She spun around and adjusted the reflector screen upward, casting Claudia in soft light from her right side. An idea for an image was taking shape in her head.

"I'm doing this photo for you. What do you want it to say?" Claudia too had grown calm and pensive.

"I liked the way you put it at Nepenthe." Though her voice was unsteady, she kept up her professional visage as much as possible, eyeing her light meter reading instead of Claudia. "That you feel close to me."

"I do." Claudia shifted sideways and rested her foot on the platform. The shirt was so large that it draped across her thigh. "I guess I'm ready whenever you are."

Leo was mesmerized by how quickly the light fell from Claudia's figure once she turned. The shirt drew most of the light, with the side nearest the reflector bathed in white radiance. Everything else was shadowed. "It means a lot that you trust me to do this."

It was a fine line in every session to balance the professional with the personal but never had it seemed more imperative than now. Doing her best to concentrate on the technical aspects of the shoot, Leo scooted her lighting assembly farther from the platform, effectively lowering its intensity. Still, the lines were sharper than she wanted, but she could blunt them with a filter over her lens.

"You'll be coming down to visit Sandy and Maria, won't you?" Claudia asked in what seemed an obvious attempt at distracting conversation. "And there's no reason I can't come up for a weekend every now and then. I know you usually do weddings on Saturday, but…"

The words fell into Leo's head but her attention had shifted to the inverted image in her viewfinder. Too much light on Claudia's legs drew the eye from the center of the frame, where the white shirt glowed. "Can you turn a little more to your left? Imagine you're trying to hide something in your lap."

"Like this?"

"That's good. Are you comfortable?"

"Mostly…but I feel like I'm going to fall off this little perch."

The strain of keeping her balance would show in the portrait, likely in the form of another wrinkle on her brow, albeit nuanced. Leo abandoned her camera and stepped onto the set, shuddering to realize that her angle gave her full view of Claudia's dark pubic curls, though they were shrouded in shadows.

"I'll make a few adjustments and you tell me when it feels better. I want you to feel relaxed." Her hands trembling, she knelt at Claudia's feet and nudged her leg into a support position. With her handheld light meter, she monitored the contrast of the shadows in order to attain the overall image of an oval shape. "Now rest your other foot on your knee and see if that isn't more stable."

"It is, but I feel like a stork," Claudia said with a nervous chuckle.

Leo stood back to take it all in. Even with the shirt on, it was amazingly intimate. "This is a gorgeous shot." She made one final adjustment, lifting Claudia's arm to drape over her knee, and stepped behind the camera to confirm her settings. "Remember that first time we went walking down by the wharf?"

Claudia flashed a gentle smile and Leo clicked the shutter.

Claudia relaxed as Leo blew out the last of her breath, wondering if that signaled an end to their session and therefore a retreat from shooting something more intimate. She was relieved and at the same time oddly disappointed, as she had gathered her courage to remove her shirt without hesitation once Leo gave the word. There wasn't a lot of difference between the photo they had just finished and the one they had done last week with the shirt off her shoulders. If anything, the other one had been more revealing, even though she'd had the security of knowing she was wearing panties underneath. Not so today, since she had been fully exposed when Leo crouched at her feet during the final adjustments.

The erotic look in Leo's eyes had thrilled her. It was obvious she was trying to maintain her professional manner, yet there was no mistaking the quiver in her voice or the shaking of her usually steady hands. They were more than model and photographer, and this was more than just an artistic sitting.

"I think that will be the new favorite in my Claudia Galloway collection," Leo said, sliding toward her on the stool. One hand brushed the shirtsleeve while the other gently nudged the bent knee farther into the shadows. "This white shirt throws off a lot of light. Your skin won't do that, so I'll need to move the light closer. It should only take a few minutes to meter it again. Will you be okay with that?"

Claudia shuddered with the realization they were pressing ahead. "Do you want me to take off my shirt now?"

"If you're ready. Or we can talk some more about how we're going to do this. I want to keep the same pose, but I'm thinking"—she lightly tipped Claudia's head forward—"it might be more sensuous if we stayed with the hiding theme. If you hold your chin down I can't see your face. It really shows off the line of your neck, though."

"But if my head's down, you won't be able to tell it's me."

"There's no way I'll forget it's you," she said softly.

Claudia found her own hands shaking as she fumbled with the buttons on the shirt. It was incredible how right Leo had been that their relationship made this more than just a photo shoot. When she first was tempted by the prospect of posing nude for Leo she had rationalized it as a chance to do something daring. Now it had become an exercise in erotica, a flaunting display of forbidden sensuality that was safe only because Leo respected the boundaries. Claudia didn't trust herself, especially as she sensed Leo's growing determination to follow through. It would be easy to cross the line, breaching not only the ethical limits of her agreement with Leo, but her commitment to Mike as well.

As she released the last button, Leo swept the shirt from her shoulders, leaving her totally nude. She could feel the eyes on her, but didn't dare turn.

A warm, trembling hand caught her arm and repositioned it on her knee. "Now lower your head until you can't see the light anymore."

She complied and saw that her right breast was fully illuminated, its areola pebbled by the cool air and excitement of being exposed. Willing herself to relax with deep, controlled breaths, she sat perfectly still as Leo held the light meter to her shoulder, hip and leg. As promised, the adjustments took only minutes and silence ensued when Leo stepped behind her camera. Several seconds passed before the shutter clicked.

"Was it okay?" she asked anxiously.

"It was absolutely breathtaking."

Chapter 21

Present Day

Leo returned to the terrace and handed Eva a diet cola from the minibar. For a bride, she didn't seem the least bit anxious that things were running so far behind schedule. On the contrary, she seemed grateful for the quiet reprieve while she waited for her mother and grandfather to arrive for their photo sessions.

"I was hoping to see Maria and Sandy today," Leo said.

"Maria's doctor won't give her a walking cast because he knows she'll be out biking again the next day." Eva covered her mouth too late to stifle a belch, and her eyes went wide with embarrassment. "Oops."

"Better now than later."

"No kidding. Todd would die laughing if I did that in the middle of my vows."

Leo chuckled at the image, thinking Marjorie Pettigrew would probably faint.

"Maria said you guys had been friends for a long time."

"About twenty-five years. In fact, if it weren't for her, I might still be taking baby pictures at the mall. She talked me into taking a lighting workshop a long time ago and it turned out to be a pivotal event in my career." As she talked, she dragged her stepstool behind Eva and held her dress out so she could perch on the top step.

"Why haven't I heard this story before? Maria's talked about you ever since I was a little girl."

Leo was surprised, not only that Maria talked about her so much, but that she apparently had spent a lot of time with Eva while she was growing up. "There isn't much more to it. I took the workshop, and one of the instructors was a retired photo editor from *Left Coast*."

"The magazine?"

"Right, and a couple of years later I got this call out of the blue. He had recommended me for an article they were doing on women business leaders in the Pacific Northwest. That was my first layout for the big shots, and it helped me get noticed by the right people." When the jobs started piling up, the first thing she had dropped was the contract for school pictures. It was only a few weeks in the fall, but she couldn't afford to be tied up that long, not if she wanted to say yes when the more lucrative offers came her way.

"I'd say you definitely got noticed. Maria said you even made the cover of *Vanity Fair*."

Leo smiled with pride. That job had fallen into her lap like this one, when a friend of hers came down with meningitis. "That was a stroke of luck—good for me, bad for somebody else. It was pretty exciting."

"What job was your favorite?"

"Probably the most fun I've ever had was back in 2004 when Gavin Newsom started marrying gays and lesbians in San Francisco. I went up with all my equipment and took portraits on the steps of City Hall. Those ended up all over the place...books, magazines, even the newswires. In fact, I did an exhibit at Maria's gallery."

"She has a couple of your photos at her house. They're on the wall going up her staircase. You know which ones I'm talking about?"

Leo chuckled as she envisioned the pair, one a voluptuous breast centered inside an oval spotlight, and the other a penis with a slim line of hair tracking up to the navel inside a diamond. "That was a whole series of geometric shapes on various body parts, nineteen photos in all. For some reason, those were the only two that made it to mass market. No shoulders, no chins…"

"Imagine that," she said, rolling her eyes. "I remember them specifically because I used to stare at them when I was a horny twelve-year-old. I hadn't seen a penis before."

"I'll never forget that shoot. The guy really enjoyed posing for it. In fact, we had to stop and wait a few times for him not to enjoy it so much."

Eva roared with laughter. "That's hilarious."

"Yeah, one minute he was a diamond, the next, a triangle. Then a diamond, then a triangle."

"So this is where the party is."

The voice was deeper and more mature, but to Leo, unmistakable. Fighting the churn in her gut, she turned and almost gasped at the woman in the doorway of the bridal suite.

Chapter 22

December 1986

Claudia closed the door in her father's study and tiptoed behind the desk. Her mother, who had been lurking around the corner all day trying to learn what was afoot, wasn't above picking up the extension phone to listen in on her call.

In her twenty-three years, she couldn't remember a more miserable Christmas holiday than this. Mike had shared with his parents his hope of her coming to Taiwan, and the two mothers had already begun planning a June wedding in San Simeon. As far as they were concerned, it was a done deal—a ceremony on the terrace of the magnificent seaside mansion followed by a catered reception in the main hall. Mike had even promised an extra week off work for a honeymoon in Phuket, the beach resort they had enjoyed two years ago in Thailand.

With every new idea for the nuptials, Claudia felt her resistance grow. No one seemed to hear her reservations about moving to Taiwan, or especially her interest in finding a job for the next school year. In fact, she had yet to receive a word of congratulations from her mother or Mike for completing her degree. Only one potential ally had emerged—her father—and even he had gotten caught up in the prospect of giving her away in marriage in such a grandiose setting. At least he had listened when she voiced her reluctance to live in Asia for a year and a half, and for losing the chance to find a teaching position next year.

As the pressure mounted for her decision on when—not if— she would move to be with Mike, she came to grips with a pull in a different direction. It was equally tumultuous and fraught with barriers, but what she wanted most was on the other side—a life of her own making in Monterey. Even more than pursuing her career and establishing her independence, she wanted to be with Leo and to explore the sensations their time together had awakened. It was too soon to know if what she felt was love, but she couldn't deny that Leo had supplanted her feelings for Mike, and the decision on whether or not to allow her emotions free rein grew more urgent as the time drew near to leave for the rendezvous in Hawaii. There was no point in traveling that far to deliver the news to him in person. It wasn't as if he could change her mind.

She paged through her travel documents and located the number for the hotel on Waikiki Beach, where it was a few minutes after noon. Mike was supposed to be there already, but she wasn't due to arrive until late tonight.

Her stomach roiled as the call rang through, and she almost lost her nerve and hung up. But then a cheerful operator greeted her and asked how she could help. Claudia drew a deep breath for courage. "Mike Pettigrew, please."

Leo dropped her pencil onto the desk and pressed the heel of her hand to her brow. A whole evening spent hunched over paperwork had produced little in the way of progress toward closing out her books for the year. Aspirin only upset her empty stomach, doing nothing for her head, which had started pounding after two nearly sleepless nights. She didn't need a doctor to diagnose her condition. She was heartsick over Claudia.

The photographs were anything but a solace, especially the two she had made on their last day together. She vacillated from one minute to the next on which was her favorite. The nude was so erotic it made her want to touch herself, but the smile she had captured in the one before made her want to touch Claudia. She would give anything on earth to be the one who got to do that all the time.

It hadn't been so bad in the days immediately after Claudia left because work had kept her busy right up through a wedding on the day before Christmas. In the three days since, she'd had only one portrait appointment and nothing else on her calendar until a formal wedding on New Year's Eve. Now she was consumed with anxiety and grief about Claudia's imminent rendezvous with Mike in Hawaii. It made her physically ill to envision them together, whether holding hands as they walked along the beach, or having heated sex amidst tangled sheets.

Mike was self-absorbed and controlling, at least that's how she saw him given his insistence that Claudia set aside her dreams for his. Though Claudia claimed he was sweet and attentive when work issues weren't plaguing him, Leo thought he was a workaholic who would always give her the short end of the stick. If her heart had been purer, she would have wished for him to stop being an asshole and treat Claudia with the love and devotion she deserved. Instead she hoped his narcissism escalated to the point where Claudia realized what was in store and broke things off for good.

A sharp pain pierced her temple as she recalled Claudia's intention to get away from the distractions so she and Mike could sort things out. If anyone could smooth a difficult situation, it was she. Leo had gotten a convincing demonstration of that the first day they met, and it made perfect sense that reasoning with third graders and with Mike required the same skill set, since both behaved like children.

From the corner of her eye she caught a glimpse of Madeline slithering from the studio through her office and into the parlor, her belly low and her steps purposeful.

"Hey, you! I know that walk. What's in your mouth?"

She tore off in pursuit, spotting the cat underneath the davenport. Though the room was dark, she could clearly see a small mouse squirming between Madeline's teeth.

"Don't you dare drop that rodent in my house."

Luckily for Leo, Madeline had no intention of letting go of her prize. She dashed around Leo's legs and back through the office.

Leo made a beeline to the kitchen and closed the door behind her. Next she sealed off the staircase, thinking the last thing she needed was the thought of a mouse in her bedroom to keep her awake.

Madeline huddled under the small kitchen table with her prey, her eyes wide and coal black. She let out a low growl when Leo grabbed her around the middle.

"Growl all you want, but don't let go." She marched across the kitchen and kicked open the back door, where the porch light illuminated her small backyard.

As Madeline dangled precariously over a bush, she released the creature, which promptly ran for its life.

"In the future, would you kindly just chase them out the door?"

She turned and dropped the cat back inside, and was startled by the sound of a car as it crunched the gravel around the corner. Who would be dropping by at this hour? It was too late for a walk-in, and Patty was visiting her sister in Houston. She listened as a car door closed and footsteps drew nearer.

"Leo?"

The familiar voice sent a shockwave down her spine. Confusion gave way to joy as Claudia rounded the corner and rushed into her arms.

The outpouring Claudia had rehearsed on the drive back to

Monterey evaporated as Leo tightened their embrace. In silence under the porch light, she basked in the relief of knowing she had done the right thing by coming back to Monterey tonight. Only her father knew that she had canceled her trip to Hawaii, and though he usually stood by her decisions, her need to "be with her friends" was one he didn't understand at all. She couldn't bring herself to tell him about her feelings for Leo.

"Is everything all right?"

"It is now. I've broken things off with Mike."

"I love you," Leo murmured, planting a tender kiss on her brow.

Claudia lifted her eyes to something she had never seen in Leo outside of her studio—unbridled certainty. Suddenly their lips were sliding together like satin.

Leo whispered, "I think I've wanted to do that since the first day I saw you."

She pulled Leo into another kiss, fascinated by the sublime sensation. With her tongue, she teased Leo's lips apart and delved into the softness again and again, marveling at how seamlessly they interchanged dominance and submission. It was her first taste ever of sensual parity.

With one hand wildly caressing her back, Leo used the other to open the door. They clumsily climbed the three steps into the back hallway, and Leo locked up without ever breaking their kiss. "I could kiss you all night."

Her body wanted more than kisses and she boldly led Leo upstairs to the second floor, where the light over the landing cast a beam into each room. It was their moment of decision, and Claudia never wavered as she steered toward the bedroom. She had to feel Leo's skin next to hers.

As they fell entwined across the quilt, her emotions hit a fever pitch that matched the lustful sensations erupting all over her body. This didn't feel like anything she had ever experienced, and it wasn't because Leo was a woman. It was because she was Leo, whose aura of vulnerability she found more alluring than all the self-confidence in the world.

She felt no hesitation or inhibition as they lay together, and no feeling that she had to wait for Leo to set the pace. Without ever breaking their kiss, they explored one another in a continuous give-and-take that inched steadily toward intimacy. She was first to venture past the meager barrier their clothing provided, prying Leo's jeans open to brush her fingers into her warm, wiry curls.

"Oh, God." Leo blindly kicked off her shoes and pushed her jeans and panties to the floor. Then she sat up to strip off her shirt and bra as Claudia too disrobed.

In the fleeting window before they came together again, she stole a glance at Leo's lanky body, noting the small breasts with high dark nipples. She trembled in anticipation of feeling them press against her own. When they did, her body reacted with a surge of heat that caused her hips to writhe upward and their smooth skin to slide together.

Leo's hand was on her in an instant, caressing her mound with tantalizing pressure.

In only moments it was too late to savor the sweetness and excitement. Pulsating waves rolled slowly at first, then erupted through her clitoris, spreading in all directions. She cried out shamelessly as Leo slid inside and held her from within.

Leo caught her breath as the throbbing subsided around her fingers. Claudia's leg, wrapped snugly around her thighs, held her in place. She hadn't expected things to happen so quickly, but Claudia's insistent touch had signaled not only permission but urgency. Not once had it felt reckless or uncertain.

Even as she relished their intimate embrace, her thoughts gave way to invading doubts about why Claudia had come back. Now that they crossed this bridge, she couldn't let her leave again.

"I couldn't stop thinking about you," Claudia murmured after a long silence, her nails trailing softly over Leo's back.

Leo disentangled and pulled down the quilt, shivering as the sheen of sweat cooled her skin.

They fell together again under the covers, hands crawling in continuous exploration. Claudia surprised her by urging her onto her back, and with tantalizing slowness, started a fingertip journey from her collarbone to her sternum and across her abdomen and hips, as if deliberately avoiding the places that screamed for her touch. Then she stopped her tickling and clutched Leo's hand. "You have the softest hands. That was one of the first things I noticed when we started shooting." She pulled it to her face and inhaled the faint scent of her essence. Then she returned to her methodical touching, finally reaching Leo's nipple. After circling it several times, she nudged the covers back to let the light from the hallway stream across Leo's chest.

Leo measured each breath as Claudia moved delicately from one nipple to the other and back. The significance of the moment—Claudia had never touched another woman before— heightened her sensitivity, stirring not only her breasts but all of her sexual senses.

Claudia didn't exhibit even the slightest bit of trepidation or doubt about what she was doing as she lowered her face and took a nipple between her lips. As she gently sucked, her hand eased lower and through the wetness that had gathered.

Leo was anxious at first about how her body would answer, because no one had touched her intimately since Melissa. Over the past few years she had honed her sexual response with her own hand, but that didn't hold a candle to the way it was reacting now. She was pulled into a rhythm of rising and falling as they both hissed with pleasure. When the tingling started between her legs, she drew a deep breath, releasing it slowly as she rode the wave over the top.

As her climax ebbed she seized Claudia's face and pulled her into another kiss. "I love you," she said again, not caring whether or not Claudia answered in kind. She was past the point of guarding her feelings.

Claudia did answer, but not in words. Moaning as she rolled onto her back, she pulled Leo on top and lustfully clutched handfuls of the flesh on her backside and shoulders.

Leo took charge, lowering her mouth to the breast she had

worshipped in the photograph. It was all she could do not to devour it. She tugged on the nipple with her teeth as Claudia cried out, and rolled the other between her thumb and forefinger. When Claudia's hips bucked into her chest, she shifted lower still, settling between her thighs where the first swipe of her tongue elicited another moan. Looping one hand over Claudia's thigh, she spread the labia and fervently lapped deeper into the folds. This time she was patient, backing off twice when Claudia's climax seemed imminent.

When she finally allowed Claudia to release, it came with a muffled scream as she thrashed against the pillows.

Leo held on and kept up her voracious assault on the swollen knot of nerves until a hand forcefully pushed her away.

"You're killing me," Claudia rasped.

"I thought it was the other way around," Leo answered, her head collapsing in Claudia's lap. "That's the most wonderful thing I've ever done."

She managed to drag her body alongside Claudia's and pull the quilt to their chins where they kissed for what felt like hours. Then with one arm under Claudia's neck and another around her waist, she closed her eyes and surrendered peacefully to sleep for the first time in three nights.

Chapter 23

Leo heaved the suitcase onto her guest bed and popped the latches. The toiletries were right where Claudia had said, beneath the shoes and zipped inside a vinyl pouch. She dumped the items out on the bed, shuddering to see the diaphragm in a clear plastic bag, along with a tube of spermicidal cream.

"Did you find it?" Claudia called from the shower.

She raced back into the bathroom and passed a small bottle around the curtain. "Here."

"Thanks. I'm worried about you, Leo. What kind of woman doesn't keep conditioner in her shower?"

"Why would I have conditioner? I hardly have any hair." She toweled her short locks, which had dripped down her shirt as she dashed from the shower to retrieve Claudia's suitcase from the car. Her own wide grin greeted her from a circle on the steamy mirror. Everything in her life that mattered was nearly perfect.

"Do you need anything else I don't have?"

The pipes in the old house groaned as Claudia turned off the shower. "Towels?" She flung aside the curtain and wrung the water from her long hair.

Though a fresh towel was already in her hand, Leo froze as she took in Claudia's naked form. She was even more gorgeous dripping wet. She helped her dry off and followed her into the guest room. "I have a sweatshirt if you want it."

"I'll take you up on that. All I have in my suitcase are shorts and floral dresses."

"I like you just fine in that towel." She retrieved the sweatshirt and stared indulgently as Claudia got dressed. "Do you want to hit one of the after-Christmas sales and pick up a few things?"

Claudia's face fell. "I don't think so. I can only stay a couple of days. I'm sure the shit's already hit the fan because Mike probably called his mother, and now I bet his mother and my mother are having it out over whose fault this is. Except if I know Mom, she's probably blaming it all on me too. I'll have to go back and face the music."

Leo's spirits plummeted as it crossed her mind this might only have been a fleeting escape for Claudia. "But you aren't going back to Cambria to live?"

"Let's go talk."

With a sinking feeling, she took Claudia's hand and allowed herself to be led into the den. Though they slumped side by side on the couch, Leo was anything but relaxed.

Claudia laced her fingers through Leo's. "You remember that first day we walked along the wharf and you talked about your dreams? You said you planned in your head all the things you wanted to do and how you were going to make it happen. That's what I need to do now."

Leo squeezed her hand and swallowed hard. "This is part of your plan, though…right?"

"Of course it is, but I have to warn you that I don't have my head on straight yet. I screwed up with Mike and I've wasted the past two years trying to arrange a life that never really had a chance. I should have realized a long time ago that it wasn't going to work because we had different expectations."

"Right, he expected you to do things his way."

"And I expected him to do things my way. But the real problem was that neither of us was willing to put the other one first...which is something people are supposed to do when they really love each other. It hit me on Thanksgiving Day that I felt that way about you, not him."

Leo pulsed with relief to hear Claudia admit her feelings. "I feel that way about you too."

"I know you do," she said, her smile breaking the tension. "But our dreams are bigger than who we're going to love. You want to do magazine layouts and I want to watch kids light up whenever they learn something new. We need those things to be happy, and what really matters is that we help each other get them."

"You've done that already for me."

"And I'm sure you'd do it for me. But I can't make all of these changes overnight. I've totally destroyed the trust of my family. I have to show them I'm not doing this just on a whim." She lifted Leo's hand and brushed her lips across her knuckles. "And I need to prove it to you too."

From a purely rational perspective, Leo understood what Claudia needed and why. Her whole life had turned on its head overnight. It didn't matter how long it took for her to be certain of what she wanted, as long as they stayed close. What scared her, though, was the uncertainty of Claudia's resolve should her family not approve, which seemed likely. Then there was the matter of Mike. What if he had a change of heart and decided to give her the support she needed? "What do you need from me?"

"Just some patience and time. I need you to keep doing what you're doing. Chase your own dreams, but help me with mine. I'm definitely going to apply for one of the jobs at Melrose next year. Until that happens, though, I might have to stay in Cambria with my folks."

"You can stay here."

Claudia shook her head. "No, I can't. That's the other part of my dream. All my life, I've wanted to show that I could make it by myself. I can't reject that kind of life with Mike and then turn around and accept it with you."

"But what's the difference between staying with your family and staying with me? You'd have a lot more independence here."

"Maybe, but if I moved in here while I waited to get a job, how could I ever justify moving back out? You'd feel like I didn't love you."

Claudia was right that she would move heaven and earth to persuade her to stay if she ever came to live here. And that was the second time Claudia had mentioned love, though neither reference had been direct or unequivocal. Still, Leo took comfort in the roundabout insinuation. "So you'd move to Monterey if you got a job?"

"In a heartbeat."

"But what if you didn't?"

"If I didn't"—Claudia spun so that she could wrap her arms around Leo's neck—"I'd wear out the road between here and there and keep trying until I did."

With tears streaming down her face, Claudia stepped around Leo in the kitchen to drop the onion peels into the trash. "Okay, what else can I do?"

Leo tossed the chopped onions into the bowl of ground beef, eggs, tomatoes and bread crumbs, and mixed it with her hands. "Everything else is ready. I just have to bake this for about an hour."

"I've never made meat loaf in my life. If it weren't for the school cafeteria, I'm not sure I ever would have eaten it either."

"Did you have Cornish hen every night at your house?"

"That was actually my father's favorite and one of the few things my mother made really well. She didn't like to cook but she was always trying these recipes her friends gave her. Except she'd skip the tedious parts, like taking the seeds out of the tomatoes or

166

flipping something in the marinade every half hour."

"That's funny. The way you describe her, I thought she would be a meticulous cook."

"No, she just wants to look that way. When she has dinner parties she buys most of it already prepared, puts it in her chafing dishes and takes credit for it. My dad says people figured that out years ago."

Leo chuckled and patted the mixture into a loaf. She checked her watch as she closed the oven, then washed her hands. "We have time for a walk if you want to get out of the house for a while."

They had been holed up for two straight days, either making love or lounging lazily on the couch to give their bodies a rest. Claudia had talked exhaustively about how she expected to handle the uproar once she returned home. While her parents digested the news she would proceed with getting her application on file in all of the school districts around Monterey. In the meantime, she would go back to her high school and summer job, which was typing up medical records from her father's handwritten patient notes. At least she would be free on the weekends to visit Leo, which she planned to do every two weeks.

On their familiar route down to the wharf, Claudia wore Leo's smallest jacket, a flannel-lined barn coat that swallowed her. "I can't believe you're going to make me wait two more weeks to see the pictures."

"I still haven't done the application. I couldn't concentrate because you were gone, and now I can't concentrate because you're here."

"Are they good?"

"They're fantastic."

"Even the nude?"

Leo sighed dreamily. "Especially the nude."

"You said shooting nudes wasn't sexual."

"I said it wasn't sexual when I didn't have a relationship with the subject. It so happens I have a relationship with you."

She squinted and feigned her best accusatory glare. "Maria

167

was right."

"It was your idea!"

"You tricked me, though. You got me all hot and bothered talking about seeing those other women naked."

The wharf wasn't as busy during the holiday week, but several tourists strolled about.

A man's voice called from behind. "Miss Galloway?"

It was the Eriksons from Melrose, Andrew and Susan, and their son Jeremy. Claudia was delighted to see them together again. "Hello."

Leo shot her a worried look, obviously aware this was a boy from her school. "I'll meet you in the art gallery."

"No, stay here," she whispered, turning back to the family. "Nice to see you all again. How are you, Jeremy?"

"Fine." The boy beamed at her, his ears turning redder by the second. Sandy had warned her about the children getting silly whenever they saw her outside of the school, as if amazed to realize teachers actually had lives.

"Do you remember Miss Westcott? She took our pictures at school."

He grinned at Leo and nodded, but was too bashful to speak.

"We just got his school pictures last week," Mrs. Erikson said. "They were wonderful."

"Thank you," Leo said, "but I can't take credit. He's a handsome fellow."

The praise was Jeremy's undoing, and he buried his face in his mother's side.

"Someone's being bashful," his father said. "Jeremy really enjoyed having you as his teacher. He told us they had a party when you left."

"That's right. I finished my internship about three weeks ago."

"Will you be teaching around here?"

"I hope so. I'll have to see what comes open next year."

Mrs. Erikson piped up, smoothing her son's hair. "Jeremy

168

would love it if he got to have you in fourth grade. So would we."

Claudia pictured herself in Joan Palmer's classroom and leaned down to smile at the boy. "There's nothing I'd like better than to have you in my class again next year."

Mr. Erikson moved next to his wife and put his arm around her waist, a loving gesture that seemed entirely natural. Obviously, they had worked out their differences, at least for now. "We don't want to keep you from your afternoon, but Jeremy was really excited to see you again."

"I'm very glad I got to see you all. Take care, and Happy New Year." She gave a final wave to Jeremy, who showed a burst of excitement when he skipped ahead of his parents.

"Was that who I think it was?" Leo asked.

"I can't believe it. They're back together."

Leo chuckled. "I wonder if Jeremy ran away like you did."

She elbowed Leo but laughed along. "I don't care how it happened. Did you see how happy he was? What could be more important than that?"

"I think you're going to be one of those special teachers people remember when somebody asks them who made an impact on their lives."

Claudia experienced a rush of warmth so strong she couldn't keep from planting an abrupt kiss on Leo's cheek. "That might be the nicest thing anyone ever said to me."

Leo puffed out her chest and grinned. "Good to know. I'll say anything if it gets me a kiss."

Chapter 24

Leo deposited the suitcase in the trunk and slogged back up the steps to the second floor. She heard Claudia saying goodbye to someone on the phone, which meant she was now ready to head back to Cambria. The only thing that saved Leo from misery was knowing she would return in two weeks, and that it wouldn't be the longest two weeks of her life. That distinction belonged to the period right before Claudia had showed up at her back door.

Claudia met her at the top of the stairs dressed in khaki slacks, a white silk blouse and navy vest, the same outfit she had worn the night she arrived.

"I put your suitcase in the car."

"Thanks." She took Leo's hand and led her to the couch in the den. "I just want a few more minutes with you before I go."

"A few more minutes…a few more decades. It's all good."

"What time do you have to go to that wedding?"

"Six o'clock. You'll be back in Cambria by then. Did you talk to your dad?"

"Yeah." She sighed and laid her head on Leo's shoulder. "He said Marjorie has called Mom at least a dozen times since I left. Apparently Mike told her he thought I was cheating on him with somebody here."

"That's absurd. Nothing happened between us until you got here three nights ago."

"I don't know, Leo. I think he's right." She sat up and turned, her brow creased with serious concern. "I let myself fall in love with you while I was engaged to somebody else. That's not supposed to happen."

"People can't help their feelings. What matters is that you controlled your actions."

"Did I? I blew off Mike's parents so I could be with you at Thanksgiving. And that last time in your studio, I was playing with fire and I knew it."

"Do you wish you had stopped yourself?"

"No, but I wish I'd had the guts to call it what it was. I would have ended things with Mike sooner. Instead I strung him along until I was sure and I'm not very proud of that." She held out her hand, which was now devoid of the diamond ring. "His ring's in my dresser drawer. I have to figure out how I'm going to get it back to him."

"Can't you ask your mother to give it to his mother?"

"My mother! Talk about a disaster," Claudia said, sighing heavily. "Breaking up with Mike is going to kill her. Marjorie Pettigrew will turn her into a pariah. I'll have to take my own medicine on this one and march right up to her front door."

She already knew Claudia's reservations about coming to live with her, but she had to offer the safety net one last time. "If it gets too tough for you down there, you can turn around and come back. I know you want to get your own place and you can do that whenever you're ready"—she held up both hands—"I promise not to pressure you about staying here. But there's no reason to be down in Cambria if you don't feel comfortable there."

"I have to stay there until things are smoothed out, Leo. If I go back and tell them I've decided to move to Monterey and be a lesbian, I could end up like Joyce with my family turning their backs on me."

"What are you going to tell them?"

"I don't know, but it'll be a whole lot easier to leave if I have a job here."

Leo couldn't help but be disappointed that their feelings for one another weren't enough to bring Claudia back to Monterey. On the other hand, Claudia hadn't been willing to move to Taiwan for Mike either. She had a fierce, genuine need to stand on her own two feet and Leo wouldn't make the mistake Mike had by suggesting she give that up. This was the opportunity to show her support. "My offer stands, but so does the offer to help in any other way I can. I won't put pressure on you, but anything that means I'll see more of you is a good thing."

"And that's why I'm going to talk to the principal at Melrose as soon as they get back from the holiday. He said he could probably keep me busy on the substitute list through the rest of the year, and that might be enough if I could get my old apartment back. It was pretty cheap."

Leo bit her tongue to keep from saying it would definitely be enough if Claudia lived with her. "So all you want from me is patience?"

Claudia fell into her lap and hugged her fiercely. "All I want from you is everything. I wish all of this drama was behind us, but I can't undo the last two years in just a few days. One of these days—whatever it takes—I want us to be able to sit down with my family or yours and feel like everyone in the room loves us and wants us to be happy."

Once again, she relished Claudia's reference to their love, and she tightened her grip as Claudia moved to get up. "Don't go."

"I'd do anything to stay, but I can't. I have to go face the music." She sat up and looked at her watch. "And you have a wedding in three hours."

Though she dreaded their separation, Leo felt only traces of

172

the angst that had eaten her up after the last time Claudia left. They had spent the past three days talking tentatively of how surprised and happy their friends would be, how they would handle things in public, and how they would make the most of Sundays, their only full day together. Making those plans gave their relationship a serious and permanent feel. Best of all, they had sealed it with lovemaking as tender as it was thrilling. Leo was convinced she had found her one true soul mate.

They headed back downstairs hand in hand. "Just remember what I told you," she said. "If it doesn't feel right turn around and come back. I'll keep the bed warm."

Claudia threw her arms around her neck. "I love you."

Finally hearing the words she wanted, she folded Claudia into a bone-crushing kiss.

Chapter 25

Present Day

"Oh, my God," Eva murmured. "Mom, you're gorgeous."

That was an understatement. From head to toe, Claudia Pettigrew was a vision of middle-aged elegance. Her once-dark hair, now dramatically short, had gone silver and her face was faintly lined, but to Leo she was every bit as striking as she had been in her youth. Small pearls adorned her ears and neck, daintily accentuating a simple, black strapless gown with a slit to mid-thigh. Claudia's hazel eyes darted briefly in her direction but settled once again on her daughter. Nothing in her glance had suggested she was surprised by Leo's presence.

"No one's going to notice me once they get a look at you, honey. You're the most beautiful bride I've ever seen."

The pride in both faces triggered a groundswell of emotion in Leo. Theirs was a beautiful bond, mother and daughter as best friends. She shook with excitement as Claudia walked past, somehow managing to steady her hands in time to capture their embrace in a candid photo with her handheld Nikon.

After a long emotional embrace they parted, and Claudia turned to Leo and smiled. "It's so wonderful to see you again, Leo."

Hearing the unmistakable tremor in Claudia's voice, a sheepish nod was all Leo could muster. It hadn't even occurred to her that Claudia would also be nervous about seeing her.

"You two know each other?"

"We sure do."

When Claudia spread her arms in welcome, Leo walked into a hug and returned it with force. "You look amazing."

"So do you."

"Wait a minute. Time-out." Eva gently pulled their shoulders apart. "Mom, you didn't say a word about knowing Leo when I told you Maria had arranged for her to fill in."

Claudia stepped away and flashed a tentative smile. "Leo and I go back a long way."

"Is she"—Eva faced Leo—"Oh, my God. You're the one from Monterey."

The one from Monterey? It was clear Eva knew something about their past, but Leo doubted seriously that Claudia would have shared all the details. "That's right. I knew your mom back when she was teaching."

"That was before I was even born."

"Which makes it a whole lifetime ago," Claudia said softly. "And we haven't seen each other in a very long time."

Leo studied her expression to no avail. There was something wistful about her tone, but it was impossible to discern if it was more than simple nostalgia for their youth.

Eva saved them from the awkward silence. "Something tells me there's a lot more to this story, and I can't wait to hear it."

Claudia nudged her daughter out to the terrace. "You're the story today, lady. Let's get you married so the rest of us can have a life again."

Despite her anxiety, Leo was giddy with joy as she returned

to her tripod, thrilled just to be in Claudia's presence after all these years. She desperately wanted a chance to talk privately, but that would have to come later, if at all. Now was the time for her best work.

She framed the corner of the terrace against the sunset, mentally ticking off the mother-daughter shots she wanted. "Why don't we start with the corsage?"

Eva and Claudia took their positions against the balcony rail, where Eva fumbled with her mother's lavender orchid. As they clowned around and giggled, Leo snapped one candid photo after another. Those, she predicted, would be among the best in the collection.

"I have only a couple of formal poses in mind," she said, trying her best to sound aloof and professional. "But I'd like to shoot them from two or three different angles."

"I know all about that," Claudia said. "Got to have those shadows just right."

A poignant ache filled Leo as her mind filtered through memories of Claudia in her studio. "I'm sure the camera will love you both."

Touching her subjects to pose them precisely was usually a mindless exercise, but not so with Claudia. The sensations were amplified—the warmth and texture of her skin, and the delicate scent of her perfume. She was relaxed and pliable, just the way she had been at her photo sessions more than two decades ago.

"Eva, do you have any idea how lucky you were to snag Leo for this?"

"Of course I do. That's exactly what I told Grandmother."

Leo snorted from her position atop a ladder. "Your mother-in-law didn't care for my gown."

Claudia laughed. "That's okay. She didn't care for mine either."

"She probably wanted you in a veil, Mom."

"I'd say she wanted me in Europe. You do realize you're my last link to the Pettigrews, don't you? As soon as you take Todd's name, I'm going back to being a Galloway."

"Are you serious?"

"Of course she is!" a man's voice boomed from the doorway.

Leo turned to see a tuxedoed gentleman who was without doubt Claudia's father, Raymond Galloway. Like her, he was slightly built, with bright hazel eyes and silver hair. A pediatrician, she recalled, probably retired by now. And if his deep tan was any indication, he enjoyed the outdoors.

"Grandpa!" Eva walked past her to embrace him. "You look so handsome."

"And you're the loveliest creature I've ever seen." As they hugged, he looked over her shoulder at his daughter. "Just like your mother on her wedding day."

Claudia had always spoken fondly of her father, and it was easy to see why. He was as warm as Marjorie Pettigrew had been prickly, and Leo liked him instantly. It wasn't just the familial bond he so obviously shared with his daughter and granddaughter, but his unpretentious manner, which seemed almost out of place in this setting.

Several minutes passed while the three of them chatted animatedly, as if they hadn't seen each other in weeks. Mindful of their shortened schedule, Leo cleared her throat and gestured toward the terrace. Her routine set, she quickly added two portraits of Eva with her grandfather to the album. "How about just one more with all of you?" she asked, gesturing for Claudia to stand beside her father.

Eva looped her arm through his as they clustered for the final photo. "Isn't this where you tell me you have a car waiting out back in case I've changed my mind?"

He chuckled and leaned around to wink at Claudia. "I made your mother an offer like that and she asked me for the keys. I thought your grandmother was going to faint."

Fighting back a sudden wave of nausea, Leo zoomed in to capture their laughing faces. Even after all these years, thoughts of Claudia's wedding still caused her heart to pine, especially hearing now that she had almost changed her mind. How different their lives would have been if she had.

Chapter 26

January 1987

Leo checked her watch for what felt like the zillionth time and craned her neck for any sign of the familiar white sports car. Her heart had been caught in her throat since Friday night, when Claudia had called to say she wasn't coming but wanted to meet at noon on Sunday here at Nepenthe. She wouldn't say why she had changed her mind, only that they needed to talk in person.

In the first week after Claudia left, they had chatted cheerfully on the phone several times. Then last Monday something in her voice had changed. She was anxious, and Leo could only guess she had finally told her family of her desire to move to Monterey, and met the predicted resistance. Leo had spent every day since preparing a list of arguments to persuade her to make the leap. A life together would certainly have bumps at first, but love was the strongest force on earth. She had plenty to give, and from everything Claudia had said about her father, he would come

178

through as well even if it took some time. She also had compiled a list of concessions—they could back up and take things slowly if Claudia had doubts, they could keep their relationship secret, or they could see each other long-distance until their future was secure—whatever it took.

It was twenty after twelve when Claudia turned into the parking lot at Nepenthe, and Leo jumped immediately from her car to meet her as she pulled into a space. Even through the closed window she could see an unmistakable look of anguish, and when she sprang from the car Leo enveloped her in a fierce embrace. Her heart nearly burst at the sound of a muffled sob. "Whatever it is, we'll fix it."

"Leo, I'm pregnant."

The words hit her chest like a sledgehammer, and her attempt to pull back so she could see Claudia's face was met with a strong grip and a deeper burrow into her shoulder.

"I'm so sorry," Claudia whispered. "That time at his house…I just wasn't prepared."

Leo stroked her hair as a sickening jealousy roiled inside, her mind's eye recalling the image of Claudia's diaphragm among her toiletries. The last thing she wanted was a vivid description of how this had happened. She needed to turn it from a crisis to a solution that meant they would still be together. "This doesn't have to change anything about the plans we've made, sweetheart. I promise it will be okay."

Claudia finally pulled away and heaved a sigh. "I told Mike yesterday. He wants to get married right away. He says he loves me."

"But you don't love him." Leo was determined not to let Claudia put Mike's feelings first. "You want this baby, right?"

"Of course!" she answered emphatically. "I couldn't do something like that. I wouldn't be able to live with myself."

"Right, but it doesn't mean Mike gets to call the shots. This is your life, Claudia. You get to make these choices all by yourself." She looked up as a sedan took the space next to the Z and four people got out. "Let's go where we can talk."

She waited as Claudia retrieved a black cashmere blazer, which she wore over faded blue jeans and a gold turtleneck. It was her usual elegant look, but dashed this time by swollen eyes and splotchy red cheeks. She gripped Claudia's hand and they followed the stone path toward the restaurant. After a few yards, they took the fork along the cliff to an overlook, where they stood side by side at a rock wall gazing at but not really seeing the ocean.

Leo put her arm around Claudia's shoulder and tipped her head close in hopes that passersby would get the message this was a private conversation. It seemed to work, as people who started down the path to the overlook turned back before getting too close. "I'll help you with everything, Claudia. Come live with me."

"I can't raise a child without a father. It wouldn't be fair."

"Please don't buy into that. What matters is that we love each other, and that we're both committed to be there for a child." If this turned on gay versus straight, she couldn't compete. "You saw it for yourself with Zack. He loves his mother and Sharon too, and he's turned into a great kid."

"But he deserves to be with his father too."

"He is. Lydia and Zack's dad share custody and everybody makes it work. This is one of those times I was trying to tell you about. If the adults aren't happy the kids won't be either." From Claudia's hopeful look, her arguments were gaining at least a hint of traction. "I love you. You're the most important thing in the world to me, and now this baby is too. I promise you we'll have a fantastic life."

"What are we going to live on? You said you didn't have money for extras right now. No one's going to hire me like this, and certainly not next fall when I have a newborn baby and no husband."

"We'll make it. My house is paid for and business is good. I can put off the workshop for a couple of years until—"

"No, that's your dream."

"You're my dream. Don't you understand that?"

All the fight and frustration left Claudia's face in that instant, replaced by the first smile Leo had seen today. "Do you have any idea what you're getting yourself into with all these crazy promises?"

"Yes, I do." Oblivious to anyone who might see them, she lowered her lips for a kiss. "All you have to do is love me like I love you."

"Oh, Leo. I already do." She held Leo's face in her hands. "You're my dream too."

"This is going to be a lucky baby." She folded Claudia into her arms, where they swayed gently for several minutes sealing their pledge.

"I have to go break the news to my parents."

"I'll go with you."

"No, I can't tell them about you yet. They'll just make it that much harder for me to leave. You have to give me a little time."

"I'll give you the whole world."

Mike was going to be hurt, and probably furious, Claudia acknowledged as she neared her parents' home. When she had called him the day before with the news, he accepted responsibility without even a hint of protest, ready to do the right thing. In his mind that meant getting married right away, and it went hand-in-hand with her moving to Taiwan so they could be a family. It was fate, he said, as he professed his love and even vowed to support whatever career she wanted when they returned to the States. She reminded him of their talk a month ago when she explained that her feelings for him had changed. He countered that they could change again, especially with a child to bring them closer. Through it all, he kept up his calm, caring tone, never once invoking the types of demands or threats he sometimes made to get others to bend to his will. In the end, though clearly discouraged by her reluctance, he promised not only to help her financially, but to charm her until she changed her mind, even from halfway around the world. She had to admit it was one of the sweetest moments of their two years together.

Still, it didn't diminish her feelings for Leo or her certainty that she wasn't the straight woman Mike had fallen in love with. Moving to Monterey—and out from under the microscope of her parents and the Pettigrews—was her chance for a clean break between the old Claudia and the new. Best of all, she would go to sleep every night in the arms of someone who not only loved her, but believed in her dreams.

Her stomach knotted at the sight of the luxury sedan and its chauffer in her parents' driveway. No doubt Mike had called his mother, despite her plea that he wait a couple of days until she'd had the chance to break the news to her parents on her own terms. At least it was out in the open now, and this would spare her the intimidating visit alone to Marjorie's house to return the ring.

The two-hour drive from Big Sur had been exactly what she needed to set her resolve, and she ran through it once more in her head to fortify her steps to the door. Since talking with Leo and reaffirming their love, there was nothing less that could make her happy. Once her family got to know Leo, she would come clean about their relationship. Sure, life in Monterey would be a struggle financially at first, but she could probably count on a little extra from her father, and would accept Mike's offer of help, at least for medical expenses and child support. He was just as responsible for this as she was, and she wanted him to be a strong presence in their child's life.

With a deep breath to steady her nerves, she entered the foyer, immediately spotting Marjorie Pettigrew on the sofa in the formal living room. She was dressed in a gray tweed skirt and black velour jacket, a teacup and saucer poised daintily on her knee.

"Where have you been, darling?" her mother asked.

Claudia shook off the endearment, which she heard only in the presence of her mother's social friends. "I drove up the coast to talk to someone."

Her father came to the doorway and put his hand gently on her shoulder. "Marjorie tells us you and Mike have news."

She met his eye with trepidation and nodded slightly. "It's true."

Relief filled her as he broke into a genuine smile. "So when do I get started on this grandfather business?"

"The doctor says the third week in August."

"So you've already been to the doctor. That's good." He hugged her tentatively as if she were fragile.

She looked over his shoulder at her mother, who was clearly torn between excitement and foreboding. "Oh, Claudia, why didn't you tell us?"

Marjorie cleared her throat, set her cup and saucer on the coffee table, and pushed herself clumsily to her feet. "I think the more interesting question is whom did she have to see before even talking to her parents. I'm beginning to suspect my son might not be this baby's father."

"That's absurd," Claudia said, pulling abruptly from her father's embrace. "Of course Mike's the father. He doesn't doubt that so why should you?"

"Because he doesn't know you ran off all day to see someone else."

"He knows I don't want to get married," she stated forcefully. "I've decided to move back to Monterey and live with a friend until the baby comes. When the time is right, I'll find a teaching job there." She turned toward her mother. "It'll be better if I'm not here. I don't want this to be a problem for you."

"No, Claudia," her father said. "You belong with your family. You'll need someone with you."

"I'll have someone, Dad. My friends will help." She pleaded with her eyes for his support, which he acknowledged with an almost imperceptible nod.

"Surely you don't think you're going to run off with my grandchild," Marjorie huffed. "If this baby belongs to my son, then it also belongs under his roof."

"With all due respect, that isn't your call," Claudia said. "Mike and I have already talked this over and he understands how I feel. I have no intention of cutting him out of this baby's life."

"Don't assume to know anything about what Mike understands. He is on his way here as we speak. You will get married and return with him to Taiwan while he finishes this project."

Claudia's father drew himself into a defiant pose. "You don't have the right to dictate our daughter's life, Marjorie. There isn't going to be a shotgun wedding."

"Suit yourself, but know this." Marjorie stepped boldly into his personal space. "I will hire the very best attorneys money can buy to raise that child as a Pettigrew, and you can forget that cute little grandpa fantasy. When they're finished dragging your daughter's name through the dirt, she'll be lucky if she ever sees this baby again." She cast a menacing look at Claudia. "And that goes for anyone else who's involved in this, so be sure you tell that to all of your little friends in Monterey."

Stunned by the viciousness of Marjorie's threats, Claudia stood speechless as the woman whisked through the door to her waiting car.

"I'm sure this will all work out," her mother called after her in a cheerful tone that seemed to Claudia almost surreal.

She charged up the stairs to her room with her father in pursuit.

"Claudia, wait. Talk to me." He caught her door as it started to close and followed her inside. "Sweetheart, you're having a baby. No matter what else is going on, this is a time to be happy about that."

"How can I be happy, Dad? Marjorie Pettigrew's controlling my life and threatening my friends." She slumped onto her bed and buried her face in her hands as tears filled her eyes.

"We won't let her do that. She's not the only one who can hire attorneys. We'll sell the house if we have to, but you have to tell me what's going on. What's all of this business about you moving back to Monterey?"

Though she wasn't yet ready to share the news of Leo, secrets weren't an option with so much at stake. "I'm in love with someone else," she whispered.

Her father's face fell in unmistakable disappointment. "Does that mean…" He gestured toward her stomach.

"No, this is Mike's baby." She crossed the room to close the door, since her mother had left little doubt about her loyalties. Then with all the courage she could muster, she met her father's eye. "It's a woman."

"I don't understand. You aren't…"

"It doesn't matter now, Dad. I won't go back to Monterey and let Marjorie Pettigrew ruin her life. And she isn't going to take my baby."

Chapter 27

Present Day

Claudia pasted a smile on her face and took the offered hand of Todd's uncle Richard. This was her ninth dance in a row, and by her count she had at least four to go. Her feet felt like bloody stumps, swollen and blistered from over five hours in high heels. She should never have allowed her daughter to marry into a family with so many men.

All around her, excited wedding guests celebrated with drink, feast and dance. As much as she detested her mother-in-law, she had to admit Large Marge threw a helluva party. Even Big Jim, now eighty-nine years old and confined to a wheelchair, seemed to dance with his eyes, the only expression he had shown since his last stroke four years ago.

Mike would have been pleased…but who knew if he would have been able to squeeze it in. Social engagements were never high on his priority list.

"Todd's a very lucky man," Richard said as he struggled with the swing beat.

"I think we're all pretty lucky tonight. There's just something about young love that brings out our fun side, don't you think?"

He twirled her awkwardly under his arm so that she now faced the stage, where Todd and Eva slow-danced with their foreheads pressed together, oblivious to the band's upbeat tempo. The ceremony by the sea had been visually stunning, perfectly scripted—except for Eva's spontaneous decision to have her mother join in the traditional walk to the altar—and mercifully brief. The pomp was a striking contrast to the simplicity of the civil ceremony at City Hall on Wednesday. Today's event had only been for show—Marjorie's show.

"I sure hope Corinne doesn't get any ideas from this," Richard said, nodding in the direction of his teenage daughter. She and her boyfriend had been joined at the hip all day.

"You should have said something earlier. We could have made this a two-fer."

"Wish I had known. That's an event I'd like to be looking at in the rearview mirror."

She joined their hands, palms pressed together, and swung her hips close. "Don't go wishing this time away, Richard. It passes before you know it and you're going to miss her like crazy when she's gone."

The music switched abruptly and so did her dance partner. Todd's grandfather, a charming gentleman who was also an incorrigible flirt, had promised all day to literally sweep her off her feet. To her chagrin, he made good on his word, lifting her in a dramatic spin that severely tested her tired bones.

"Stop showing off, Karl," she admonished firmly. "This isn't a polka."

He laughed heartily, his eyes twinkling from behind his wire-rimmed spectacles. "I'm just warming up for Marjorie Pettigrew. Think I can get her to do the Dirty Dog?"

The image of her mother-in-law grunting on the dance floor in front of all her friends was both hilarious and disturbing.

187

"If you do, be sure you get my attention so I can alert the photographer."

Leo.

Claudia had been in knots since learning from her daughter about the last-minute switch. If she hadn't known better, she would have sworn Maria had broken her leg on purpose just to orchestrate the reunion. It shocked her that Leo had accepted the job. They hadn't even spoken to each other since before Eva was born.

Not that Claudia minded how it came to be that Leo was here. Any excuse to see her again would do as far as she was concerned, though having it happen in the midst of her daughter's wedding wasn't exactly the opportunity she had dreamed of for more years than she could count. Seeing Leo in her element behind the lens stirred memories and feelings that seemed a hundred years old and stronger than ever.

Leo had changed little since their days together, though her black hair was now streaked with gray. It still fell the same way across her brow, framing those unforgettable green eyes. Everything else—from her introverted demeanor to her slow exhale as she captured a stream of photos—was just as Claudia had remembered. That slow exhale jogged another memory, one that made her smile.

"...but I think I'd have more fun dancing with Big Jim."

"Excuse me?" She hadn't realized Karl had been talking to her.

"I said Eva's Aunt Deborah looks like she gargles with quinine. I think I'd have more fun dancing with Big Jim."

Claudia had grown so accustomed to her sister-in-law's sour disposition that she hardly noticed it anymore. At least she no longer had to put up with Hardin, her overbearing brother-in-law, who had been kicked to the curb five years ago after an affair with Marjorie's housekeeper.

The music stopped and she spun to snatch a flute of champagne from the tray of a passing waiter, hoping it would ward off the next invitation to dance. If she didn't sit soon, she would fall flat on her face. As she raised the glass to her lips, her eyes landed on a familiar sight across the room—Leo zooming in on her from behind a tripod—and she felt a surge of warmth and longing. She tipped her drink in a silent toast and smiled directly into the camera.

Leo followed through her lens as Claudia took a sip of champagne and discreetly ducked out of the ballroom. All night she had been at the center of the celebration, making introductions between the two families and dancing gamely with everyone who approached her. She was overdue a few moments of escape.

There was no denying that all two hundred guests—with the possible exception of the dour, skeletal woman who turned out to be Claudia's sister-in-law—were having the time of their lives. Two bands, a comedian and the most lavish buffet she had ever seen guaranteed it. The price tag for an event like this was well into the six figures, but that was mere pocket change to the Pettigrews. According to the newspaper, their development corporation had sold in 2001 for three hundred million dollars.

It was gut-wrenching to be physically close to Claudia yet on the periphery, and it pierced her heart to realize that so many of these people at the wedding knew Claudia better than she did. They had shared holidays, special occasions and years of milestones. She doubted anyone in the room knew she and Claudia had once been lovers, although Eva's reference to her as "the one from Monterey" had been intriguing.

All night she had hoped for a private moment, and while she suspected she might find Claudia now in the ladies' room, she had more tact than to follow her there. That didn't preclude stepping into the hallway in hopes of catching her on the way back to the reception. Since Claudia had made no attempt of her own to personalize their encounter, Leo had dim expectations about what any conversation would bring. All she wanted was a few minutes, seconds even, to tell Claudia she was happy for the wonderful life Eva had so obviously given her. She would hide her longing and regret, and continue to fulfill the promise she had made to both of them long ago—to support the decisions Claudia had made in pursuit of her own dreams. And she wanted to prove that she had managed to have a good life as well, despite her prediction long ago that she wouldn't, not without Claudia.

She slid her camera off the mount and sauntered through the crowd to the door. Expecting to see clusters of people milling about, she was surprised to find the hallway deserted. As she turned back to the ballroom, a movement from the corner caught her eye—a hand holding a champagne flute was peeking out from a large wingback chair. Tiptoeing closer, she spied a pair of black high heels on the floor…size six was her guess.

The significance of the moment almost overwhelmed her. It was their first moment alone together since leaving the parking lot in Big Sur so many years ago, when she had been so anxious that her promise of love would not be enough to overcome Claudia's uncertainty. Though her fears had proven true, her love had never diminished and she wondered if the woman before her—now mature and confident—shared even a trace of those feelings.

Claudia's eyes were closed and her bare feet were tucked beneath her, a pose that if not for her silver hair would have made her look younger than her forty-six years. Leo had always thought her a lovely woman, but in repose she was especially beautiful. Any photographer worth her salt would see this as a scene worth saving.

The flash of the camera caused Claudia to blink.

Leo lowered the camera and smiled apologetically. "Sorry. It was too good to pass up."

"It's okay. I just had to get out of there for a few minutes."

"I don't blame you. Believe it or not, I caught your daughter out here about an hour ago in the same chair."

"The poor girl's been running on pure adrenaline for the last three days. I hope they don't sleep through their honeymoon."

"Where are they going?"

"They've signed up to work three weeks at a village in Kenya. They've both gone there for projects with their friends before, but they never had time to go together." The pride on her face was obvious.

"Sounds like something you would have done." Eva had obviously taken after her mother in that vein, just as Claudia had followed her grandmother.

"I appreciate the compliment, Leo, but Eva's her own girl. She runs circles around me with all of her causes and volunteer work." She straightened out her legs and wiggled her toes. "My feet are killing me."

"I'm not surprised." Leo picked up one of the patent leather heels. "I don't believe human beings were meant to wear shoes like this."

"I probably shouldn't have taken them off. I doubt I'll be able to get them back on."

"Keep pouring the champagne and no one will notice if you're barefoot." Leo set her camera on the coffee table next to the empty glass, fighting the urge to sweep Claudia's feet into her lap for a massage as she took a seat on the adjacent sofa. "It was a lovely wedding—one of the most beautiful I've ever done. And I've done at least a thousand."

"I'd drink to that but my glass is empty."

"You want me to get you another? I can walk back in there easily because I'm wearing sensible shoes."

Claudia chuckled. "Thanks, but I'd better not. I'm already dangerously close to telling my sister-in-law that her earrings make her ass look big. She'd probably rip them off so fast she'd hurt somebody."

Leo joined her in a conspiratorial laugh, appreciating that Claudia trusted her enough to share an inside family joke. Now if they could just get past the superficial small talk. Even after twenty-three years, a part of her felt closer to Claudia than to anyone else on earth and what she wanted to talk about was deep and personal.

"Did you get a chance to eat? There's an obscene amount of food in there."

"Yes, I did. Thank you."

Shifting suddenly, Claudia leaned over and picked a stray hair off Leo's pants. "I see you got another cat."

"No, actually I didn't. Madeline lived to be almost twenty-two. I lost her just last year, but I've discovered that her fur lives on forever."

"Twenty-two years old!" Claudia shook her head in amazement.

"Most of it was on the windowsill in the parlor. I had to put a stepstool there when she was about eighteen. And I carried her upstairs to bed every night."

"I bet it broke your heart to lose her."

It had, and as she thought back on their years together, it had occurred to her that she had gotten Madeline the same year she met Claudia. "We've all had losses."

Claudia nodded solemnly. "I got your card. Thank you. I'm really sorry I didn't write back. I just…"

"It's okay. I didn't send it for you to answer. I just wanted you to know I was thinking of you."

"It meant a lot to me. All of my friends came through."

Leo didn't want to dwell on a difficult time, especially not on such a joyous occasion. "Speaking of your friends, I was hoping Maria and Sandy would be here, but Eva said Maria wasn't able to get around yet. I haven't seen them in a couple of years."

"I don't see them as often as I'd like, but we still have Thanksgiving together every year. Even Dad comes with me now that Mom's gone."

When Maria and Sandy had first moved to San Luis Obispo, Leo had struggled with jealousy to know they remained in close contact with Claudia. By mutual agreement they withheld their secondhand updates, though Maria had passed on from time to time that Claudia was doing well. That had turned out to be something of a consolation.

Their silence extended for almost a full minute, but it felt more restful to Leo than awkward.

Finally Claudia released a deep sigh and leaned forward to brace her elbows on her knees. "I think I've used up all my chitchat for today."

The words cut like a knife, but Leo was determined not to let it show. Instead, she transitioned into professional mode and pushed herself up from the couch. "It's okay. I should probably go back inside and get some more pictures for your daughter."

"No, that's not what I meant at all." She placed her hand on Leo's knee to stop her from standing, her eyes shining with emotion. "This is the first time I've seen you in twenty-three years and all I meant was that I can't seem to say anything of substance. Before we know it the wedding will be over and you'll be gone again."

Leo's eyes darted between Claudia's pleading look and the hand on her leg, the latter like a brand burning through to her bones. "I'm not the one who leaves."

"There you are!" A middle-aged woman emerged from the ballroom. "I thought I might find you hiding out here."

Claudia groped the floor with her feet for her shoes and gripped the arms of the chair to stand. "You caught me, Lena."

"Don't get up. You deserve to take it easy. I just wanted to say thank you for everything. Bob's saying goodbye to Todd and Eva. They are such a lovely couple."

"Thank you. Have you met our photographer? This is Leonora Westcott. She does the most incredible work, and she happens to be one of my oldest and dearest friends."

"How do you do?" Leo said as she jumped to her feet, skeptical of Claudia's sentiment. It was more likely she was making excuses for why they were in the hallway talking.

"Lena and Todd's mother are sisters," Claudia told Leo.

"Yes, I remember from the photos after the wedding."

"Are you staying in the hotel?" Claudia asked.

"No, we're driving back to the city. Bob thought we should leave now to beat the fog." Her husband emerged from the ballroom and joined her.

Claudia walked barefoot with them to the exit.

Leo sat glued to the couch, angry with herself for her cynicism. Why had she assumed the worst about Claudia's intentions? She would never have said something so cutting. And just like the allusion to chitchat, her own words had come out like a careless retort. She had meant to offer reassurance that she would always be there to listen, not to throw it in Claudia's face that she had left.

"Damn it," she muttered under her breath. She needed just another minute or two of privacy to clear that up, but it was too late. The guests had begun trickling out of the ballroom to leave, and all of them seemed to want one last word with the mother of the bride. Leo was determined to wait them out so she could at least finish their night on an up note.

Unfortunately, it wasn't to be. When the overnight guests headed for the elevator as the last band said goodnight, Claudia had been swept up in the crowd. Her only signal to Leo had been a furtive glance cut short by Todd's grandfather, who had been clamoring for her attention all night. The wedding breakfast offered another small window to talk to each other, but there was no reason to think it would be any different from tonight. This weekend was supposed to be about Eva and Todd, not her and Claudia. But if Claudia was serious about saying something "of substance," she was just as serious about listening.

With a check of her watch, she returned to the ballroom. It was after midnight and she had a two-hour drive home to Monterey—in the fog—and then back to shoot the breakfast at ten a.m. Why on earth had she turned down the offer of a room in the hotel? Not that she would be sleeping. Her head would race all night with the uncertainty about where she and Claudia stood.

A leather pouch containing her two cameras sat by the door of the ballroom with her tripod. Throughout the evening, she had ferried her equipment to her car, and had only this final load. She took one last look around for a stray lens cap, light filter or anything else she might have overlooked, dragging out the packing process for as long as she could in hopes Claudia would return after getting her guests off to bed. Not even a goodnight, she thought morosely.

The hotel staff had begun to strike the ballroom, breaking down tables and carting off dishes and used linens. An industrial vacuum cleaner drowned out most of the banter among the workers.

Leo shouldered her heavy bag and grasped the tripod, keeping one hand free for her car keys. The valet had allowed her to park her Volvo station wagon in the circle so she could load, and he helped her stow the last of her gear in the back.

She swallowed hard to calm the lump in her throat as she slid into the driver's seat and buckled up. Mindlessly she put the car into gear and started forward, almost hitting a bellman who suddenly appeared in her headlights.

"Miss Westcott, I have a note for you."

With shaking hands, she took the envelope and reached for a bill.

"Not necessary," he said. "Mrs. Pettigrew took care of me already."

In the light from the dashboard, she recognized Claudia's hand. *Sunset Suite, fourth floor.*

The hotel's luxurious foam slippers felt like clouds on her feet.

It had taken forever to get Karl on his way so she could send for Leo, but now that twenty minutes had passed, it was likely she had already gone. Eva had said Leo declined the invitation to stay at the hotel, which meant she was on the road back to Monterey. Claudia wanted to think she had left before the bellman reached her. Otherwise it meant she had waved off the invitation. She also wanted to believe she was part of the reason Leo had come to Eva's rescue at the last minute, and not only as a favor to Maria. Even if she had, it was clear she harbored resentment about how things had ended for them so long ago.

Tomorrow would be another circus but she had to try again to finish what they had started in the hallway. Except now the problem was bigger than just her inability to articulate all the things in her head. From Leo's abrupt reminder of which one

195

of them had walked away, a thousand apologies might not be enough to heal the chasm between them. They had lived whole lives apart. True healing would take the impossible—winding back the clock so she could choose again—but choosing Leo had never been an option thanks to Marjorie. All she could hope was that Leo would let her back into her life, no matter what the terms.

Once she decided Leo wasn't coming to her suite, she scrubbed her face and changed into silk pajamas and the hotel's soft terrycloth robe. The eight o'clock alarm would come very early, and she had to keep up a cheerful mood until the last guest left. Then she could get plastered in the bar and put it on Marjorie's tab.

The king-sized bed, turned down and stacked with six plush pillows, looked inviting, even as she doubted she would do it justice once she closed her eyes. What she needed tonight was to shift her thoughts from worrying about Leo to being happy for Eva and Todd. They'd had the wedding her mother had hoped she would have, but her own situation back in 1987 had called for a bit more decorum. With her baby bump showing in a pale green dress, she and Mike had married on the veranda of his parents' home with only their immediate families in attendance. If a miserable wedding meant an equally miserable marriage, then she had high hopes for her daughter and son-in-law after today's extravaganza.

Finally convinced she could fall asleep, she turned out the lights in the parlor and retreated to her bedroom. A faint knock at the door barely caught her ear.

Through the peephole she could see Leo shifting nervously from one foot to the other. She flung open the door.

"Am I too late?"

Their eyes met and held for several seconds. Then Claudia opened her arms as joy erupted inside her. "Never."

Leo hugged her fiercely, cradling her head against her shoulder. It was neither romantic nor sexual, but it was the most intimate sensation Claudia had felt in years.

"I'm so glad you came back."

"I'll always come back," Leo whispered.

Claudia tightened her grip, fighting the urge to risk a kiss. It was enough for now just to hold each other like this, and her heart would break if Leo rebuffed her. "I have so many things to tell you."

"Just tell me this feels good."

"Nothing else has ever felt like this." They had so much ground to make up, but this was exactly where she wanted to start, with both of them admitting their feelings were still alive. "I can't tell you how many times I've wished I could go back and choose again."

"No, Claudia." Leo broke their embrace to look her in the eye. "You can't second-guess yourself now. Look at the woman your daughter has become. That's all because of the choices you made. Would you change anything about her?"

"No, of course not." But that didn't mean she had been right.

"Then don't look back." Leo drew her again to her chest. "Those years are gone for us, but it doesn't mean we have to give up whatever's ahead. That's what I was trying to say before, but it came out all wrong. I was trying to tell you that I never left you then and I won't leave you now. We'll just have to start over and see if what we had is still there."

"It is." As far as Claudia was concerned, they didn't have to begin anew. Her feelings for Leo were as alive as ever. "We're going to get it right this time."

No one else had a claim on her, especially after today. She was free to follow her heart's desire, without the myriad pressures and demands that had held her captive since the day she had discovered she was pregnant. Though she had a whole life back in Cambria—a house, a job and a loving father nearby—there was nothing she wouldn't trade for even a glimmer of what she had shared with Leo.

Leo sighed dramatically and stepped back to grip Claudia's shoulders. "I can't believe I'm saying this, but I have to go. I have to leave or I'll never make it back here by nine o'clock."

"You're insane. It's a quarter to one."

"I can't help it. I was taking all the reception photos with a new camera and it quit on me, so I need to go back home for my Mark III."

"But you had another camera."

"That was for stills. I'm supposed to shoot candids at the wedding breakfast."

"Then I'm riding with you. I can keep you awake." She started toward the bedroom but Leo caught her arm.

"Believe me, Claudia. I'm way too excited right now to sleep. Besides, you're the one who needs to get some rest. I saw how everyone was pulling on you tonight. Tomorrow's going to be more of the same."

As much as she hated to admit it Leo was right. Eva was depending on her to smooth the ridges between the McCords and the Pettigrews, and she couldn't do that if she was exhausted. "Will you have some time to talk after the breakfast?"

"I'll have years."

Chapter 28

February 2001

A line of private prop planes parked in front of San Luis Obispo's general aviation hangar flashed by Claudia's window as the charter jet braked sharply. By her watch, which she had kept on Pacific Time, it was seventy-four hours since her journey to Kuala Lumpur began on Thursday afternoon. She had spent most of the time in quiet solitude in the executive cabin, stepping out of the plane only a few times during the dozen or so refueling stops.

The wail of the engines slowed as the jet swung into place in front of the Pettigrew Construction hangar. Next to the bay a uniformed chauffeur held an umbrella for Marjorie Pettigrew as she waited beside her new black Bentley.

"Ma'am." The copilot who had flown the last leg from Vancouver interrupted her thoughts as he opened the door and lowered the folding staircase.

"Thank you, Jeff." She stood and stretched before brushing the wrinkles from her pleated navy slacks. On her way to the exit, she stopped to don her London Fog raincoat. Marjorie detested her taste for the ordinary labels she wore so as not to appear snooty among the other teachers. But then her mother-in-law looked down her nose at the idea of her working at all.

The stairs already glistened with rain, prompting her to grip the handrail tightly as she descended. The cold drizzle was a fitting touch to the dismal day, made worse by the realization that her daughter wasn't present. "Where's Eva?"

"I delivered her to your parents. A thirteen-year-old child doesn't need a memory such as this," Marjorie answered brusquely.

Claudia tamped down the familiar surge of rage she felt whenever Marjorie inserted herself into decisions that weren't hers to make. Eva had been adamant in her desire to come to the airport, and Claudia had left explicit instructions with Big Jim that she be allowed to greet the plane.

Without another word she took up her position beside her mother-in-law, standing ramrod straight as a mahogany casket was unloaded from the rear of the plane. She heard a faint whimper and glanced to see Marjorie's anguished face. For an instant she tried to comprehend the pain of losing a child but it was more than she could bear. Though she sympathized with the woman's heartbreak, she believed any words of condolence would stir only agitation.

Marjorie dabbed a handkerchief to her cheek. "We've arranged for a private service at three tomorrow afternoon. He'll be buried in our family plot."

Though it wasn't the Pettigrews' place to do so, Claudia didn't particularly mind that they had assumed command of the funeral arrangements. She had already mourned her husband's passing privately during the long hours over the Pacific. The gulf between her and Mike, present since even before their marriage, no longer mattered. For better or worse, he had been her husband and the father of her child. Her priority now was to support her daughter and to guide her through this loss. Her first act would be to invite Eva's two closest friends to the "private" service, along with Maria and Sandy. Marjorie could huff all she wanted.

"Mike left a trust for Eva that should take care of your living expenses until she graduates from college. At that time, she'll inherit her father's estate directly. It's all contingent, of course, on the two of you remaining in Cambria."

Claudia gritted her teeth. There wasn't a doubt in her mind that her mother-in-law had engineered that caveat in order to keep her under her thumb and Eva under her influence. For a woman of such high social status, Marjorie was classless when it came to respecting others. "I'm sure we'll have plenty of time to discuss Mike's estate. Can we just get through this please?"

The men solemnly loaded the casket into the waiting hearse. When it pulled away, Marjorie primly waited for her chauffeur to open her door. "Jim is waiting at home to discuss his ideas for a memorial."

"Not today, Marjorie. I asked Jeff to call ahead for a taxi, which should be out front by now. I need to be with my daughter."

Leo slammed her backseat door and slung the strap of her garment bag over her shoulder. Her three-day photo shoot at the luxurious Bellagio hotel and casino in Las Vegas had been exciting and fun, but she was glad to be home.

The first thing that met her as she strode through the back door was definitely not the smell of fishy cat food. More like spaghetti, which she had made the night before she left and put in the refrigerator. She dropped her bag in the kitchen and stepped over a five-gallon bucket of paint that propped open the door into what used to be her studio. From the looks of things, the crown molding was in place and the room had gotten its first coat of paint on its way back to becoming a dining room.

She had expected the remodel of the old Victorian to be obtrusive, but with her new studio and office on Cannery Row she had been able to avoid most of the ruckus, if not the mess.

It was worth it to convert her house into a home, even with her planned renovations slated to take more than two years.

A small stack of unopened mail sat on her desk and she quickly thumbed through it, confirming to her satisfaction there was nothing that couldn't wait until tomorrow. This room was next on her remodel list. With the help of one of her new magazine clients, an interior designer from LA, she had ordered custom furniture that would turn the space into a comfortable gathering place for her growing circle of friends.

She turned off the desk lamp and followed the sound of the television to the second floor. Patty Clemons's long frame stretched from one end of the couch to the other. She was sound asleep, which allowed Madeline to help herself to the remnants of her spaghetti. Whether startled or glad to see her, the cat meowed loudly, causing Patty to stir.

"I was just resting my eyes," she said as she sat up and stretched. "How was Vegas?"

Leo took the empty seat beside her and leaned into a warm, slow kiss. "Crazy as ever. One of the models caught a stray cigarette with her boa and burst into flames. Peter doused it with gin and the designer nearly had a seizure."

Patty frowned, still looking a bit groggy. "How come nothing like that ever happens where I work? I'd give anything to see some of the people I work with catch on fire."

She chuckled and fell against Patty's strong shoulder. "I was glad to see your car still here. Are you staying tonight?"

"Can't." She tugged on her sneakers and laced them. "I have an eight o'clock meeting with the team from Austin to go over our new application. If I fall asleep they'll probably screw around with the code and break it."

"Did Maddie give you any trouble?"

"Not unless you count eating off my plate faster than I could." Patty gave the cat an affectionate scratch. "But she took her pills without biting me this time."

"What's the matter with you, Maddie? You going soft on me?" Given the fifteen-year-old cat's thyroid problems, it was a godsend that Patty was willing to stay over on the nights when Leo's work took her out of town. She usually went home when Leo returned, ironic considering they had been lovers for four years. Neither seemed to need the closeness of everyday contact or the intimacy of sharing a bed, at least not from one another. To this day Patty still seemed to need it from Joyce, who had left her abruptly after six years for someone at work. Leo understood the pain of a broken heart, and the comfort they found in their companionship seemed natural. What they lacked in passion, they made up for in friendship.

"We're still on for Wednesday, right?" Patty asked as she slipped on her jacket.

Leo stretched out in the spot Patty had vacated. The last Wednesday of every month was always a potluck dinner with their lesbian friends. When her renovations were finished, she would host it more often at her house. "Sure. What am I supposed to bring?"

"I can throw something together."

They both snorted. "Like what? Noodles and wallpaper paste?"

"You'd better hope you never get sick and have to depend on me." She gave Leo a parting peck on the lips and started out. "Oh, I almost forgot. Maria called this afternoon. She thought you might want to know that Mike Pettigrew died."

Just the name was enough to send a shockwave through her. "How?"

"Heart attack, apparently. He was working somewhere in Asia."

"When did this happen?"

"Three or four days ago. She said Claudia had to fly over and bring his body home."

Leo's heart raced with emotions, chief among them a cavernous ache that she had missed so much of Claudia's life, and the likelihood that an offer of condolences would be perceived as distant or run-of-the-mill, lost among those from Claudia's real friends.

"I'll call you tomorrow," Patty said, returning from the doorway to drop a kiss on Leo's forehead. She wore a tacit look of understanding, not unlike the one Leo sported whenever Joyce's name came up. It was an unspoken acknowledgment that somewhere deep inside each of them, a torch burned for someone else.

Chapter 29

Present Day

The long table held two dozen guests from the bride and groom's immediate families. The breakfast dishes had been cleared, but the families lingered over coffee as though not ready to have the occasion officially end. Eva and Todd had set the casual tone by appearing in jeans and T-shirts in preparation for their long journey to Africa.

Raymond Galloway, looking dapper in slacks and a sport coat, had apparently been tasked with stewardship of the Pettigrews at the far end of the table, where his persistent smile was a stark contrast to Marjorie's upturned nose, Deborah's scowl and Big Jim's vacant gaze. Most of the women were clustered around the center of the table, except Claudia, who sat at the other end with the McCord men. Eva and Todd walked around the perimeter to speak personally with each of their guests. They were due to depart for the airport soon.

From her discreet position in the corner of the banquet room, Leo clicked off a series of photos as Claudia and the McCord men laughed. She was too far from the table to hear what was so funny, but it amused her to see the men competing for Claudia's attention. Best she could tell Claudia was doing all the charming.

They hadn't spoken this morning, but Claudia had shot her a wink when she walked into the banquet room. As far as Leo was concerned, that confirmed where they had left things last night when she finally dragged herself out the door of the Sunset Suite. If she had stayed thirty seconds longer she would have stolen a kiss, which might have opened the floodgates for more. In the light of day that notion felt like too much too soon, but she couldn't decide whether she was guarding her own feelings or Claudia's. It felt safer to let Claudia define the parameters, as well as set the pace.

"Leo, can we talk a minute?"

She had been so consumed with watching Claudia that she hadn't seen Eva approach. "Sure."

"I just wanted to ask how you felt about the album. Did you get all the photos you wanted?"

"I got exactly what I wanted. The question is did I get what you and Todd wanted?" She pulled two memory cards from her pocket. "We'll have a couple thousand to choose from."

"Wow."

"I got some great shots at the reception."

"That's fantastic. I can't wait to see them." She looked over her shoulder, where the guests were starting to rise. "Granddad said you and Mom were talking out in the hallway last night."

"Just for a minute. It's been good to see her again." Dozens of people had seen them together outside the ballroom, but she doubted anyone knew about her late visit to the Sunset Suite.

"It's been good for her too."

The comment took Leo by surprise at first, but then she recalled Eva asking her mother if she was the one from Monterey. "What makes you say that?"

Eva grinned slyly and shrugged. "I know my mom. When she decided at the last minute that she wanted a strapless dress with a slit in it instead of the formal gown she'd picked out a year ago, I knew there had to be a reason."

Leo could feel the heat rising on her neck, and there was no way to hide it under her open-collared shirt.

"Anyway, I just wanted to say I'm glad it worked out for you to do this. I appreciate you jumping in at the last minute and doing such a good job."

"It was my pleasure." In every way imaginable, she thought.

"Eva!" Todd pointed to his watch. "Limo...plane...Land Rover."

Leo followed the family en masse as they exited to the circle at the front of the hotel where a Town Car waited. Marjorie Pettigrew shook her head at the vehicle with unveiled disdain and glanced at the nearby valet lot, which held an array of luxury cars. Leo figured the Bentley was hers. She also spied one she was willing to bet was Claudia's, a black Nissan Z convertible.

She picked off a superb photo of Eva bending over Big Jim's wheelchair to give him a kiss on the cheek, and then several more as she and Todd walked the line to the car. She zoomed in to capture Eva's final hug with her mother, a long one in which Claudia beamed with happiness and pride. Then as the limo pulled out, Leo caught the shot of the day—the Pettigrews sulking scornfully away while everyone else celebrated.

That moment marked the end of her job, and she began the methodical task of stowing her equipment. There wasn't much else to do, since her tripod and camera bag were already locked up with the bell captain.

Claudia sauntered over after the others left, her arms folded casually across her chest. "What's up next for you, Photographer Lady?"

"Since I canceled my plans to be at a magazine shoot in Tucson all weekend, I find myself free."

"So you have until..."

"Tuesday noon. Then I have a meeting in San Francisco."

She considered offering to share the ride down to Cambria but getting back to Monterey would be a bitch.

"I don't suppose you'd be willing to stick around here for another day."

"You aren't going home?"

Claudia shook her head. "No, I promised to pack up the bridal suite. The bathroom alone could take me all day."

"Why didn't you ask your sweet sister-in-law for help?"

That earned her a guffaw. "In the first place, she would have said no. In the second place, I'm done with Deborah and her little dog too. And I'm also done with Marjorie, at least until Eva decides to have children. By then it'll be up to Eva whether or not she wants her children to grow up with that kind of influence."

"Maybe she'll put it off a few years."

"We'll see. Family planning isn't exactly our forte, you know."

Leo snorted.

"Just sayin'." She hooked her arm through Leo's unabashedly and steered her back into the hotel. "So what do you say? Are you going to help me or leave me stranded?"

She looked down at Claudia's arm and noticed for the first time a woven bracelet containing the Vulcan jade pendant she had given Claudia for her college graduation. "I could never turn down a beautiful damsel in distress. But I can't promise I won't fall asleep if you let me sit down."

The bridal suite looked like a tornado zone. Eva's billowy dress covered the entire sofa, and all her accessories were scattered about.

Claudia eyed the bedroom door, which was partially closed. "If this outer room is any indication of what's behind that other door, I don't even want to see the rest of it."

Leo tiptoed over and peeked into the bedroom. "I see pieces of a tuxedo and a couple of suitcases. Not too bad...except I spotted a sports car out there that had your name all over it. I don't think there's any way all this stuff will fit in it."

"Very funny." Claudia shouldered past her and removed a garment bag from the closet. "I'm only responsible for the wedding dress. Todd's parents are taking everything else back to San Francisco so it will be in their apartment when they get back from Africa. But I promised to pack it up."

"Shouldn't take long."

She eyed a pair of men's designer briefs on the floor next to the bed. "Do me a favor, would you? Pack all the boy things in that black suitcase. I don't want to know my son-in-law that well."

Leo laughed and set about picking up Todd's belongings.

Claudia entered the bathroom, where cosmetics and hair styling tools occupied every square inch of the counter. "God, it seems like it was just yesterday that she was getting into my stuff. Now she has enough to open a store of her own."

They worked diligently for over an hour getting things packed and ready for the McCords, folding each crumpled item with far more care than it had been shown the night before. It took both of them to stow the flowing wedding dress inside the clear plastic bag. Then Claudia called Todd's mother to report things were ready to go.

With their task done, her anxiety grew about what would follow. No one but Leo had ever sparked the giddy feelings that gripped her now. Over the years it had happened whenever Maria mentioned her name, or when she had driven up the coast through Monterey, and it had built steadily in anticipation of seeing her again at the wedding. What was different now was that Leo seemed to be feeling it too. There had been a moment the night before when she almost thought Leo would kiss her, and undoubtedly they would have tumbled into the bedroom to rediscover their lost love. Then something had stopped them, something that felt more like caution than denial. Now they had to chart the course for what would happen next.

"I need to drop this off in my room," she said, hoisting the dress over her arm. "Then if you have the energy, maybe we can just sit and talk."

"What do you want to talk about?" Leo sported a tiny smile, a look more confident than Claudia could remember seeing away from the camera.

"I want to know everything you've done since the last time I saw you."

"That's a lot of photo shoots."

"I can read your bio on your Web site...which I've done, by the way, so I already know what a hotshot you are."

Leo laughed as they reached the Sunset Suite. "I don't know about being a hotshot, but I'm doing the kind of work I always dreamed about."

"I remember those dreams." She hung the dress in the closet and gestured for Leo to sit on the couch. "Is this okay, or do you want to go out to the bluff?"

Leo answered with a familiar gesture by taking a seat and propping her feet on the coffee table. "Since you've already read my bio, why don't you tell me yours? You don't have a Web site."

Claudia sat across from her in an ornate wingback chair, remembering how special it had felt the first time she saw Leo let down her guard and relax. "Nothing really to add to my story, except that I got part of my dream too. I've been teaching third grade now for eighteen years, ever since Eva started school."

"I remember that. I almost called you when Maria told me you were back from Taiwan."

It was bittersweet to think they might have reconnected so long ago and kept at least a friendship alive. "I wish you had. I didn't have many friends back then besides Maria and Sandy." The smile left her face as she recalled one of the darkest times of her life. "What stopped you?"

"I didn't want to disrupt your life. Besides, I was going cold turkey on my Claudia Galloway addiction. If I'd gotten just a little bit, it would have made me want more."

It was an unusually candid statement from someone who kept her cards so close to her vest, Claudia thought.

Leo continued, "If you had talked to me on the phone, I

would have wanted to meet you at Maria's, and then I would have asked to see you alone. Sooner or later you would have told me no and it would have been like losing you all over again. The only way to resist you was not to see you at all."

She had no trouble wrapping her head around that explanation. The temptation to contact Leo had been intense at times, but she always backed down out of fear she would be rejected, or that Leo would welcome her and it still wouldn't be enough. "Maria talked about you every now and then. Nothing specific, just that you came down, you looked good, that kind of thing. It was vague unless I asked her something point blank."

"She kept me up with you too, especially when you first got back. I was really glad to hear when you got the teaching job."

Claudia shook her head to recall that particular episode in her life. It was the first time she had defied Mike to do something for herself and there had been consequences. "Maria said you quit asking about me."

"It made me miss you too much," she said matter-of-factly. "She called me when Mike died, and then again a few years ago when your mother died, but other than that I just had to keep telling myself you were doing fine and that you were happy."

"Happy isn't necessarily the word I would use, but between Eva and my job I had some good things going on in my life."

"I found one of those good things on the Internet once."

"What are you talking about?"

"There was an article in the *Tribune* when your class won the award for reading the most books."

Her mind ticked off the years as she tried to remember that class, and she smiled to realize Leo had kept up with her that way. "That was ages ago."

"I almost didn't recognize you because you'd cut your hair. But back then it was still brown," she added with a smirk.

"That's because Eva wasn't a teenager yet. These are all hers." She ran a hand through her white hair. "Actually, that's my dad's line about me, and you can see that I took after him in the hair department...except for the goatee, of course."

211

"I remember the goatee. You were obsessing about your pointy chin."

"And now I have an extra chin to obsess about."

Leo shook her head. "You don't have a double chin and your hair is gorgeous. In fact, you're even more beautiful than I remember."

A feeling of tenderness overtook her as she relished Leo's words. "I bet the last time someone said something that sweet to me, it was you."

"I find that pretty hard to believe."

"It's true." She sighed and let her gaze wander to the window where the mid-afternoon sun put a sparkle on the ocean. It was difficult to talk about Mike with Leo, because Leo's pain was obvious. There was no other way, however, to catch Leo up on her life. "Mike and I never really recovered after I broke our engagement that Christmas. Getting married was about Eva, not us. I thought we might do better when we all came back from Taiwan, but once I insisted on going to work, he took off without us for a new project in Jakarta. I didn't care by that time. Eva was all that mattered."

"Was he a good father?"

"He wasn't there much, but you'd have to ask her to know for sure. Even when he was home he was working. Marjorie smothered her though, once she saw how much she looked like Mike. She had to stop whispering to everybody that he probably wasn't her father. Once she came to grips with that, we couldn't get rid of her. I put up with it because I always believed Eva deserved the chance to know her father's family, but she can make her own choices about them now."

"I remember when you got upset about that boy in your class when his parents were splitting up. You said parents should do whatever they had to do to keep the family together until the kids were old enough to make it on their own."

"Yeah, that was what I expected of everyone else, but not myself." Even her daughter didn't know she had given up on that particular principle. "The irony is that Mike and I had been

212

separated for four months when he died. He didn't care whether he was married or not and he certainly didn't care about me. He had already signed papers giving me physical custody of Eva. His mother was the only one who knew and she threatened to tie up Eva's trust if I took her away from San Simeon before she finished college."

"Just like she threatened you when she learned you were pregnant."

"Exactly." And all of her friends in Monterey, but Claudia had never told Leo that part. She would have wanted to fight and there was no beating Marjorie Pettigrew. "But I couldn't risk giving Marjorie any ammunition. Besides, I considered moving back up this way when Eva started at Stanford, but then Mom died that year and I didn't want to leave my dad alone."

Leo flashed a gentle, poignant smile.

"What?"

"Nothing."

"Bullshit." She kicked at Leo's foot. "What was that look for?"

"I was just thinking how so many of the decisions you've made have been for other people. I wish you had made one for me...or rather for us."

The words stung, but Claudia had no comeback. It was undeniable that she had forced Leo to share her sacrifice.

"I didn't say that to be cruel, Claudia. I know it's pretty selfish of me to feel that way, but I've always wished things had been different."

"It isn't selfish to want love, Leo. What was it you said last night? We can't change the past. All we can do is go forward."

"I've beaten myself up with what-ifs." She dropped her head in her hands and groaned with unrestrained frustration. "You can't imagine how many times I dreamed about you coming back. I'd sit out on the porch and watch every damn sports car that came down the road, hoping it would be you."

Claudia moved to the space beside her and put a hand on her back. They had to get past the old hurts before they could look ahead. "I did the same thing, Leo. I drove by your house at least a dozen times. Every time I'd see a car parked in your spot, I'd get a rush out of knowing you were just on the other side of that door. It was so tempting to stop just so I could see your face again."

"You should have."

"I drove by one time and saw Patty on the porch. Maria said you were with her for a long time...until what? Just a couple of years ago?" That news had made her burn with envy. "I have to admit I was surprised. I couldn't really picture the two of you together."

Leo folded her arms across her chest in an obviously defensive pose. "We were there for each other when it mattered. I can't say that about everybody."

Claudia couldn't help but squirm as she noted Leo's accusatory look. "I didn't mean to say anything bad about her, just that your personalities didn't seem to fit like that."

She relaxed visibly, dropping her elbows to her knees as she leaned forward. "Joyce left her for somebody at work. Kind of tough on the old self-esteem, if you know what I mean. After a couple of years I started making her do things with me because I was worried about her, and the rest of it just happened out of the blue. We never lived together though. In fact, when we stopped being lovers about seven years ago, nobody noticed because we stayed friends. People probably wouldn't have known at all if Patty hadn't started seeing somebody else."

"Were you in love with her?"

Leo frowned and Claudia thought she had her answer. Realizing now that Leo hadn't been involved with Patty all these years made her want to kick herself. She would have called years ago.

"I loved her and I always will, but I don't think either of us was ever in love. It's hard to have a life with one person when you're still in love with someone else."

The words resounded between them like wind through the room. "All this time?"

214

"Nobody was ever going to measure up to you, Claudia. We were lovers for three days so all my memories of you are perfect." She rose abruptly and started to pace the small living room. "We were young, everything was new and we made love like a house on fire. We never fought or even had to deal with each other on a bad day. I was driving home last night and it hit me that if I lost you again, it would spoil the way I've always thought about us."

Panic gripped her as she saw Leo's agitation rise and she stood for a face-off. She couldn't let Leo back away now that they were free to be together. "Are you telling me you'd rather have a perfect memory than a future that might have ups and downs? Because that's some serious bullshit, Leo. I don't know who taught you about love, but it doesn't mean you get to be happy all the time."

"Nobody knows that better than I do," Leo said defiantly, her eyes smoldering with resentment. "Because everything I know about love I learned from you."

"If you learned it from me then it's still there, and it's as strong as it ever was."

Leo's fiery gaze suddenly softened and she closed the distance between them.

Gasping for breath, Leo gave herself over to the euphoria of Claudia's lips on hers. Though her heart raged with fear and doubt, she was powerless to resist the fantasy that had visited her every day for the last two decades. "Please don't break my heart again."

In an unspoken assurance, Claudia tightened her arms around her neck and her kiss grew more intense.

It didn't matter if Claudia denied her a verbal promise. She would put today with the other memories if it was all they had. Her hands traveled over Claudia's back, settling on the curve of her hips. "You have the sweetest body in the world."

"It's not the same body you remember," Claudia demurred, brushing her nose against Leo's shoulder.

It was too sappy to say aloud, but all Leo could think was

that this body held the heart of the woman she loved, and that was all that mattered. She dipped her fingers beneath the hem of Claudia's shirt and tickled the warm flesh of her back. They kissed again, deep and slow, as her hands wandered higher and released the bra's clasp. She could feel Claudia respond, allowing her hips to be pulled forward as her head fell back. Emboldened by the surrender, Leo grasped a breast and kneaded its nipple to a peak.

Claudia hissed with pleasure.

With mounting fervor, she tugged at the fastener on Claudia's slacks and thrust her hand inside.

"You've got to let me lie down, Leo, or I'm going to fall."

She released her prize and led the way into the bedroom, where Claudia tossed the comforter into a pile at the foot of the bed. Leo kicked off her shoes and dropped all of her clothes onto the floor. Claudia did the same, and they met on the cool white sheets and fell together in a heap.

Leo was inside her instantly, covering her moan with a kiss. With every stroke Claudia grew wetter, and Leo gave in to her lust and lowered her mouth to its source. It was exactly the taste that had been burned into her memory.

Claudia groped for her hand and squeezed it hard as she came with a shudder. Panting from exertion, she tugged Leo upward and grasped her face with both hands. "I love you. Give me another chance and I promise I'll put you first every time."

Chapter 30

It was daybreak when Claudia awoke. A chilly breeze wafted the cloth curtains, but Leo's warm body covered most of hers. Their lovemaking had been intense, both physically and emotionally, as they poured themselves into each other. It was unbelievable she had lived so long without it.

They had rediscovered one another throughout the night, getting out of bed only to wolf down cheesecake from room service. It was decadent, like the half dozen orgasms she'd had at Leo's touch.

"You were wrong about your body," Leo murmured, nuzzling her head under Claudia's chin. "It's as amazing now as it was the last time I touched you."

"How long have you been awake?"

"About ten minutes maybe. I was thinking about Maria and wondering if she expected this to happen."

Claudia rumbled with a low laugh. "I think she staged the whole thing. I didn't actually see her broken leg."

"Are you going to tell anyone about this?"

She struggled to sit up. "Of course I'm going to tell people. What kind of question is that?"

"I didn't mean ever. I just wondered if you were thinking about waiting awhile to see what happens. It isn't something you can un-say."

Obviously, it wasn't going to be easy for Leo to trust her. "Look, if my feelings for you were going to go away, don't you think they would have done that already? The people who care about me need to know about you. And I think some of them might notice when I move to Monterey."

"Mmmm," Leo said, wriggling with satisfaction. Apparently, the commitment to move was just the thing she needed to hear. "I think Eva already knows."

"Yeah, I think I might have told her but I'm not sure."

Leo sat up in bed beside her. "Might have?"

"It was on her twenty-first birthday. I went up to Stanford that weekend. I remember something vaguely about sitting in her apartment and sharing a bottle of tequila. I'm pretty sure I spilled my guts." And it had brought her the worst hangover of her life. "I definitely spilled them the next day."

"What did you tell her?"

"That was the weekend she told me she was in love with Todd. I remember saying that I'd only been in love once, and it was with a woman I'd met in Monterey."

Leo thinned her lips and nodded. "That explains what she said. She doesn't seem to have a problem with it."

"My daughter? Are you kidding?" Claudia stretched and swung her feet out of bed. She had a robe out in the sitting room, but it was silly to fetch it so she could wear it into the bathroom. "She thought it was cool as hell. Turns out she had a girlfriend her freshman year. Believe me, that was an eye-opener. It finally hit me what my father must have thought about me."

"You told him about us?"

"Not specifically, but he knows I was in love with a woman when I married Mike. Wait till he finds out I still am. He's going to love you, by the way."

"What makes you say that?"

Claudia cranked the shower handle until it flowed hot. "Because I do."

Leo nodded. "I'll buy that. I liked him for the same reason."

As she stepped into the shower, she saw that Leo had come to stand in the doorway naked with her arms folded casually across her chest. She was as lanky as ever, and gravity had been kind to her small breasts. Lots of things about seeing her again were bittersweet, she thought, like feeling so comfortable with someone after not having this level of companionship in her life. "I never asked about your mother."

"Eighty-one and still going strong."

"Will I get to meet her?"

"Sure. She probably won't get the lesbian thing, but she'll treat you a lot better than your last mother-in-law." Leo handed her a towel and stepped into the shower as she was getting out. "I'll have to tell Patty. She's going to say I told you so."

"Did she really know you were in love with me, or was she just guessing?"

"We talked about everything. And one time she caught me looking at the portfolio we did for that workshop."

Claudia smiled at her memories of their attic sessions. She had thought of the photos several times, but had decided they might be a sore subject, since Maria had told her Leo wasn't accepted into the workshop that year. She assumed that meant they didn't pass muster, but she still wanted to see them eventually, especially the nude. "You promised to show me those, you know."

"And then you left me to get married to somebody else," Leo said, shaking her head with incredulity. "I refuse to feel guilty about not crashing your wedding to show you a photo album."

"Do you still have them?"

"Of course I still have them. They're locked up in my cedar chest. No one's ever seen them but me."

219

"And the judges."

"Not even the judges. I ended up not applying that year. My heart wasn't in it but I hired a model over the summer and shot them again in the studio downstairs."

Claudia was stunned. "Are you serious? We did all of that work and you never even sent them in?"

"I didn't want to give them up." She finished rinsing her hair and turned off the shower. "They were all I had left of you. I used to sit and stare at them for hours thinking about all that time we spent in the attic."

She tossed Leo a fresh towel and started filling her toiletry bag. "Hurry up and get dressed. I want to see those pictures now."

Claudia made one last sweep of the suite for her personal items. The bellman had carted away all but her purse and Leo's camera bag.

"I think we should drive straight to Cambria and pack your things," Leo said seriously, pulling her into an embrace at the door. "Otherwise I'll have nightmares about you never coming back."

Claudia understood that she had to earn Leo's trust but she couldn't speed up the process. It would come only with the passage of time. "I'm under contract for next year in Cambria. I'll break it though if you really need me to."

Leo's jaw twitched before she finally shook her head. "I won't make you do that. But it's going to be a long year."

She recalled wistfully what Leo had said the night before about wishing she had chosen for them. "You know what? Forget it. I'm going to call my boss on Monday and tell him he has six weeks to find someone else. Life's a lot shorter than it was twenty-three years ago and I don't want to wait another year to sleep with you every night."

Leo's face lit up in a bright smile. "Does that mean you'll live with me?"

"I told you I always wanted a Victorian house." She wrapped

her arms around Leo's neck and pulled her down for a kiss.

"And I always wanted you," Leo said, guiding her into the hallway toward the elevator.

Claudia was still grinning when the doors parted on the ground floor.

Marjorie Pettigrew stood beside Big Jim, whose chair was being pushed by a bellman. In typical fashion, she looked past Claudia as she spoke, as though making direct eye contact was beneath her. "I had presumed you would have departed already."

"I'm leaving now." Claudia pulled Leo forward and grasped her hand. "Did you have a chance to meet our photographer?"

"Of course I did. Miss Westcott, isn't it?" Marjorie's eyes dropped to their joined hands and she shrugged her shoulders uneasily. "I'm quite surprised to see you today as well."

"Leo stayed the night with me in my bed," Claudia said smugly. "In fact if you ever see me again, you can expect to see her too."

As realization dawned, her mother-in-law's face contorted with fury. "Don't think for a minute that I'm going to allow—"

Claudia lowered her voice but leaned in to make certain the woman heard every word. "You don't *allow* a fucking thing in my life, Marjorie. Eva graduated from college last month. That means her father's trust is vested, so you don't get to pull our strings anymore."

With Leo's hand still firmly in her grasp, she marched to the exit, exhilarated to finally be free of Marjorie Pettigrew.

Leo grinned to see Claudia's sports car alongside hers in the parking area next to her house. The wedding dress was buckled into the passenger seat, where Claudia had adorned it with sunglasses and a scarf.

"I can't believe you made fun of my car and you're still driving a Volvo station wagon that's older than Miley Cyrus. For an artist, that doesn't say much for your creativity."

"It says I'm practical," Leo said, hoisting the camera bag over her shoulder. After a burglary several years ago in which she had lost over a hundred thousand dollars worth of equipment—fortunately insured—she had installed an alarm system on her house and car, and placed security lights around the perimeter. "You should bring the lovely lady inside, along with anything else you want to keep."

"I still love this house."

Leo looked with pride at her yard, which she'd had professionally landscaped after completing the last round of interior renovations. "Wait till you see the inside." She usually entered through the back door, but since she wanted to show off the new look they walked around to the front porch.

"I see you still have your porch swing."

"I sit out here and read sometimes…and watch for sports cars."

She opened the door into the parlor, where the first of many renovations leapt out. A long staircase led to the second floor.

"Oh, my goodness. It doesn't even look like the same house." Claudia twirled slowly in the parlor, taking in the other changes. The seating area was smaller, its centerpiece still the antique davenport that had always adorned the entry.

The living room, which had once been the office and showroom, was now formally appointed with contemporary classics, a simple leather sofa with a matching loveseat and chair. Colorful rugs and throw pillows gave the room a modern flair.

Opposite the fireplace, which was centered on the outside wall, was an archway. "You remember my studio." A teak table with eight place settings sat beneath a bright chandelier. The far wall was a picture window that looked out onto a tree and narrow strip of yard.

"You put in a window."

"No, it was here already. I just uncovered it."

Claudia walked around the table, her fingers trailing along the tops of the chairs. "Do you even know seven other people?" she teased.

Leo laughed. "Believe it or not, I hosted Thanksgiving dinner last year, and we had to drag in two more chairs from the kitchen."

"You're right, I don't believe you."

"It's true."

"What happened to that bashful introvert I used to know?"

One by one, Leo had expanded her circle of friends—real friends. It was easier now that the lesbian community was more visible, and it didn't hurt that her best friend was the most outgoing person she knew. "Patty keeps me in the thick of things. She likes to throw her parties here because she still lives in a one-bedroom condo out near Pebble Beach."

Claudia went ahead into the kitchen, which had been remodeled in granite and mahogany. An island with two barstools stood where the small table had once been. "You got rid of the back staircase."

"It's the laundry room now. I had to move the second-floor bathroom over to where the guest room was because the front stairs came up on that side."

"This was a huge job."

"It took about two years to do it all, but it was worth it. I was working out of the new studio by then and I took Madeline with me every day." She led the way back into the parlor and up the stairs. The door leading into the turret room was gone, giving the whole floor an open feel. It was still her den, but it now doubled as an office. Another staircase led to the attic.

"No more ladder?"

Leo laughed and shook her head. "I'm too old to climb a ladder. Go on up."

A king-sized brass bed sat before the front window of the turret. A dresser, cedar chest, side table and loveseat completed the ensemble. The floors were polished oak, as was the wainscoting that met the sloping ceiling. Toward the back end of the house, a hallway separated a row of closets from the master bath.

"Leo, this is stunning."

"I might never have done this if not for you. My bed's right where you used to sit."

Claudia walked around and sat on the edge. "You can see the

223

ocean from here."

"I wake up to it every day. Go sit on the loveseat." She groped in her bottom dresser drawer and located the key to the cedar chest. The portfolio holding the photographs of Claudia was on top, as she had studied them for hours during the week leading up to the wedding. She opened to the first.

"God, I look so young."

"It was half a lifetime ago. Do you remember what we were trying to do with this one?"

With the tip of a manicured nail, Claudia traced the outline of the stark shadow across her face. "Something about hard light."

"That's right." Leo flipped to the next one. "And here we have the same pose in soft light. See that?" She touched the line of Claudia's brow. "I saw this in the darkroom and thought about where it came from. You were talking that day about your engagement ring, how it was too big…something Mike wanted but you didn't."

"Wow, it showed up even then."

"The camera finds little things." She flipped to the next two, both taken in natural light. "You were very angry that day. See the lines around your eyes?"

"Amazing."

She paged through the album, stopping again at the photo of Claudia's profile and shoulder. "This was the day I realized my crush on you had gotten out of hand. You had the most exciting body I'd ever seen."

Claudia cocked her head and gave her an accusatory look.

"You still do. Next time I'll add that without prompting." She turned to the first photo she had made on their last day together, just before the nude. Claudia was smiling and looking directly into the camera. "This one is my favorite because you were thinking about us."

"How do you know that?"

"Because I'd just asked you something about when we walked on the wharf. It made you smile."

Leo grasped the next page with her fingertip but held it still.

"You ready for this one?"

"Is it good?"

"It's still the best photo I've ever taken."

Claudia gulped and nodded once. "Oh, my God," she murmured as the page opened to the nude photo. "Is that really me?"

"In the flesh," Leo said. "And lovely flesh it is." Every time she looked at it, she remembered how thrilling it had been to have Claudia's total trust.

"This is exquisite. I can't believe you never showed it to me."

"I hoped to give it as a gift someday, but you always said you didn't want to risk anyone else finding it."

"Oh, Leo," Claudia said as she leaned over and planted a kiss on her cheek. "This is far too beautiful to hide in that cedar chest. It should be hanging in a gallery somewhere."

"I thought about hanging it up here, but I never wanted anyone else to see it."

"You've had someone up here?"

"You know how nosy some people are. They push through the door and demand to see your whole house." She laughed at Claudia's shocked response.

"The truth's finally out. There I was reaching out in friendship and all you saw was someone being nosy."

Leo set the book aside and pulled Claudia into her arms. "Thank God you were. You gave me the biggest gift of my life just by coming into it."

"But then I took it away."

"I held on to the best part, Claudia. Your love stayed inside me all these years, and now we get to share it again."

Epilogue

※

"You artist types are so hot," Claudia whispered, her eyes dancing with flirtation.

Leo put an arm around her waist and pecked her on the lips. If anyone was hot, it was Claudia. The plunging neckline of the deep green cocktail dress had tantalized her all evening. "It's usually tradition for the artist to get laid after a successful showing."

"I'm a big believer in tradition."

Maria caught her eye from across the gallery and pointed to a tall gentleman who had just entered. He looked out of place in his worn tweed sports jacket and polo shirt, but Leo recognized him as the photo editor for *Golden Shores*, a California-themed magazine. He had expressed interest in contracting her services for a series on powerhouse couples in Hollywood, and Maria had promised to make the introductions.

226

"There's David Kent," Leo said.

"Do you want me to leave so you can talk to him?"

She shook her head. "No, I like you right where you are."

The annual fall gallery walk in San Luis Obispo always brought out a crowd, and tonight was no exception. Leo shared space in Maria's gallery with several other artists representing four media. Hers were the only photographs, and she had chosen a handful of her favorites. She was a regular exhibitor in San Luis Obispo, something she did as much to honor her friendship with Maria and Sandy as to network with potential clients.

Sandy squeezed between them to deliver two flutes of champagne. "Thought you'd be interested to know Maria's gotten two inquiries on the naked ladies."

"Not for sale," Leo answered, not hesitating for an instant. With Claudia's encouragement, she had toyed with the idea of including her nude portraits in a published body of work, but in the end decided she preferred the real-time display, especially with Claudia at her side only vaguely unrecognizable as the model.

With a hand over her mouth, Sandy playfully taunted, "I'm just waiting for some kid to come in here and say, 'Hey, Mom, look! It's my third grade teacher.'"

Leo grinned at Claudia, who was rolling her eyes. "All the little third-grade boys will be dreaming about you. And probably half the girls."

"Oh, my God! Look who it is," Claudia exclaimed.

Leo followed her eyes to the door, where a lovely woman— mid-fifties with graying brown hair and wide dramatic eyes—had entered on the arm of a much younger man Leo would have bet was gay.

"That's Christina John," Claudia said animatedly. "I've seen every movie she's ever made. What's she doing here?"

"I think she lives here."

"Maybe she'll come over and look at your work. Wouldn't you just die if she said something about it?"

Leo was delighted at Claudia's fan-girl zeal. From the corner

227

of her eye, she watched as the couple drew closer. When they stopped to study the nude photo and its description, Claudia nearly burst with excitement.

The actress suddenly whirled to face them. "Leo?"

"Hello, Chris. Good to see you again." They traded kisses on the cheek. "And you're looking marvelous, as usual."

"Thank you. It takes a little longer than it used to, but the minute I don't do it some rude asshole takes my picture." She motioned to the man to continue on without her and he did so.

"Let me introduce you to someone." She guided Claudia forward. "This is my wife, Claudia Galloway. I think she's a fan of yours."

"How do you do?"

"Miss John, I'm so pleased to meet you. I can't believe Leo didn't tell me she knew you."

"She's probably still having nightmares about my dogs."

Leo laughed. "Not true," she explained to Claudia. "I had the pleasure of doing a magazine layout with Chris and her dogs about three years ago. I wish all my jobs were that much fun."

The actress pointed over her shoulder at the nude portrait. "I bet *that* was fun. Any chance I could get you to do one of those for me?"

"Are you serious?"

"Of course. I've done nude scenes in film, but I'm always playing someone else. I'd like to have something more personal for myself."

"I'd be honored." Leo fished a calling card from her pocket. "Have someone get in touch and we'll set something up."

"You have to promise to make me look like that, though. Brush away all the wrinkles."

"Walk around and have a look at the other side." She and Claudia followed as Christina found the updated photo, same lighting and pose, taken last year in her studio on Cannery Row.

"This one's you!" she said, looking at Claudia with astonishment.

"So is the other one," Claudia said, beaming with pride. "Leo

228

does amazing work."

"I'll say." She looked directly at Claudia while leaning in to speak to Leo. "For that, I think I could be a lesbian too."

Leo grinned at Claudia's stunned look as Christina walked away. "I think you just got a huge compliment."

"I'm going to faint."

"I want to hang these in our bedroom when we get home."

True to her word, Claudia had moved in with her for good in Monterey only three weeks after Eva's wedding. Leo's perfect memories of their time together long ago were still intact. They even had a few disagreements under their belts, but they were mostly minor adjustments to sharing personal space with someone else. Disagreements or not, Leo intended to share everything in her life with Claudia for as long as they lived.

"Here comes Maria with David Kent. I'm going to go stalk Christina John."

Leo caught her hand as she started to leave. "Don't forget about that tradition…you know, the one where I get laid."

"Not a chance."

WALTZING AT MIDNIGHT by Robbi McCoy. First crush, first passion, first love. Everybody else knows Jean Harris has a major crush on Rosie Monroe, except Jean. It's just not something Jean, with two kids in college, thought would ever happen to her. $14.95

NO STRINGS by Gerri Hill. Reese Daniels is only in town for a year's assignment. MZ Morgan doesn't need a relationship. Their "no strings" arrangement seemed like a really good plan. $14.95

THE COLOR OF DUST by Claire Rooney. Who wouldn't want to inherit a mysterious mansion full of history under the layers of dust? Carrie Bowden is thrilled, especially when the local antique dealer seems equally interested in her. But sometimes secrets don't want to be disturbed. $14.95

THE DAWNING by Karin Kallmaker. Would you give up your future to right the past? Romantic, science fiction story that will linger long after the last page. $14.95

OCTOBER'S PROMISE by Marianne Garver. You'll never forget Turtle Cove, the people who live there, and the mysterious cupid determined to make true love happen for Libby and Quinn. $14.95

SIDE ORDER OF LOVE by Tracey Richardson. Television foodie star Grace Wellwood is not going to be golf phenom Torrie Cannon's side order of romance for the summer tour. No, she's not. Absolutely not. $14.95

WORTH EVERY STEP by KG MacGregor. Climbing Africa's highest peak isn't nearly so hard as coming back down to earth. Join two women who risk their futures and hearts on the journey of their lives. $14.95

WHACKED by Josie Gordon. Death by family values. Lonnie Squires knows that if they'd warned her about this possibility in seminary, she'd remember. $14.95

BECKA'S SONG by Frankie J. Jones. Mysterious, beautiful women with secrets are to be avoided. Leanne Dresher knows it with her head, but her heart has other plans. Becka James is simply unavoidable. 14.95

PARTNERS by Gerri Hill. Detective Casey O'Connor has had difficult cases, but what she needs most from fellow detective Tori Hunter is help understanding her new partner, Leslie Tucker. 14.95

AS FAR AS FAR ENOUGH by Claire Rooney. Two very different women from two very different worlds meet by accident— literally. Collier and Meri find their love threatened on all sides. There's only one way to survive: together. $14.95

NIGHT VISION by Karin Kallmaker. Julia Madison is having nightmares. So are all the lesbians she knows. What secret in the desert could be responsible? $14.95

AFTERSHOCK: Book two of the Shaken series by KG MacGregor. Anna and Lily have survived earthquake and dating, but new challenges may prove their undoing. $14.95

BEAUTIFUL JOURNEY by Kenna White. Determined to do her part during the Battle for Britain, aviatrix Kit Anderson has no time for Emily Mills, who certainly has no time for her, either, not when their hearts are in the line of fire. $14.95

MIDNIGHT MELODIES by Megan Carter. Family disputes and small-town tensions come between Erica Boyd and and her best chance at romance in years. $14.95

WHITE OFFERINGS by Ann Roberts. Realtor-turned-sleuth Ari Adams helps a friend find a stalker, only to begin receiving white offerings of her own. Book 2 in series. $14.95

HER SISTER'S KEEPER by Diana Rivers. A restless young Hadra is caught up in a daring raid on the Gray Place, but is captured and must stand trial for her crimes against the state. Book 6 in series. $13.95

LOSERS WEEPERS by Jessica Thomas. Alex Peres must sort out a possible kidnapping hoax and the death of a friend, and finds that the two cases have a surprising number of mutual suspects. Book 4 in series.
$13.95

COMPULSION by Terri Breneman. Toni Barston's lucky break in a case turns into a nightmare when she becomes the target of a compulsive murderess. Book "C" in series. $14.95

THE KISS THAT COUNTED by Karin Kallmaker. CJ Roshe is used to hiding from her past, but meeting Karita Hanssen leaves her longing to finally tell someone her real name. $14.95

SECRETS SO DEEP by KG MacGregor. Glynn Wright's son holds a secret that is destroying him, but confronting it could mean the end of their family. Charlotte Blue is determined to save them both. $14.95

ROOMMATES by Jackie Calhoun. Two freshmen co-eds from two different worlds discover what it takes to choose love. $14.95

WHEN IT'S ALL RELATIVE by Therese Szymanski. Brett Higgins must confront her worst enemies: her family. Book 8 in series. $13.95

THE RAINBOW CEDAR by Gerri Hill. Jaye Burns' relationship is falling apart in spite of her efforts to keep it together. When Drew Montgomery offers the possibility of a new start, Jaye is torn between past and future. $13.95

TRAINING DAYS by Jane Frances. A passionate tryst on a long-distance train might be the undoing of Morgan's career—and her heart. $13.95

CHRISTABEL by Karin Kallmaker. Dina Rowland must accept her magical heritage to save supermodel Christabel from the demon of their past who has found them in the present. $13.95

ROOT OF PASSION by Ann Roberts. Grace Owens knows a fake when she sees it, and the potion her best friend promises will fix her love life is a fake. But what if she wishes it weren't? $14.95

KEILE'S CHANCE by Dillon Watson. A routine day in the park turns into the chance of a lifetime, if Keile Griffen can find the courage to risk it all for a pair of big brown eyes. $14.95

SEA LEGS by KG MacGregor. Kelly is happy to help Natalie make Didi jealous, sure, it's all pretend. Maybe. Even the captain doesn't know where this comic cruse will end. $14.95

TOASTED by Josie Gordon. Mayhem erupts when a culinary road show stops in tiny Middelburg, and for some reason everyone thinks Lonnie Squires ought to fix it. Follow-up to Lammy mystery winner Whacked. $14.95

NO RULES OF ENGAGEMENT by Tracey Richardson. A war zone attraction is of no use to Major Logan Sharp. She can't wait for Jillian Knight to go back to the other side of the world. $14.95

A SMALL SACRIFICE by Ellen Hart. A harmless reunion of friends is anything but, and Cordelia Thorn calls friend Jane Lawless with a desperate plea for help. Lammy winner for Best Mystery. #5 in this award-winning series. $14.95

FAINT PRAISE by Ellen Hart. When a famous TV personality leaps to his death, Jane Lawless agrees to help a friend with inquiries, drawing the attention of a ruthless killer. #6 in this award-winning series. $14.95

STEPPING STONE by Karin Kallmaker. Selena Ryan's heart was shredded by an actress, and she swears she will never, ever be involved with one again. $14.95